Ian McFadyen was born in Liverpool and has enjoyed a successful career in marketing. He lives in Hertfordshire with his wife and his retired greyhound. He has three grown-up children. *Deadly Secrets*, featuring DI Steve Carmichael, is the fourth novel in the series, all published by Book Guild.

DEADLY SECRETS

Ian McFadyen

Book Guild Publishing
Sussex, England

First published in Great Britain in 2013 by
The Book Guild Ltd
Pavilion View
19 New Road
Brighton
BN1 1UF

Typesetting in Baskerville by
Nat-Type, Cheshire

Printed in Great Britain by
CPI Group (UK) Ltd, Croydon, CR0 4YY

A catalogue record for this book is available from
The British Library.

ISBN 978 1 84624 849 8

I dedicate this book to Gerard Barton, my great friend. We shared a lot of laughter.

Acknowledgements

With my sincere thanks to the burgeoning group of people who provide valuable encouragement and in many cases the basis for some of my best characters!

In particular:

- Carol Biss and her marvellous team at the Book Guild
- Paul and Sue Yerby (guardians of Sarkozy Bank)
- The Bears (Graham, Alison and Hilary)
- The October racing ream (Paul, Heather, Steve and Pat)
- Dorothy (my favourite Aunt)
- Jamie and Emma (the graduates who recently fledged)
- Lauren (PA extraordinaire)
- The rest of the McFadyen and Worman Clans (scattered all over UK)

But most importantly to Chris, for her unwavering support and inspiration!

Chapter 1

Friday 13th August

Geraldine Ramsey took down her lime-green, linen jacket from the coat hook by the front door and slipped her tiny, pale arm into the right sleeve. 'Unless there's anything else I can do for you, I'll be off now, Marcus,' she shouted up the staircase as her left hand struggled to locate the sleeve opening.

'That's fine, Geraldine,' came back the muted, almost disinterested reply from upstairs. 'Have a great time in Italy.'

Geraldine eventually managed to successfully slide her left arm into her jacket and spent a few seconds checking herself in the hallway mirror. As soon as she was happy that her appearance was up to her normal, exacting standards, she allowed herself a small, self-righteous smile before she made her way to the front door.

'Oh, actually, you could do something for me,' announced Marcus, who by now was at the top of the stairs. 'You couldn't pop some letters in the post box for me on your way past, could you?'

'Certainly,' replied Geraldine with a kindly smile. 'Although you do realise that the last collection went about twenty minutes ago. They won't get picked up now until the morning and won't be delivered until Monday, even if they have first-class stamps on them.'

'Blast it,' replied Marcus who gazed intently at his

1

wristwatch. 'I didn't realise the last collection was at five o'clock; I thought it was five thirty.'

'No,' replied Geraldine authoritatively. 'It's most certainly five and has been for years.'

'They'll just have to arrive on Monday then,' replied Marcus with an air of despondency in his voice. 'They're on the writing desk in the front room. There are three of them in white envelopes.'

Geraldine walked through the open door that led to Marcus Ardleigh's front room.

Carefully placed on the desk were three envelopes addressed in her old friend's distinctive handwriting. Geraldine picked them up, nosily looked to see whom they were addressed to and placed them in her handbag.

When she emerged back into the hallway she glanced up the staircase, expecting to still see Marcus looking down from the landing, but he had disappeared. Geraldine smiled to herself and shook her head before turning to her left and walking over to the front door. How such an intelligent, highly qualified and incredibly successful man could be so scatty was beyond her, but that was Marcus. His absent-mindedness was one of the many quirks that made him such an interesting, unique individual and, for Geraldine, someone she still found as fascinating to be around as she had twenty years ago, when they had first met.

'I'll see you in two weeks,' she shouted up the stairs.

* * * *

With a smug simian grin on his face, Marcus Ardleigh watched from the upstairs window as Geraldine Ramsey wandered slowly down the main street. Although the post box was only a matter of 200 yards away, it took her almost fifteen minutes to get there, since she stopped first to engage in conversation with Mrs Savage, an old friend, and then with

2

Helen Parkes, who managed one of the hairdressing salons in Moulton Bank.

Throughout the whole of this time Marcus Ardleigh patiently kept watch on her progress. As soon as he could see that the letters had all been safely despatched into the bright-red pillar box, Ardleigh turned away from the window, leaving Geraldine to make the rest of her way home unobserved.

* * * *

Twenty-three miles away at Kirkwood Police Station, Inspector Steve Carmichael decided to call it a day. It had been a quiet week, with little going on to occupy his naturally inquisitive mind, and with the weather being so warm and sunny, he decided to finish work early and get himself home. The prospect of having a beer or two in the garden, before the sun finally went down, seemed a perfect start to the weekend.

As Carmichael was opening his car door, he spied Chief Inspector Hewitt across the car park getting into his large black Lexus.

'Enjoy your holiday, sir,' he shouted. 'I hope you have a relaxing time.'

'I'm not sure "relaxing" is the right word to describe my vacation this year,' replied Hewitt as he clambered into his car.

Carmichael opened the rear passenger door and placed his bulging briefcase onto the seat. As he did so, Hewitt's car pulled up beside him.

'I'm leaving the station in your capable hands for the next two weeks, Inspector,' he announced through his open window. 'I'll have my BlackBerry with me for emergencies,' he continued. 'But I'm sure you'll be able to manage while I'm in Kenya.'

'I'm sure I will, sir,' responded Carmichael. 'But I'll certainly call you if I need your help or advice. Enjoy the safari.'

As he watched his boss disappear out of the station car park, Carmichael shook his head. 'Not my idea of a holiday,' he quipped to a PC who happened to be passing. 'Traipsing across the African savannah taking photos of elephants and crocodiles. I reckon he thinks he's Dr Livingstone.'

The PC laughed. 'Is that where the Chief's going on holiday, sir?' he asked.

'Yep,' replied Carmichael as he climbed into his car.

'And God help the poor bloody crocodiles,' he muttered to himself as he sped off in the direction of his home in Moulton Bank.

Chapter 2

Monday 16th August

Number 28 Station Road was an imposing, detached, double-fronted, three-storey, red-brick house that stood proudly between two smaller dwellings in the heart of Moulton Bank's main street. From any one of its five front-facing windows, pretty much everything that happened in the centre of the village could be easily observed. Conversely, its location also meant that the comings and goings at 28 Station Road were just as noticeable to the adjoining residents.

So, when an ambulance, two police cars and two unmarked cars were brought to rest in quick succession outside, and uniformed officers hurriedly cordoned off the house, the fact that something was amiss at Marcus Ardleigh's home was clearly evident to the inhabitants of that part of Moulton Bank.

Inside, Steve Carmichael looked up at the motionless body that dangled on the end of a thick, blue nylon rope. 'Was it suicide?' he asked Dr Stock, the able pathologist whom Carmichael had come to respect so much.

Stock had only arrived at the scene a few minutes before Carmichael and had not yet had enough time to come to any firm conclusion.

'I'm not sure,' he replied, without once taking his eyes off the corpse. 'It certainly looks like suicide, but I'd like to look at this a little more thoroughly before jumping to any hasty conclusions.'

Carmichael smiled. 'I understand,' he replied, then turning to Cooper he asked, 'Who is he?'

'His name's Ardleigh,' replied Sergeant Cooper in astonishment. 'I'm surprised you don't recognise him. He's quite a prominent figure in the village. He's regularly in the local papers giving his views on all sorts of things.'

Carmichael moved nearer the lifeless corpse to take a closer look.

'Oh yes,' he said when it dawned on him who the dead man was. 'I do recognise him now. I've seen him around the village a few times but had no idea who he was.'

Dr Stock shook his head in disbelief. 'Marcus Ardleigh is, or rather was, an eminent mathematician,' he said firmly. 'He had a first from Oxford, he had written countless books on mathematics and was an advisor to Thatcher's government in the late 1980s. Surely even a philistine like you, Carmichael, will have heard of Marcus Ardleigh!'

Carmichael glanced sideways in Cooper's direction. 'I'm clearly moving in the wrong circles,' he remarked glibly.

For the first time, Dr Stock took his eyes from the body of Marcus Ardleigh and, with a despairing look in Carmichael's direction, shook his head once more before turning back to continue his examination.

Carmichael looked upwards at where the nylon rope had been tied. 'He wanted to make sure it was fastened tightly,' he said to Cooper. 'It's certainly been fixed firmly.'

Cooper gazed up at the top of the staircase landing where the rope had been secured using four of the spindles on the upstairs hallway. 'Those knots look unusual, too,' he observed.

'They look to me like they were tied by someone who's had some form of sailing experience,' commented Stock.

'Why do you say that?' enquired Carmichael inquisitively.

'I've not had a chance to look at them closely yet,' replied Stock. 'But from what I can see whoever tied them has used a bowline, an anchor hitch and, if I'm not mistaken, a stopper knot used to tie jib sheets. That's the figure-of-eight knot at the end of the rope.'

'I didn't know you were a seafaring man,' remarked Carmichael in bewilderment.

'I'm not,' responded Stock resolutely. 'However, against my wishes my parents made me to go to sea cadets when I was young; and my father was a member of our local sailing club for many years, so I have a little knowledge of knots. Until now it has been of no value to me whatsoever.'

'Well, all I can say, Stock,' replied Carmichael with a grin, 'is thank goodness your parents were so insistent. Those knots may well prove to be important.'

'So what are we saying here?' enquired Cooper. 'If we can prove that Ardleigh was a sailor, are we then saying this was a suicide?'

'Maybe not,' interrupted Stock, with more than a hint of excitement in his voice. 'Look at this!'

Carmichael and Cooper moved nearer to Ardleigh's suspended torso. 'See those abrasions?' said Stock as he pointed at some pronounced grazes on Ardleigh's wrists. 'They look like rope marks. If I'm not mistaken, poor Mr Ardleigh looks like he has had his hands tied.'

'In your opinion, could they have been tied when he was hanged?' Carmichael asked.

'It's possible,' replied Stock. 'We'll have to check for fibres, but the cuts look fairly fresh and are certainly consistent with him being tied up very recently.'

'So, he could have been tied up by someone, then hanged,' said Cooper, who was now starting to consider the possibility of this being more than a simple suicide case.

'Yes,' replied Stock. 'Then, after he died, the ropes that

bound his wrists could have been untied and taken away to try and make it look like he had committed suicide.'

'Is that what you think happened?' Carmichael enquired.

Stock considered the question carefully. 'I wouldn't like to commit myself just yet,' he replied. 'I need to do much more work, but I wouldn't rule it out.'

Carmichael continued to look at the lesions on Ardleigh's wrists. 'And what's your estimate of the time of death?' he asked the pathologist.

'That's a bit easier to deduce,' replied Stock. 'He's been dead for at least twelve hours but no longer than twenty-four.'

'So, some time on Sunday?' confirmed Cooper.

'Yes,' replied Stock. 'And once I get him back to the lab and do a proper post-mortem, I'll probably be able to be more specific about the time of death, but it was certainly yesterday some time.'

'We'll leave you to it then,' announced Carmichael before turning with Cooper and walking slowly away from the lifeless body. 'Who discovered Mr Ardleigh?'

'It was an old friend of his called Hugo Lazarus,' replied Cooper. 'He's with Rachel in the kitchen. He was in one hell of a state when we arrived.'

'He's still here!' said Carmichael with surprise. 'In that case I better have a word with him.'

The two officers walked briskly into a large modern-looking kitchen, which was situated at the rear of the house overlooking Ardleigh's beautifully maintained back garden.

Inside the kitchen, facing each other across a large pine table, sat DC Rachel Dalton and a distinguished-looking, albeit ashen-faced man, whom Carmichael estimated as being in his late fifties or early sixties.

On seeing her boss enter the room Rachel stood up. 'This is Inspector Carmichael and Sergeant Cooper,' she said to the dazed man sitting opposite her. 'Sir, this is Hugo Lazarus. It was Mr Lazarus who found Mr Ardleigh this morning.'

At first Hugo Lazarus made no attempt to acknowledge Carmichael and Cooper. After a few seconds he half turned his head to face them, but said nothing.

'I totally understand that all this must have been a huge shock for you, Mr Lazarus,' said Carmichael, trying hard to sound as sympathetic as he could. 'However, I would like to ask you a few questions. Is that OK with you?'

Hugo Lazarus nodded.

'What time was it when you found Mr Ardleigh?' Carmichael asked.

'I'm not sure,' Lazarus replied softly, his accent more in keeping with the Home Counties than with mid-Lancashire. 'It must have been around eight this morning.'

'And what were you doing here at such an early hour?' continued Carmichael.

'We were supposed to be meeting up last night for a drink in The Railway Tavern, but Marcus never turned up,' explained Lazarus, who was still quite clearly very shaken by the whole ordeal. 'I thought I'd come round to make sure he was OK.'

'And at what time were you supposed to meet yesterday?' asked Carmichael.

'We had arranged to meet at nine,' explained Lazarus. 'I waited until about nine forty-five and then phoned him here and on his mobile, but he didn't answer.'

'So, what did you do then?' Carmichael asked.

'I just went home,' replied Lazarus. 'I thought that Marcus had simply forgotten our arrangement.'

'Forgotten!' Carmichael exclaimed with astonishment. 'Is it typical of Mr Ardleigh to be so forgetful?'

Lazarus looked into Carmichael's eyes. 'Oh yes,' he replied. 'That is quite characteristic of dear Marcus. He could be extremely absent-minded at times.'

'I see,' replied Carmichael. 'But you clearly had some concerns; otherwise you wouldn't have come round this morning.'

'That's correct,' replied Lazarus. 'Although at first I just thought it was Marcus being his normal scatter-brained self, when I was in bed last night I couldn't help thinking that I should have popped in to make sure he was all right.'

'What made you think that way?' Carmichael enquired. 'If missing a meeting was pretty normal behaviour, what made this particular missed appointment cause you so much anxiety?'

Lazarus thought for a short while before answering. 'Because Marcus was so insistent that I should meet with him when he rang me on Saturday evening. He sounded very agitated and was very keen for us to get together. He said he wanted to discuss something very important with me. So when I got home last night and thought about everything, I did start to get a bit worried about him.'

'But not concerned enough to pay him a visit last night?' remarked Cooper.

Lazarus wearily shook his head. 'You're absolutely right – I *should* have come over last night. Maybe if I had, I could have stopped him hanging himself.'

'Have you any idea what Mr Ardleigh wanted to discuss with you, Mr Lazarus?' Carmichael asked.

'No idea at all,' replied Lazarus. 'But he was very insistent that we should meet up at the pub.'

'How long have you known Mr Ardleigh?' Carmichael asked.

'For over thirty years,' replied Lazarus. 'We were at Oxford together in the mid-70s.'

'I see,' replied Carmichael as he rose from his seat and smiled down at Hugo Lazarus. 'As I say, I'm sorry about your friend, but if you can give DC Dalton a full statement that would be most helpful.'

Lazarus nodded his head gently. 'Of course,' he replied. Carmichael and Cooper were almost through the kitchen doorway when Carmichael suddenly turned back to face Lazarus. 'One last thing,' he said with a note of bewilderment in his voice. 'How did you manage to get into the house this morning?'

Lazarus's sombre face cracked slightly to show the faintest of smiles. 'Oh, Marcus left a spare key under the front doormat,' he replied. 'I was forever telling him to find a less obvious hiding place but he never took any notice of my advice.'

'So who else knew about this hiding place?' Cooper asked.

'Just about all of his friends I would imagine,' replied Lazarus.

'I see,' replied Carmichael again. 'Then can I ask you to also give DC Dalton a list of all of Mr Ardleigh's friends. That would be very useful to us.'

* * * *

Sergeant Marc Watson had woken up that morning with the mother of all hangovers. It had been his wife Susan's birthday the day before, and the surprise barbecue that he had arranged for her and a few close friends had been a great success. That Sunday had been one of the hottest for some time, and the party, which had started at noon, continued well into the evening. Marc had intended to take it easy and pace himself, but by seven thirty, having already consumed at least six or seven bottles of strong lager and half a bottle of red wine, he then made matters worse when he decided to get out a bottle of his favourite malt whisky.

Neither he nor Susan had heard the alarm go off at 6:30 and had it not been for Susan's mother's refusal to put down the receiver when she called them at 8:15, it's unlikely that they would have stirred for at least another hour.

11

Despite living no more than a five-minute walk from the crime scene, the exceptionally dishevelled and decidedly delicate Watson could only manage to make his appearance at Ardleigh's residence just as Carmichael and Cooper were making their way down the path away from the house.

'Nice of you to join us!' remarked Carmichael sarcastically.

'Sorry I'm late, sir,' replied Watson. 'I overslept.'

Carmichael shook his head slowly to emphasise his displeasure.

'Better late than never, I suppose,' he said, doing his best to make the already pained sergeant feel even more uncomfortable. 'I suggest you go and help Rachel out in there.'

'Right you are, sir,' replied Watson as he brushed passed Cooper and headed towards the door.

'Then, when you've done that, go down to the path lab with Dr Stock and wait there until he's completed the post-mortem examination,' continued Carmichael with a mischievous grin.

'Do I have to?' replied Watson, who on hearing the latest order had stopped dead in his tracks.

'Yes,' replied Carmichael mercilessly. 'I want to know the full details as soon as Stock has completed the autopsy.'

Watson ambled slowly through the front door, not bothering to reply.

'Do you think the autopsy will throw up something important?' enquired Cooper with some bemusement.

'God, no,' replied Carmichael with a wicked smile. 'But looking at poor Marc, I suspect something may be thrown up at some point this morning.'

Chapter 3

Within the space of thirty minutes a trio of white envelopes with Marcus Ardleigh's unique handwriting dropped through the letterboxes of their three respective recipients. In her deluxe riverside apartment the elegant middle-aged woman, dressed in a thin silk dressing gown, placed her coffee cup on the glass breakfast table and lit her first cigarette of the day.

'There's a letter for you, my dear,' announced the suave voice of the muscularly built young man, dressed only in his boxer shorts, who joined her from the hallway.

'Just put it down here,' she replied, blowing a thick funnel of smoke into the bare tanned midriff of her young lover. 'I'll read it later, when you've gone.'

The young man placed the letter on the table as instructed and then, bending down slowly, placed a long lingering kiss on her smoky moist lips. 'So you're sending me away,' he said with a grin.

'Of course,' she teased. 'You're no use to me in the daytime.'

'As you wish,' he said as he walked slowly towards the bedroom. 'I know when I'm not wanted.'

As he reached the bedroom door he half turned. 'Shall I come round again this evening?'

'Maybe,' she muttered, her attention having been completely taken by the envelope lying in front of her, written in the hand that she knew so well. 'Actually, no,' she said, her interest in her young companion now having left her completely. 'I'll call you next week.'

* * * *

Gordon Napier picked up the small pile of letters that had landed on the doormat. It was just after ten thirty, and although his tiny village antiques shop had been open for over an hour and a half, he had yet to hear the tinkle of the doorbell that signified the arrival of a potential customer. Regrettably this was not an unusually quiet day. In each of the last three months the shop had failed to make a profit; and in the last two weeks on almost half of the days when he had been open, Napier had failed to make any kind of sale at all.

The portly antiques dealer looked at the envelopes one by one as he walked back towards his imposing mahogany writing desk.

'Bill, bill, circular, bill,' he muttered under his breath as he flicked through the day's post.

Suddenly he stopped in his tracks as he saw the familiar handwriting of his old friend Marcus Ardleigh on the pure-white envelope.

Without even bothering to open the clutch of letters that he had already identified as being either invoices he could not pay or junk mail, he despatched them all into the waste-paper bin by the side of his desk.

He sat down in his leather chair and placed the white envelope on the desk in front of him. He looked at it closely. It was certainly from Marcus, the unmistakeable script could not have been written by anyone else. However, the very fact that he had received a letter from Marcus puzzled the antiques dealer. In the thirty years he had known Marcus, he had never known him to correspond by mail. Text messages occasionally, emails quite often, but letters never.

Assuming that whatever was inside must be of very great

14

importance and with his curiosity now heightened, Napier slit open the envelope with one swift stroke from his razor-sharp, silver letter opener. His chubby fingers extracted the single white sheet of paper from inside which he then started to read.

* * * *

It would be much later that morning before the third of Marcus Ardleigh's letters was opened and its disturbing contents read.

Chapter 4

When eighteen years earlier, Penny Carmichael had suggested to her husband that that they named their only son Robbie, without any hesitation Steve agreed. He had wanted his son to have a Scottish-sounding name and Robbie seemed perfect, especially as his own father's name was Robert. It had never occurred to him to ask his wife why she liked the name. Had he done so, he would have discovered that his wife was actually naming their son after the nickname of a boy she had known in the village where she had grew up. For her part, Penny had not thought it necessary to tell Steve how the name had come to her. At that time they were then living 200 miles away from her childhood home in Moulton Bank so it never occurred to her that her husband would ever meet the man his son had been named after. However, fate had conspired to not only allow the two men to meet, but also uncannily to become such great chums. In the three years that they had lived in the quiet Lancashire village, Steve had never mentioned the strange coincidence to either his wife or Robbie Robertson, the landlord of The Railway Tavern. He had sometimes wondered whether there was a link and it had crossed his mind that maybe in their youth, Penny and his new friend had dated, but this curiosity had never been strong enough for him to broach the subject with his wife.

Robbie Carmichael, on the other hand, had twigged that he had been named after the pub landlord the very first time he had met Robbie Robertson. It wasn't something he was altogether happy about and it had played on his mind to the extent that he had experienced quite frightening dreams in which he would discover that his real father was actually Robbie Robertson rather than Steve Carmichael. Being now nearly eighteen, Robbie felt that he was far too grown-up to mention these nightmares to either of his parents; however he secretly longed to have the opportunity to discuss the origin of his name with his mother and get her to tell him the truth.

On that particular Monday morning Robbie Carmichael's alarm had woken him early. He was very tired having spent a restless night being tormented by the reoccurring dream of his parentage. It was now midway through the school's summer holidays and to his relief young Robbie had secured himself a few weeks' work at Mr Hayley's chicken farm at the end of Wood Lane. The work was very hard but Mr Hayley paid well and Robbie enjoyed this job and had made good friends with a few of the farm labourers. In particular, Robbie had become mates with a bloke they all called 'Spot On'.

Spot On was big strong lad about ten years older than Robbie who had originally hailed from Cumbria. He had a thick Cumbrian accent, and whenever anyone asked him how he or anything was, he would reply with a broad smile, 'Aye, spot on.'

Robbie was not sure what Spot On's real name was, but thought it was Chris, or maybe Carl.

Robbie was keen to earn as much as he could, given that he'd now found himself a girlfriend called Brooke. Having his own money allowed him to pay for the two sweethearts to take themselves off on the train for the day to either Southport or Wigan, when they wanted to escape from the suffocating small-village setting of Moulton Bank.

* * * *

17

Robbie Carmichael had already been working for three hours when his father's car pulled away from Marcus Ardleigh's house and headed off in the direction of The Railway Tavern, where Steve Carmichael and Sergeant Cooper intended to speak with the landlord to check out Hugo Lazarus's claim to have been in the pub on the previous evening.

'So what did you make of Ardleigh's death?' Cooper asked as they made the short car journey to The Railway Tavern.

'I'm not sure,' replied Carmichael honestly. 'My initial impression when we arrived there this morning was that it looked like a suicide, but those rope burns on his wrists are a bit baffling and there was no suicide note, which I also find quite strange.'

Cooper nodded to register concurrence. 'And if Lazarus is telling the truth, it makes no sense for Ardleigh to have set up that meeting last night, not turn up and then kill himself.'

'I agree,' replied Carmichael as they pulled into the pub car park. 'Let's see what Robbie has to tell us. If Lazarus was in the pub last night I'm certain he will remember.'

The two officers clambered out of the black BMW and sauntered over to the front door of The Railway Tavern.

* * * *

Marc Watson's first act when he entered Marcus Ardleigh's house was to go straight to the kitchen and, ignoring both DC Rachel Dalton and Hugo Lazarus, the dishevelled sergeant took an empty glass from the draining board, filled it to the top from the cold tap and in one long gulp drained the vessel dry.

'Morning,' said Rachel, whose dismay at her colleague's behaviour was engraved across her furrowed brow.

Bleary-eyed and unaware of the look that Rachel was giving him, Watson turned to face Hugo Lazarus. 'So what sort of person was Ardleigh?' he asked, trying hard to sound like a man in control.

'He was a fine man,' replied Lazarus, who was still clearly shaken. 'As I've been telling your colleague here, I've known him for over thirty years and I just can't understand why he would take his own life.'

'Is that what you think happened?' remarked Watson.

'Well, of course,' responded Lazarus with surprise in his voice. 'It was suicide, wasn't it?'

Watson shrugged his shoulders. 'Probably,' he replied, making no attempt to acknowledge the feelings of the dead man's friend. 'But let's wait for the pathologist's report before we jump to any conclusions.'

Lazarus nodded. 'I fully understand,' he replied. 'I've already promised your inspector to give your colleague here a full statement, and it goes without saying that I'll try and help you all as much as I can.'

'Great,' replied Watson, who was feeling no better after drinking the glass of water and once more started to fill the empty glass from the kitchen tap. 'In that case I'll leave you two to get on with it,' he commented, before again downing the glass in one go and starting to walk back towards the hallway.

Rachel stared at Watson in astonishment, with her mouth wide open. Although she could feel her cheeks reddening, Rachel tried her hardest not to allow Lazarus to see how embarrassed she was by her undeniably hung-over colleague.

'I'll be outside with Stock when you've finished,' continued Watson, who appeared to care nothing about what sort of impression he was creating on Hugo Lazarus and seemed equally oblivious to the look of utter horror that was imprinted on his young colleague's face.

* * * *

19

Despite the fact that as a publican he was rarely in bed before midnight, Robbie Robertson was an early riser and at 10:30 when Carmichael and Cooper knocked on the front door of The Railway Tavern, the jovial landlord was on hand within seconds to open the door.

'Steve!' he said with surprise in his voice. 'What brings you here at this time?'

'Hello, Robbie,' replied Carmichael with a faint smile. 'Cooper and I need to ask you a few questions. Can we come in for a few minutes?'

'Of course,' responded the publican in his familiar booming Lancashire accent. 'Come on through. I was just having a coffee – why don't you both join me?'

'That sounds excellent,' replied Carmichael, who strode through the open doorway and into the pub, followed closely by Sergeant Cooper.

'Sit yourselves down,' Robbie said, pointing to a group of tables and chairs in the main lounge. 'Do you both take milk and sugar?'

'Milk and one sugar in mine,' replied Carmichael as he plonked himself down in one of the large wooden chairs.

'Same for me, too,' added Cooper who sat down opposite his boss.

In the twenty years he had been in the police force, Carmichael had reason to visit countless pubs in the early morning before lunchtime opening. Out of hours they all emitted the same feel – one of emptiness – and invariably in the daylight, with the stale smell of beer from countless spillages the night before, they always seemed shabby places in desperate need of some tender loving care. The Railway Tavern was no exception and, as the sun flooded through the high open windows, it served only to expose the age of the threadbare carpet and the tired appearance of the vacant tables and chairs which littered the deserted room.

Within an instant the gloomy surroundings were lifted

with the entrance of the cheery landlord, who burst through the door holding a tray of hot drinks. 'Here you go, gents,' he said as he placed them down on the table in front of them. 'Two coffees both with sugar.'

'Thank you,' replied Cooper, as he grabbed one of the mugs off the tray.

Carmichael didn't pick up his mug. He was keen to see if Robbie Robertson could help corroborate Hugo Lazarus's claim to have visited the pub the night before. 'We need your help,' he said. 'We need to verify the whereabouts of someone who said he was in the pub here last night.'

'Who's that?' enquired Robbie after finishing his first swig of coffee.

'A man called Hugo Lazarus,' replied Carmichael. 'Is he familiar to you?'

Robbie smiled. 'Oh I know old lah-di-dah Lazarus,' he replied. 'He doesn't come in that much, but yes I know him.'

'Was he here last night?' Carmichael asked.

'Yes, he was,' replied Robbie. 'He came in at about nine. He sat over there on his own with his glass of wine and then after about an hour or so he left.' The landlord pointed to the table in the farthest corner of the room.

Carmichael and Cooper exchanged a look. 'So he was here from about nine o'clock to ten?' Cooper confirmed.

'That's right,' replied Robbie. 'Is he in any trouble?'

'No,' remarked Carmichael. 'We just needed to confirm something he told us.'

'Well, he was certainly here,' reiterated Robbie.

'How well do you know Mr Lazarus?' Carmichael asked, as he took his first sip of coffee.

'Not very well at all,' replied Robbie. 'He's lived in the village for years, but he's not from round here. He's a rich layabout, who's never done a day's work in his life as far as I know.'

'Lucky man,' remarked Cooper with a knowing smile.

21

'And do you know his friend Marcus Ardleigh?' continued Carmichael.

'Marcus,' replied Robbie with a massive grin. 'Yes, he's in here quite a bit, but mainly at lunchtimes during the week. He's another brain. He went to Oxford you know. He's a bit like Lazarus but much more down to earth. He doesn't ram his Oxford background down your throat like the other one.'

'So Ardleigh's the most sociable of the two?' Cooper asked.

'Yes, I'd say so,' replied Robbie who was now becoming curious as to why he was being asked so many questions about the two intellectuals. 'So come on – what have they been up to?'

Carmichael saw no reason to keep the news from the landlord. 'I'm afraid that Marcus Ardleigh was found dead this morning,' he announced.

'How?' enquired Robbie, who was clearly taken aback by the news.

'He was found hanged in his house,' Carmichael replied.

'Was it suicide?' Robbie asked, his voice trembling with shock.

'We're not sure,' replied Carmichael frankly. 'But he was supposed to be meeting Hugo Lazarus here at nine last night so we just thought we'd check it out with you.'

'Well, as I said before, Lazarus was here, but Ardleigh wasn't,' said Robbie.

'That's all we needed to know,' announced Carmichael, who, disregarding the half-full coffee mug, stood up and shook the landlord's hand firmly. 'We need to be off now, Cooper. Thanks for the coffee, Robbie.'

Cooper struggled to gulp down the last third of his coffee before rushing to join his boss, who, by the time he reached him, was already outside. Robbie Robertson stood at the main entrance to the pub and watched as the two officers set off up the road. He did not notice Barry the postman until he was almost standing right next to him.

'You've quite a few today,' he remarked with a grin as he thrust the day's mail into the publican's hand.

Robbie Robertson returned the smile in Barry's direction, before retiring back into The Railway Tavern. Once inside he shut the door behind him before carefully studying the front of each of the letters in his hand.

Chapter 5

As soon as her young lover had left her lavish riverside apartment, Miranda Coyle lit another cigarette and read the letter from Marcus Ardleigh for a second time.

'You crafty old bugger,' she muttered to herself when she had finished examining his message. She took a long drag from the cigarette while she considered what to do. She did not need long to come to a decision. Picking up her mobile phone from the table she keyed in her PA's number.

'It's Miranda,' she announced. 'Cancel all my meetings today. Something's come up.'

'But, you're supposed to be at the board meeting this afternoon at two,' replied her confused PA.

'Cancel it,' replied Miranda curtly. 'I don't care how you do it or what you tell them but cancel it ... Cancel any other meetings in the diary today. Actually, cancel all tomorrow's, too.'

Miranda Coyle, entrepreneur and doyen of the high-street fashion industry, abruptly ended the call; she was in no mood to explain or debate her decisions with a mere PA.

* * * *

As soon as he had read Marcus's letter, Gordon Napier closed the door of the antiques shop and locked himself away in his small back office.

He sat there for almost half an hour before deciding that his best course of action was to call his old friend.

The phone in Ardleigh's house rang for twenty seconds before the answer machine kicked in. 'Hello, this is Marcus Ardleigh,' replied the recorded message in Marcus's distinctive Oxbridge tone. 'I am so sorry that I cannot take your call at this time, but please leave a message and I'll get back to you as soon as I can.'

'It's Gordon,' said Napier, his voice shaking so much that it was clear that he was troubled. 'I've got your bloody letter and we need to talk. I need to know who these other damn people are. I can't wait until tomorrow, so call me urgently.'

Trembling and sweating, Napier slammed down the receiver.

* * * *

Hugo Lazarus had spent over an hour giving DC Dalton a very detailed report on his movements over the previous twenty-four hours and, prompted by a variety of questions from Dalton, a whole host of information about Marcus Ardleigh. Although he was twice her age, Rachel saw Hugo Lazarus as not only articulate and very charming, but also a remarkably good-looking man. Having finished taking his statement, Rachel Dalton dutifully walked Lazarus to the front door, which was precisely when Napier's call came through. The answering machine that recorded the call was just by the door so both Rachel and Lazarus heard the message clearly.

'Do you recognise that man?' Rachel asked.

'Yes,' replied Lazarus. 'It's Gordon Napier. He's an old friend of ours from Oxford. He owns the antiques shop in the High Street. I will drop in on him on my way home and let him know about poor Marcus.'

'Thank you – you've been a great help,' replied Rachel before shaking Lazarus's hand.

'If I can be of any further help, please don't hesitate in calling,' said Lazarus as he descended the three short steps that led down to the path.

Rachel smiled and nodded gently. 'I certainly will,' she replied.

* * * *

As Carmichael had predicted, Marc Watson's condition was not helped at all by having to witness the gruesome autopsy of Marcus Ardleigh.

He started to feel queasy as soon as he stepped foot in the lab. The smell of death and disinfectant that was synonymous with path labs was never something that Watson liked, but in his already nauseous state it was almost too much for him to bear. Dressed in the customary green gown, Watson stood as far away from the body as he could. To avoid being sick he averted his gaze away from Ardleigh's lifeless torso and swallowed hard. In spite of his best efforts, nothing Watson did seemed to help and as soon as Dr Stock made his very first incision, Watson realised he could not cope anymore and hastily departed to get some fresh air. Still clad in the green gown which matched his sallow complexion, Watson would spend the next hour and forty-five minutes sitting patiently on the low wall outside the pathology lab while Stock concluded his examination.

* * * *

Carmichael and Cooper had only just pulled away from The Railway Tavern, when Cooper spotted a familiar figure getting out of an old maroon Volvo and walking towards the village antiques shop. 'Isn't that Hugo Lazarus?' he enquired.

26

'I think it is,' replied Carmichael, who watched as Lazarus surreptitiously made his way towards the antiques shop.

'I wonder what he's up to?' questioned Cooper.

'I'm not sure,' replied Carmichael. 'But whatever it is he looks like he's trying hard not to be noticed.'

'Yes, he does look quite furtive,' remarked Cooper. 'Shall we stop and find out what he's up to?'

Carmichael considered Cooper's suggestion for a few seconds. 'No,' he finally said. 'It's probably nothing. Let's get back to the station.'

* * * *

'Tell the poor, delicate sergeant he can come in now,' sniggered Stock to his young female assistant, once his autopsy had been completed. 'Let's hope he can manage to stay vertical long enough for me to give him a summary of my findings.'

The young assistant smiled and went outside to summon in Sergeant Watson.

* * * *

It took Miranda Coyle just over an hour to drive from her expensive apartment in Salford Quays to the quiet village of Moulton Bank. As her tangerine Lotus Evora glided down the High Street she tried hard to remember the last time she had been in the village. Although she couldn't precisely recall, she concluded that it must have been over fifteen years before.

As she approached Marcus's house Miranda spotted the police cordon and the small group of villagers and news reporters who had gathered on the pavement.

Miranda eased her right foot off the accelerator as her car came close to the house. She peered intently at the scene

27

through the passenger window as her distinctive sports car crawled past the police cordon. However, she couldn't see anything beyond the onlookers, and once her car had passed Ardleigh's house, she put her right foot down and sped on.

Chapter 6

News of the death of Marcus Ardleigh spread quickly through Moulton Bank and the surrounding villages. So much so, that by the middle of the afternoon it was just about the only topic of conversation in that part of Lancashire and was known by the majority of the area's inhabitants.

Ruben Kenyon – the senior partner at Ogilvy, Cave and Kenyon, one of Moulton Banks' oldest firms of solicitors – was one of the few exceptions. He only learned about Marcus Ardleigh's death at just after 3 p.m. when he returned to his office in the village. He had left early that morning and had spent the day in Kirkwood County Court, so it was only when the receptionist had mentioned the news to him on his return to the practice that he had any idea of his client's death.

'Are you sure, Mrs Osborne?' he said to the receptionist upon being told the news. 'He's dead?'

The middle-aged lady behind the smart new reception desk nodded enthusiastically. 'I'm afraid so, Mr Kenyon. And they are saying that he was murdered.'

Ruben Kenyon had been Lyn Osborne's boss for over twenty years, so he was well aware of his receptionist's proclivity to embellish an account when it suited her. Over the years he had become quite skilled at filtering out the facts from hearsay. He therefore had immediately questioned the credibility of Mrs Osborne's murder theory, but he was in no doubt that she would have her facts correct with regards to Marcus actually being dead.

'I'll not be taking any calls for the next hour,' he said as he made his way up the staircase to his office. 'I have some important work I need to do and I don't want to be disturbed.'

'Would you like a coffee?' Mrs Osborne shouted up the stairway.

She took the lack of any answer and the firm slam of her employer's office door as a no.

* * * *

Penny had been having breakfast with Steve when he had taken the call that morning, so she knew there had been a suspicious death in the village. But at that time the details were sketchy and her husband had left so quickly that she was still unaware of the full story when at 3:30 p.m. she arrived for her hair appointment with Samantha Crouch at Helen Parkes Hair Salon.

'Hello, Penny,' said Samantha enthusiastically when she saw her enter the salon. 'Have you heard about Marcus Ardleigh?'

Unlike her husband, Penny was fully aware of the illustrious Marcus Ardleigh.

She shook her head. 'No, what's happened?'

'He's dead,' whispered Sam, as she guided Penny to the chair. 'They say he hanged himself last night. Although some people are saying he was murdered.'

Penny instantly surmised that the urgent case Steve had to rush to that morning was almost certainly the death of Ardleigh. She was intrigued to hear more of the gossip from Sam, but she had been married long enough to a policeman to know that she had to be very guarded in what she said. Particularly in a small village like Moulton Bank, where she knew that anything she said could be exaggerated and misrepresented. If he was in charge of the case, the last thing that Steve would want was for gossip to be spread based upon a careless remark from his wife.

'Really?' replied Penny. 'I hadn't heard. When did this all happen?'

'Hasn't Steve mentioned anything to you?' remarked Sam, who was clearly disappointed that Penny appeared to be less informed than she was about the death. 'He's definitely the investigating officer as some of the ladies this morning said they saw him at Ardleigh's house with the rest of the emergency services.'

Penny shrugged her shoulders. 'He may well be,' she replied. 'But I've not seen or spoken to Steve since he left the house this morning.'

'Bloody hell, Penny,' sighed Sam. 'I was looking forward to you coming in to give me the true facts.'

'Sorry,' replied Penny, 'I'm afraid I'm going to be no help to you at all in that case.'

Sam shook her head and smiled. 'And I suspect, even if you did know, you wouldn't tell me. Don't worry, I understand.'

Penny smiled. 'Well, to be honest,' she remarked, knowing she was just about to say something that was less than honest. 'Steve rarely discusses his cases with me so I probably won't know much more than you do even if he is the investigating officer.'

'Helen and I were wondering how Geraldine Ramsey will take it all,' continued Sam. 'She idolises him and we reckon she'll be devastated when she comes home. Mind you, without a wife or children, our bet is that he will have left pretty much everything to her, so she won't go short of a bob or two.'

'Who's Geraldine Ramsey?' Penny asked.

'She's Marcus's friend,' replied Sam. 'Word is that they weren't lovers or anything, much to her frustration, but they had been friends for years and she was always around at his house helping him clean the place, doing all his gardening and also doing all sorts of errands for him. Helen said she met her on Friday evening and she told Helen that she was going to Italy for a few weeks on holiday. So our guess is that she won't have heard about him dying yet.'

'How sad,' remarked Penny with genuine compassion in her voice. 'It sounds like it will be a terrible shock for her.'

'I suppose it will,' replied Sam, who was now starting to feel a little guilty for not treating the idea of Geraldine's almost inevitable feeling of loss more sympathetically. 'I suppose someone should really try and contact her.'

'Well, I'll mention it to Steve, when I see him this evening,' replied Penny.

'Anyway,' remarked Sam after a short pause in the conversation. 'Let's get started on your hair.' The stylist beckoned over the salon's trendy, well-groomed but lacklustre young trainee. 'Can you get Mrs Carmichael a coffee and wash her hair for me please, Sophie?'

Penny had often wondered why Helen Parkes continued to employ such a miserable and lethargic trainee. In all the time that she had been coming to the salon to have her hair styled, Penny couldn't ever remember seeing Sophie smile or look in the slightest bit interested in her work. Worse still, she was a very clumsy girl. Regrettably for Penny, today would be no exception. When eventually Sophie managed to bring a cup of coffee over to Penny, she'd already spilt much of it in the saucer. And when the hapless young junior ultimately started to wash her hair, Penny could feel the customary heavy spray of warm water cascading over her face and arms, which was now almost routine when she was left in the incapable hands of Sophie.

'Anyway, Sam Crouch,' Penny shouted across the salon, 'we've spoken enough about poor Mr Ardleigh. What other gossip can you share with me? Let's face it – nothing happens in this village without it sooner or later being discussed in here.'

*   *   *   *

Miranda Coyle sat down on the comfortable armchair in the executive room that she had booked at The Lindley Hotel. She had the TV turned on to the news channel, which was already starting to reveal to a wider audience the sketchy details of Marcus Ardleigh's death.

She knew that sooner rather than later she would be dragged into the media frenzy and required to make a comment. However, she was hoping that her whereabouts would not become common knowledge for at least another forty-eight hours, which would allow her to take control of the situation. She lit up another cigarette and once more read the bombshell of a letter that she had received that morning.

Chapter 7

It was almost four o'clock by the time Carmichael and his team managed to assemble in his small office.

'OK, Marc,' Carmichael proclaimed, 'what has the good doctor to say about Ardleigh's death?'

The team all turned to face Watson, who at long last was starting to feel like he was human once more. He opened up his pocket notebook and looked intently at the comments he had scribbled during his meeting with Dr Stock earlier in the day.

'Well, he has confirmed that Ardleigh died as a result of his neck being broken, which he maintains is totally in keeping with him being hanged. He put the time of death at between 9:30 p.m. and midnight last night.'

'That's quite specific,' remarked Carmichael. 'How can he be so sure?'

Watson shrugged his shoulders. 'I didn't ask and he didn't elaborate on how he came to this conclusion,' he confessed.

Carmichael nodded. 'I'm sure his full autopsy will clarify why he is able to be so precise. He can normally be trusted to be thorough, so for now I'm happy to accept what he is saying and understand why he is so sure later.'

'Precisely,' replied Watson, who was relieved that the boss had not pushed him more on the matter.

'So that means he was still alive when he should have been meeting Lazarus at The Railway Tavern,' Cooper pointed out.

'So does that put Hugo Lazarus in the clear?' Rachel asked. 'I think we're getting ahead of ourselves here,' said Carmichael, who was still keen to hear more of Stock's findings. 'Does Stock have an opinion as to whether Ardleigh committed suicide or whether he was murdered?' he asked, his eyes fixed intently on Watson. 'That's where it gets less certain,' replied Watson. 'Stock says he cannot explain the rope marks on Ardleigh's wrists, but they do look like they were made close to the time of death and are consistent with him being tied up.' 'But his hands were not tied when we found the body,' remarked Rachel. 'So if he was tied up, where is the cord?' 'Good question,' replied Watson. 'The SOCOs so far have been unable to find any length of rope or cord at the house that match the marks on Ardleigh's wrists.' 'Maybe the murderer took the cord with him,' suggested Cooper.

'Or maybe he just got the marks some other way and Marcus Ardleigh did commit suicide,' interrupted Rachel. 'My hunch is that he was murdered,' remarked Cooper. 'The marks are too suspicious; there is no reason for him to take his life and there was no suicide note. I think the chances are he was murdered.'

'Well, Dr Stock had one more nugget of information that may make you change your mind, Paul,' Watson said with the air of someone about to make a significant pronouncement. 'Stock maintains that Ardleigh was in the advanced stages of cancer. It was in his lungs, liver and stomach.'

'Would Ardleigh have known he had cancer?' Carmichael asked.

'I asked Stock that,' replied Watson smugly. 'He said that, although there were no signs that Ardleigh had been having chemotherapy, he was taking some pretty strong painkillers, so he is sure that Ardleigh knew he was very ill.'

Carmichael thought for a few seconds. 'I suppose the truth

is we don't know if he was murdered,' was his straightforward reply. 'But I think we have enough concerns to continue to treat this as a suspicious death. Do we all agree?' Carmichael's blue eyes scanned the room to gauge the views of the rest of his team. When it was clear that nobody was prepared to argue against him he looked back in the direction of Watson. 'Did Dr Stock say anything else that we should know about?'

Marc looked again at his notes.

'No, that's about it,' replied Watson.

* * * *

Robbie Carmichael was a hard worker and Mr Hayley had been so pleased with the young man's efforts that day, he had told him he could go home early.

'Take a tray of eggs for your mum,' he shouted over to Robbie. 'I'll see you in the morning.'

'Where are you off to?' enquired Spot On indignantly, when he saw Robbie taking off his blue overalls.

'Mr Hayley's said I can leave early today,' replied Robbie, 'and I'm taking some eggs for my mum.'

'Make sure you knock before you go in,' muttered Spot On cruelly. 'You don't want to catch her with her lover.'

Robbie laughed. 'What the hell are you on about, Spot On?'

To his surprise his chum didn't return the smile he had expected.

'It's not my place to say, lad,' replied Spot On, 'but you should know there are rumours going round about your mam and the publican at The Railway.'

Robbie couldn't believe his ears. He scowled back at Spot On and headed off down the lane, balancing the eggs precariously in his left hand while he texted Brooke with his right hand:

Lets go to Southport tonite. Meet u at the station at 6. XX.

It took Robbie Carmichael around fifteen minutes to reach the village high street, oblivious to the drama that had unfolded earlier in the day at Marcus Ardleigh's house. As he walked, Robbie's thoughts were only on what Spot On had said. He was angry with himself for not remaining longer at the farm and for not having pushed Spot On to be more specific about his allegations. Secretly he suspected that there might be some truth in what Spot On had said, though he was not ready to know the full truth.

Under normal circumstances Robbie would not have gone near The Railway Tavern on his way home; however, for some reason that afternoon his chosen route home included a small detour. As he passed the train station, he spied two figures lurking in the dappled shadow of the tall beech trees that lined the narrow pathway between the railway station and The Railway Tavern. At first he could not recognise who the people were. However, as he got nearer to the alleyway, he realised to his horror that the silhouettes belonged to his mum and Robbie Robertson.

As soon as he realised who they were, he stopped and hid behind the colossal beech at the end of the row. He peered round the trunk, being careful not to be seen, and strained his ears to try and catch what they were saying.

'Of course I won't say anything, you silly man,' he heard his mother say in a way that was as kind and affectionate as he had ever heard her. 'We go back for ever, Robbie, and you know I'll always be there for you.'

With that Penny took hold of the landlord's head and gently kissed him on his brow.

The young man at the end of the passage could not believe his eyes. His worst fears were now confirmed. Robbie could not bear to watch anymore and turned away to march the short distance to his house. As he did, he temporarily lost control of the tray he was carrying, allowing four of the eggs to fall and splatter on the floor. 'Bugger!' he muttered before taking himself and the remaining eggs back home.

* * * *

'So if he *was* murdered, who are our suspects and what's our motive?' Carmichael asked his three trusty officers.

'I think Lazarus has to be on the list,' said Watson, mainly to see Rachel's reaction. 'He's clearly got free access to the house and we only have his word that he was asked by Ardleigh to meet him in the pub last night.'

'I agree,' remarked Cooper. 'He has to be a potential suspect, although he did look genuinely troubled this morning.'

Carmichael nodded gently. 'I agree,' he said. 'But who else did Lazarus say knew where Ardleigh kept the key?'

Rachel Dalton opened up her pocketbook. 'He was sure there would be several but could only give me names of two other people who would have definitely known,' she said as she tried to locate their names. 'A man called Gordon Napier and he also mentioned a lady called Geraldine Ramsey.'

'Do we know anything about these people and their relationship with Ardleigh?' Carmichael asked.

'Well, Lazarus didn't say much about Geraldine Ramsey, but he did say that Napier, Ardleigh and he had all met years ago at Oxford, so they clearly go back ages,' replied Rachel. 'However, I'm not sure Napier's our man – when I was leaving the house earlier today a call came through from him. He didn't sound that happy and was clearly keen to speak with Ardleigh, but unless he was putting it on he certainly didn't know that Ardleigh was dead.'

'What did he say?' asked Carmichael, his curiosity plainly evident.

'I've got the tape here,' replied Rachel, who handed it to her boss.

Carmichael took the tape out of Rachel's hand. 'Old technology,' he remarked self-righteously. 'You can't beat it!' He then removed the tape from his ancient message recording machine and inserted the tape he had just been given by Rachel.

'It's Gordon. I've got your bloody letter and we need to talk. I need to know who these other damn people are. I can't wait until tomorrow so call me urgently.'

Carmichael ejected the tape and placed it on his desk. 'I suggest we start with Gordon Napier,' he remarked. 'Do you know where we can find him?'

'He works in the village,' replied Rachel. 'He owns the antiques shop on the High Street.'

'That would be the one Lazarus was outside earlier today,' remarked Cooper.

'I wonder what he was doing there,' said Carmichael.

'Oh, he was just going to tell Napier that Marcus was dead,' interjected Rachel. 'You see Lazarus was with me when the call came through at Ardleigh's house. He said he'd call in on Napier on his way home and give him the bad news.'

Carmichael stared in amazement at the young officer. 'And didn't it occur to you that we might want to talk with Napier before he and Lazarus were able to discuss Ardleigh's death?'

Rachel's cheeks turned crimson. 'No sir, sorry sir; I didn't think,' she replied sheepishly.

* * * *

Penny gave Robbie Robertson a lingering hug. When she finally released him she stepped back a pace. 'I'll come round tomorrow afternoon,' she said gently, her eyes never leaving his.

The landlord of The Railway Tavern watched intently as Penny sauntered slowly down the passage.

When she reached the main road Penny turned and smiled back at Robertson before making her way home.

She did not notice the broken eggs until her right foot had almost come down into the sticky mess.

'Yobs,' she muttered to herself, assuming that the mess below her was the sloppy remains of some local youths having an egg fight.

* * * *

Carmichael checked the time on his wristwatch. It was 4:35 p.m.

'OK,' he said, trying hard to mask his anger at Rachel's stupidity. 'You two try and track down Geraldine Ramsey,' he continued, pointing to Rachel Dalton and Cooper. 'I want to know where she was on Sunday and find out if she has any suggestions as to the identity of the murderer – that's assuming he was murdered.'

After receiving their instructions Cooper and Dalton made a hasty exit.

'If you find out anything that you feel is relevant, call me,' Carmichael shouted at them as they disappeared into the corridor. 'Otherwise I'll see you both here again at lunchtime tomorrow, when we can have another quick team meeting.'

'Don't be too hard on her,' remarked Watson, although secretly he had enjoyed seeing Rachel being admonished by the boss. 'She's still learning her trade and I'm sure she won't make that mistake again.'

'I bloody hope not,' snapped Carmichael. 'Particularly now she's with a sergeant who will be fit to guide her a bit better than you did. Don't think your hangover went unnoticed this morning. I blame you just as much as her for that cock-up. Actually, I blame you more.'

Watson wisely elected to say nothing.

'I hope you were not expecting to be home early tonight, Marc,' continued Carmichael, who by now had given up any attempt to try to appear controlled. 'We've got two people to go and see now because of Rachel's lapse in judgement today. So get your jacket.'

* * * *

On the way home Penny's mind remained deep in thought as she replayed over and over in her head her conversation with Robbie Robertson. She was so engrossed in her thoughts that she failed to see her husband's car approaching until it stopped and she heard Steve's unmistakable voice.

'I'm going to be late,' he shouted across the road. 'We've a few people we need to talk to this evening, so it could be seven or eight before we're through.'

'That's fine.' Penny replied with a faint but unconvincing smile. 'I'll see you later.'

Carmichael wound up his window and sped off towards Gordon Napier's antiques shop, leaving his wife to walk the few dozen yards back to their house.

'Is Mrs Carmichael OK?' enquired Watson.

'Yes,' Carmichael retorted tersely. 'She's absolutely fine – why do you ask?'

'Oh nothing,' replied Watson. 'She just did not seem her usual cheery self.'

Carmichael gazed back at his wife for a few seconds through the rear-view mirror. 'She probably has a thousand things on her mind,' he remarked flippantly. 'But she's fine.'

Chapter 8

In his youth, Gordon Napier had been a fit, lean, energetic young man who cut a dash amongst his fellow Oxford undergraduates. He had played rugby and tennis for his college and, with his long blond locks trailing in the wind as he sped around in his bright red MG, he was a very popular figure in the pubs and clubs of the town. Gordon was always to be seen at parties and more often than not with a different lady in tow. However, that was over thirty years ago and the passing years had not been too kind to Gordon. He was at least four stone heavier and, whether it was his forehead increasing or his hair gradually receding, he now felt it necessary to wear a toupee. In short, he was totally unrecognisable from the brash, handsome and confident young man who had graced the Oxford social scene in the 1970s.

Carmichael and Watson clambered out of the car and made their way up the short gravel drive that led to Napier's Antiques.

'It looks shut,' remarked Watson as they approached the door.

'If he was a close friend of Ardleigh's, I suspect he will have shut the shop when he learned of his old pal's death,' replied Carmichael, trying to give some logic to the scenario.

When Watson reached the door he tried the latch, which confirmed his earlier observation. He looked at his watch.

'The sign says they are open on Mondays until five thirty,

'so he should still be open for another twenty minutes,' he remarked.

Carmichael did not reply. He had wandered over to the small green and brown van that was parked on the drive. On the side of the van was printed in bold letters:

NAPIER'S ANTIQUES Est. 1984.
Antique Silver and Furniture Specialist
Invest in the past to pay for the future
Tel: Moulton Bank 833722

'Well, look at what we have here,' remarked Carmichael, who, when Watson turned around, could be seen intently peering through the rear window of the van.

'What's that?' asked Watson, who started to walk back towards the van.

'In the back of the van, Marc,' announced Carmichael. 'Take a look.'

Watson bent down to make a closer inspection of the van's contents.

'But it's empty,' exclaimed Watson in astonishment.

'Look a bit more closely,' Carmichael told the sergeant.

Watson stared keenly through the glass in an effort to find what his boss was talking about. 'All I can see is a few small lengths of blue nylon rope.'

'Exactly,' replied Carmichael. 'Just like the rope that hanged Ardleigh.'

'Oh yes, I see,' replied Watson as he realised what Carmichael was inferring.

'Can I help you, gentlemen?' boomed out a loud voice from the other side of the van.

Carmichael and Watson straightened their backs in unison.

'Mr Napier?' enquired Carmichael. 'My name is Inspector Carmichael and this is Sergeant Watson. Could we have few moments of your time?'

* * * *

When Penny arrived back at the house the front door was open and she could tell that Robbie was home as his mucky trainers had been abandoned on the doormat.

'Hi, everyone, I'm home,' she shouted down the hallway.

'Oh hi, Mum,' replied her eldest daughter, Jemma, who appeared from the living room.

'I can see that your brother's back,' remarked Penny, pointing to the training shoes.

'Yes,' replied Jemma with a shrug of her shoulders. 'But he's in a real bad mood. He's stropped off to get a shower.'

'Oh dear,' replied Penny, who was all too familiar with her son's moods. 'Someone probably upset him at work.'

'Well, if they did there's no need for him to bring his bad temper home,' Jemma announced before stomping up the stairs herself.

'It was easier when they were toddlers,' muttered Penny to herself as she tidied up her son's shoes and walked down the hallway to the kitchen.

Penny filled up the kettle and sat down at the large pine breakfast table, her thoughts once more drifting back to the other Robbie and the dilemma she was now in. As she did, she noticed the tray of eggs that her son had deposited on the worktop beside the cooker. She immediately gathered that these would have been a gift from Mr Hayley.

'I wonder why he didn't fill the tray,' she said to herself. 'It seems a bit strange to leave four spaces empty.'

* * * *

'Do you mind if we have a look at the rope in the back of your van?' Carmichael asked.

'What rope?' replied Napier with surprise.

'The blue nylon rope there,' confirmed Carmichael, pointing through the window.

Napier sauntered down to the back of the van and opened up the doors.

'It's not locked then?' observed Watson.

'No, I never bother really,' replied Napier. 'There's nothing ever left in there to steal.' He flung back the doors. 'Oh, I don't know how that got there; it's certainly not my rope,' he remarked with genuine astonishment.

'In that case, may we take it?' enquired Carmichael.

'Be my guest,' replied Napier. 'Why is it of such interest to you?'

Carmichael didn't answer Napier. 'Marc, get it bagged,' he instructed. 'There are some bags in the boot of my car.'

Watson ran back to Carmichael's BMW and returned a few moments later with a large plastic bag. He carefully climbed into the back of Napier's van and collected the two short lengths of rope, which he then sealed up and placed in the boot of Carmichael's car.

'Thank you for that, Mr Napier,' said Carmichael. 'Can we go inside? We have few questions we need to ask you about your friend Marcus Ardleigh and the message you left on his answering machine earlier today.'

Napier ushered the two police officers to the rear door of the antiques shop. Once inside, he took them through into his office and offered them a seat. 'How can I help you, Inspector?' he asked

'I understand that you are already aware of the death of Marcus Ardleigh,' began Carmichael. 'I believe that Hugo Lazarus came around earlier and told you.'

'That is correct,' replied Napier, who was looking quite shaken and uncomfortable.

'How well did you know Mr Ardleigh?' Carmichael asked.

'We knew each other for years,' replied Napier. 'We were at Oxford together in the 70s.'

'Really?' replied Carmichael. 'So how come two old friends from Oxford University both ended up in a small Lancashire village?'

'Good question, I suppose,' responded Napier. 'When we left Oxford I worked in the City for a while, but after a few years I couldn't take it any more so I decided to have a career change. I had made a few quid as a broker and, well, it seemed an attractive idea at the time.'

'But that doesn't explain how you came to set up shop in Moulton Bank?' Carmichael enquired.

Napier wriggled in his chair. 'Well, that was Marcus's suggestion,' Napier replied. 'He had happily settled here after university and we had kept in touch, so when I said I was looking for a rural location to set up my antiques business he suggested Moulton Bank.'

'Where are you originally from?' asked Watson. 'From your accent it's nowhere near here.'

'Kent,' replied Napier. 'Tunbridge Wells to be precise.'

Carmichael allowed the pause in the conversation to linger for a few moments before he suddenly spoke. 'So what was it that made you so annoyed with Mr Ardleigh that you called him this morning and left him that angry voice message?'

Napier shuffled nervously in his seat. 'It was a private matter between Marcus and me,' he replied. 'As Marcus is now sadly dead, it is of no consequence.'

Carmichael stared angrily back at Napier. 'We are treating Mr Ardleigh's death as suspicious and we have found some rope in your van which may implicate you in his death. My advice to you is that you cooperate fully with our enquiries and explain what it was that you were referring to when you called Mr Ardleigh this morning.'

Napier was noticeably shocked at hearing that he was a murder suspect.

'You have to be joking,' he exclaimed. 'Marcus and I go back years. He was my friend.'

'Then that's all the more reason why you should be totally honest with us, Mr Napier,' suggested Watson. 'If you've nothing to hide, you've nothing to fear.'

Napier considered his position for few seconds before asking. 'Am I under arrest?'

Carmichael smiled. 'No, you are not under arrest but we would like you to help us with our enquiries. You can do that here and now, or maybe you'd like to join us at Kirkwood Police Station, where we could finish off our discussions.'

'OK,' replied Napier, who realised that he was cornered and needed to be more cooperative with the two officers. 'I got this in the post this morning from Marcus.'

Napier pulled open the desk drawer and handed over to Carmichael the letter he had received.

Carmichael took the letter out of Napier's clammy hand and started to read.

> 28 Station Road
> Moulton Bank
> Lancashire
> Friday, 13th August
>
> My dear friend Gordon,
> I posted three letters today, the one you are about to read plus two others. These letters are identical as you all have one thing in common, a unique but very damaging secret that none of you would wish to be made public.
> After careful consideration I feel I am no longer able to keep these secrets. I am hereby inviting you all to meet my solicitor and me in the Sefton Suite at The Lindley Hotel in Moulton Bank this coming Tuesday, 17th August at 8 p.m. At this meeting we will divulge to all of you the three secrets, and I

47

will explain in more detail my reasons for sharing them with all of you.

I'm sure that you are feeling uncomfortable about your own secret being exposed, which I fully understand; however, I believe this is the right time for all three of these secrets to be made public.

I sincerely urge you to attend the meeting on Tuesday. Please understand that if you feel, for whatever reason, you cannot attend, I will still reveal to those who do attend, all three of the secrets.

Yours,

Marcus.

Carmichael handed the letter to Watson. 'You better read this, Marc,' he remarked, with a look of astonishment.

While Watson studied the letter, Carmichael continued to question Gordon Napier. 'Do you have the envelope this was sent in?' he asked.

'It will be in the waste-paper bin,' replied Napier, who immediately started to rummage in the bin. 'Here it is,' he said as he pulled out the envelope, the address written in Ardleigh's unique script.

Carmichael carefully took the envelope from Napier and looked at the postmark. 'It was posted here in Moulton Bank on Saturday,' he remarked just as Watson was finishing the letter.

'So what is your murky secret, Mr Napier?' Watson asked bluntly.

'That's the thing,' replied Napier. 'I have no idea what he is talking about. And before you ask, I've also no idea who the other two people are either.'

'I find that quite hard to believe, Mr Napier,' Carmichael remarked. 'If you did not know what Marcus was referring to in his letter, why were you so angry in your voice message?'

'I wasn't angry,' replied Napier. 'I was unhappy at what Marcus had done and the theatrical manner in which he had chosen to communicate this message, but I wouldn't say I was angry. I was confused, if anything – I can assure you I had, and still have, no idea what secret he is referring to.'

Carmichael didn't believe Napier, but could sense that the antiques dealer was not about to divulge his secret. 'So where were you yesterday evening and last night?' he asked.

'I was here,' replied Napier. 'I have a flat above the shop and I was in all night.'

'Can anybody vouch for you,' Watson asked.

Napier slowly shook his head. 'No, I live alone.'

'So how do you explain the rope being in your van, Mr Napier?' Carmichael asked.

'I can't,' replied Napier. 'It certainly wasn't there yesterday afternoon when I unloaded a table and some boxes of china I bought at an auction in Lancaster on Saturday.'

'So are you trying to tell us that it was planted in your van?' remarked Watson sarcastically.

'That's what it looks like,' replied Napier. 'When it's empty, my van's always unlocked.'

Carmichael thought for a moment. 'I think you need to come down to the station tomorrow morning and make a statement,' he remarked. 'In the meantime we'll take the rope and the letter as evidence.'

'Of course,' replied Napier, who appeared relieved that he wasn't being arrested.

'I'd advise you spend a bit of time this evening thinking seriously about what this secret might be,' continued Carmichael. 'It would be in your interest if you could remember, even if it's embarrassing.'

With that, Carmichael rose from the chair, shook Gordon Napier by the hand and with Watson close behind, walked back towards the rear entrance of the antiques shop.

'Just one more question,' Carmichael asked as they reached the door. 'Do you know who Ardleigh's solicitor is?'

Napier nodded his head. 'Oh yes,' he replied, 'I know Ruben Kenyon.'

As it happened, Carmichael also knew Ruben Kenyon, as he and Penny had registered their own wills with the village solicitor only a few months earlier, but from Napier's tone Carmichael surmised that the antiques dealer was not one of Kenyon's greatest fans.

'Thank you,' replied Carmichael. 'We'll see you in the morning at Kirkwood Police Station then?'

Napier nodded. 'Yes, of course,' he replied in the most convincing voice he could muster.

'Aren't we going to arrest him?' remarked Watson as soon as they were out of earshot of the portly antiques dealer.

'On what charge?' replied Carmichael. 'Not being totally honest with us! No, we need more than just a rope that looks similar to the one used to hang Marcus Ardleigh to charge him. Let's get the rope and the letter all off to forensics tonight and see what they say. We can decide what to do with Napier in the morning when we've had some results and we've taken his statement.'

Watson nodded. 'OK,' he replied.

The two officers walked down the path to Carmichael's BMW.

'Does everyone leave their car doors open and front door keys where anyone can find them in Moulton Bank?' Carmichael remarked sarcastically.

Watson smiled. 'Not everyone, but a lot do.'

Carmichael shook his head in disbelief.

'So what do we do now?' Watson asked. 'Do you still want to go and see Lazarus again?'

Carmichael looked at his watch and then considered his options. 'It's getting on now,' he remarked. 'I guess Lazarus can wait until tomorrow, Marc. You take my car and deliver the rope and the letter to forensics. Tell them to look at them both urgently. Then you can call it a day.'

Carmichael handed Watson the envelope and his car keys.

'So what are you going to do?' Watson asked.

'I'm going to walk home, but on the way I'll see if Ruben Kenyon is in his office.'

Watson took the keys from his boss and opened the car door.

'Do you want me to drop you off at the solicitors'?' he asked. 'It's on the way.'

'Err, no thank you, Marc,' replied Carmichael, who had already started to amble away. 'The walk will do me good. Mind you, I'll be needing the car in the morning. Drop the keys through my letterbox this evening.'

Watson smiled. 'No problem, sir.'

Chapter 9

Lyn Osborne had left the offices of Ogilvy, Cave and Kenyon at 5:00 p.m. on the dot, as was her customary habit. In the space of the next 90 minutes the rest of the staff of the small village law firm had all, one by one, made their way home, too. That was, all except Ruben Kenyon, who remained cocooned in his office with the door firmly shut.

At their last meeting only the week before, he had been given a very precise directive by his client about the manner in which Tuesday evening's meeting was to be conducted and he had spent the afternoon going over these instructions. He had also been provided with a sealed envelope by Marcus that he had been told could only be opened should anything untoward happen to his friend prior to the meeting.

At the time Ruben had considered Ardleigh to be totally paranoid and had told him so. However, now that the vivid suspicions his client cum friend had expressed about being in danger had been realised, Ruben felt rather foolish at having not taken Ardleigh's concerns more seriously, though in truth he felt no real sadness at his parting. Over and over again, Kenyon read, and then re-read the short letter that Marcus had left him. As his long-serving solicitor, part of him felt that he should just carry out his client's wishes; but another part of him had other ideas. After deliberating for almost two hours, Kenyon concluded that he should do what he always did when he was unsure – that was to sleep on it.

At just before 6:30 p.m., the solicitor decided to call it a day. It was at that moment that his telephone rang.

'Ruben Kenyon,' he announced as he placed the receiver to his right ear.

He listened for a few moments before replying.

'Yes of course,' he said as he gazed up at the large clock on his office wall. 'I could be there in about twenty minutes.'

'I'm not sure that would be totally ethical,' he said, although his objection was not that forcefully voiced.

'You may be right and circumstances certainly have now changed,' he said after listening intently to his caller.

'I'll bring everything with me and we can discuss what the best option is for all of us,' he concluded. 'I'll certainly be with you before seven.'

Kenyon replaced the handset, collected the various papers that he had spread out on top of his desk and, having stuffed them all into his briefcase, quickly made his way down the stairs, out of the office and into his gleaming bottle-green Bentley.

* * * *

It was 6:45 p.m. when Carmichael finally arrived at the offices of Ogilvy, Cave and Kenyon. It was a beautiful, calm summer's evening and even at that time of the day the sun remained warm, bright and generous. As he slowly strolled up the steep path that led to the front door of the solicitors' practice, Carmichael continued to consider the events of the day. He was still quite prepared to accept that Ardleigh's death was nothing more than another sad suicide, but ever since he'd seen the lifeless body of Marcus Ardleigh that morning as it dangled from the banister, he had instinctively felt all was not quite right.

Had Carmichael taken the lift that Watson had offered him, he may have managed to just catch Ruben Kenyon before he left the office and headed off in his car towards Ambient Hill.

But, of course, Carmichael had elected to walk and as a result, by the time he tried the solicitors' door, it was patently obvious that the practice was well and truly shut for the evening.

'He can wait until tomorrow,' Carmichael mumbled to himself before setting off on the short walk that would see him home and give him ten more valuable minutes to consider his tactics for the following day.

Chapter 10

With tears in her eyes, Penny gazed uneasily out of the upstairs window. She didn't like being deceitful with Steve, but her head was consumed with thoughts of Robbie Robertson and the very personal conversation they had had that afternoon. She had never known her childhood friend to be so open about his feelings. He had always been so reserved. But it was his candour and the nature of the disclosure he had made to her that convinced Penny she must withhold the truth from her husband.

When she eventually saw Steve's unmistakeable figure ambling towards their house, she took a deep breath and, with a couple of quick dabs from her handkerchief, attempted to erase away any traces of her having been crying.

She quickly checked herself in the mirror, put on her best smile and strode along the hallway and down the stairs.

Carmichael's thoughts were still on the case as he entered the house. Although his wife was at the door to greet him, he hardly noticed her and was certainly oblivious to her reddened eyes and her unusually nervous demeanour.

'Hi, darling,' he said as he gave her a pathetically weak hug. 'Have you heard about Ardleigh?'

Carmichael fully expected his wife would know much more about the dead man than he, given that she was born and bred in Moulton Bank, and generally much more in touch with the village life and gossip than him.

'Yes I did,' replied Penny, who was very pleased her

husband was seemingly unaware that she was not her normal cheery self. 'I was in the hairdresser's today and it's the talk of the village. I assume you're leading the enquiry?'

'Yep,' replied Carmichael. 'It's mine all right.'

'So was it suicide?' Penny asked.

'We're not sure,' replied Carmichael. 'However, from what we can see, it has all the signs of being a murder made out to be a suicide.'

'Good grief,' remarked Penny. 'Let me pour you a drink and you can tell me more.'

* * * *

Ruben Kenyon's conspicuous green Bentley glided into the empty car park that lay next to the C of E church on Ambient Hill. He pressed the small button on the armrest which silently wound down the window, before turning off the engine and lighting up an expensive, thick Cuban cigar.

He had taken only a few puffs before he glanced at his watch for the first time. It was 7:10 p.m.

At 7:30 p.m. he finally finished his smoke. It was then that the passenger door opened. 'I see your timekeeping hasn't improved,' Kenyon said in an annoyingly patronising tone. 'I thought we said seven.'

* * * *

'To tell you the truth,' remarked Carmichael, as he took a small sip of amber liquid from his whisky glass, 'until this morning I'd never heard of Marcus Ardleigh.'

'You're unbelievable,' replied Penny with a look of astonishment. 'He's been a local celebrity here for ages. He was one of Maggie Thatcher's advisers when she was in number 10. He's written loads of books and he's been on the TV dozens of times. How you cannot have heard of him is beyond me.'

Carmichael shrugged his shoulders and took another sip of whisky.

'Come on, let's Google him,' continued Penny as she stood up and walked purposely over to the computer terminal in the corner of the room.

Carmichael got up slowly from his armchair and walked over to where his wife was now sitting and leaned over her as she typed the name Marcus Ardleigh into the Google search engine.

* * * *

His business successfully concluded, Ruben Kenyon remained alone in his Bentley contemplating how he should manage the meeting the following evening now that he had agreed to exclude one of the three people whom Ardleigh had invited. He knew he would have his work cut out altering all the documents to cover up this change, but he did not mind losing a night's sleep, particularly as the deal he had just made would be making him fifty grand. He turned on his mobile and dialled his home number.

'Hello, darling,' he said as soon as his wife had picked up the phone. 'I'm going to have to work late this evening. I've so much I need to get done regarding poor Marcus's estate. I'll try and be as quick as I can but it's going to be very late before I'm home. It may even be well into the early hours.'

Having finished his call, Ruben Kenyon switched on the engine and glided slowly out of the car park and down Ambient Hill towards Moulton Bank. He took no notice of the headlights of the pursuing car that would remain behind him at a constant distance of thirty metres as he returned to his office.

* * * *

57

'Here you go,' announced Penny as she pointed at the screen. 'Read this.'

Carmichael peered intently at the Wikipedia article on the life and career of Marcus Ardleigh.

'Born 30 March 1949 in Great Missenden in Buckinghamshire,' mumbled Carmichael over his wife's shoulder. 'Is a British academic, studied at Oriel College, Oxford, former professor at Oxford and lecturer of Mathematics at Harvard and Oxford Universities. From 1983 to 1987 he was an advisor to Prime Minister Thatcher and was also an advisor to Prime Minister Blair from 1998 to 2004.'

'Batted for both sides then,' remarked Penny, who had not known that Ardleigh had also been on Tony Blair's payroll.

Her husband made no comment as he was too engrossed in the very detailed synopsis on Marcus Ardleigh laid out on the screen in front of him.

'Is the author of several books on mathematics and wrote two highly acclaimed books on the use of probability analysis within business and in the military,' continued Carmichael more loudly. 'The former having sold in excess of twenty thousand copies worldwide and regarded as a must-read by many distinguished business leaders.'

'So he wouldn't have been short of a few bob then,' interrupted Penny, as she stood up and headed in the direction of the hallway to answer the phone which had just started to ring.

'I'll have to check that out,' replied Carmichael, who, without taking his eyes off the screen, sat down in the seat his wife had just vacated and continued to read. 'Marcus Ardleigh is a keen patron of the arts, an avid theatregoer and a practising Roman Catholic. He retired in 2004, but is still an active after-dinner speaker.'

'That reminds me,' announced Penny, who suddenly remembered her conversation with Sam Crouch at the hairdresser's. 'Apparently a very good friend of his is a lady called Geraldine Ramsey. According to Sam, they are very close but she's on holiday at the moment.'

'Thanks,' replied Carmichael. 'Her name's come up already today. We must talk to her as soon as we can.'

Penny did not hear her husband's last sentence as it coincided with her picking up the receiver.

Carmichael despatched the Wikipedia article off to the printer as he wanted to make sure he had a hard copy to take to the station in the morning. As he did so, he listened to try and make out whom his wife was talking to. He strained hard to hear her but was unsuccessful.

'Look,' she whispered down the phone, 'Steve's here – I can't talk now. I'll ring you in the morning.'

Penny replaced the receiver and returned to the living room where she found her husband retrieving the three A4 sheets of paper that had vomited out of the printer and fallen in an untidy heap on the living-room floor.

'Who was that?' he asked.

'Err, nobody you know,' replied Penny, trying hard to appear nonchalant. 'It was just one of the teachers from school wanting to know if I'd help out on one of the stalls at the summer fair this year.'

'And will you?' her husband asked.

'I said no,' said Penny. 'I think it clashes with the day Natalie wants me to take her to see that pop group in Southport.'

'Right,' remarked Carmichael, who could sense that Penny was quite agitated. 'Is everything OK?'

'Absolutely,' responded Penny enthusiastically. 'You know me, I'm just not that good at saying no.'

'I see,' replied Carmichael, who was not totally convinced that he was being told the whole story. 'As long as you are sure that everything is OK.'

'It is,' said Penny without any hesitation. 'Everything is fine.'

Chapter 11

Tuesday 17th August

'Good morning, young man,' proclaimed Carmichael in a jovial, albeit slightly sarcastic tone. 'It's not often I have the pleasure of your company at breakfast time.'

Bleary-eyed and still half asleep, Robbie Carmichael didn't bother to look up from his bowl of cereal to give his father the satisfaction of knowing that his comments had registered.

'What time did you get in last night?' continued his father as he filled up the kettle from the gushing kitchen tap. 'I didn't hear you.'

'Dunno,' muttered Robbie. 'About twelve I guess.'

'More like one I expect,' replied Carmichael. 'I was still up until just around midnight.'

'May have been,' retorted Robbie. 'I didn't check.'

'How's it going at the farm?' enquired Carmichael, who could see that his son was in no mood to debate his movements the previous evening.

'It's actually quite good,' replied Robbie. 'The work's really hard, but Mr Hayley's been spot on and the pay's brilliant.'

'Spot on,' aped Carmichael. 'Sounds like you've fallen on your feet there, son.'

'Yep,' replied Robbie, as he gazed up at the kitchen clock. 'But he'll not be that pleased if I'm late so I need to be off.'

'Don't worry,' replied Carmichael. 'I'll give you a lift. I

have to see someone in the village before I go to the office so I can drop you off if you like.'

'Great,' replied Robbie, who for the first time that morning took the trouble to look up at his father. 'I've got to be there in twenty-five minutes though!'

'That's OK,' said Carmichael. 'I'll just grab a quick coffee and we can be off.'

Ten minutes later, Steve and Robbie Carmichael were heading towards Mr Hayley's farm at the end of Wood Lane.

As soon as she heard the sound of the car pulling out of the driveway, Penny rushed downstairs and dialled the mobile number of the landlord of The Railway Tavern.

* * * *

Miranda Coyle's distinctive Lotus sped down the long gravel drive and out of the front gate of The Lindley Hotel. 'I've concluded my business here and I'll be at the office in about an hour,' she announced to her long-suffering PA. 'I know I asked you to cancel all my meetings for today, but that was yesterday. I will be available after all, so call around everybody and tell them they are reinstated.' As usual, Miranda did not wait for a response and ended the call abruptly by pressing the call-end button on her steering wheel.

Miranda loved speeding; it gave her a sense of power. In spite of numerous warnings from friends and family, and with total disregard of the fact that she already had nine points on her licence, Miranda's driving that morning was, in keeping with her normal habit, fast and reckless. Although the roads were winding and unfamiliar to her, Miranda drove without any regard for either her own safety or for the wellbeing of other road users. For the first two miles of her journey this was not an issue. However, when she decided to cut a tight bend doing forty-five miles an hour, she almost came to grief.

'What the …!,' shouted Carmichael as he slammed on the brakes, swerved, and brought his car to rest in the long grass on the near side of the road.

Miranda stopped about 30 yards down the road, but remained in her seat and kept the engine running. Using her wing mirror, she looked back to see if the occupants of the car that she had forced off the road were OK.

Carmichael's initial reaction was to make sure Robbie was unhurt. As soon as he was happy that they had both survived the ordeal unscathed, he jumped out of the car and marched swiftly towards the offending vehicle.

Once Miranda could see that there was no real damage, she pushed the lever hard into first gear and sped off.

'Hey, you idiot, wait!' he shouted as he waved his fist in the direction of the disappearing tangerine sports car. 'Unbelievable,' he muttered to himself.

By the time he arrived back at his own car Robbie had also clambered out and was leaning against the boot.

'Did you get the car's reg, Dad?' he asked.

'No,' replied Carmichael. 'It was too far away.'

Robbie laughed. 'You need your eyes testing – it was RE08FKX,' he replied with a smug grin of satisfaction.

'Good lad,' replied his father as he scribbled down the registration and the time into his pocketbook. 'If you're sure you're OK, I'll take you to Hayley's farm. We can call the number in on the way and get that nutcase picked up.'

Father and son then clambered back into the black BMW and headed off in the direction of Wood Lane.

* * * *

Lyn Osborne's screams could be heard within a radius of several hundred yards from the small secluded car park at the rear of the offices of Ogilvy, Cave and Kenyon. Within a matter of moments she had been joined by the village postman, an elderly man who had been out walking his dog and a couple of the residents of the adjacent houses. There was no doubt that Ruben Kenyon was dead. His blood-covered torso hung half out of the open door of his Bentley, his mouth wide open and his eyes bulging almost out of their sockets. Had it not been for the fact that his seatbelt was still on he would have certainly fallen completely out of the blood-spattered car. But the harness was in place, which made the sight that poor Mrs Osborne had found that morning even more distressing.

* * * *

By the time Carmichael reached Hayley's farm, he had already phoned through to the station the registration of the Lotus Evora.

'Quite an eventful morning,' Carmichael said as his son climbed out of the door. 'That'll give you something to tell your mum when you get home.'

'I suspect she'll be too preoccupied with other things,' muttered Robbie back at his father.

Carmichael was taken aback by what his son had just said. 'What do you mean?' he enquired.

'Nothing,' replied Robbie, who just shrugged his shoulders.

'No, you wouldn't just say what you said for no reason,' remarked Carmichael, who was now becoming quite agitated. 'What are you implying, Robbie?'

Robbie looked back at his father in total disbelief. 'You mean you haven't noticed?' he exclaimed. 'There's something going on with her and it involves your mate the landlord at The Railway Tavern. Surely you must have noticed!'

Carmichael could not believe what he was hearing. 'Robbie, what are you talking about?' he said.

'I don't know exactly,' Robbie replied. 'But something's

not right between them. My guess is it's something that goes back years.'

'Robbie!' exclaimed Carmichael with an air of total disbelief in his voice. 'That's your mother you're talking about. Are you trying to tell me that she's having an affair with Robbie Robertson?'

'You need to ask her yourself,' retorted Robbie angrily. 'And when you do, you might want to ask her how I was given his name and also what she was doing cuddling up to him yesterday afternoon. I saw them, Dad.'

Carmichael shook his head in disbelief. 'This is nonsense, Robbie,' he said firmly. 'Your mother and Robbie Robertson are just old friends.'

'Look, I'll be late for work; I've got to go,' said Robbie, who felt relieved to have at last got this off his chest, but at the same time felt dreadful for being the one to have to break the news to his father.

Before Carmichael could say anything more his son had hurried away across the farmyard. Carmichael sat in complete silence as he watched him disappear into one of the dusty wooden outhouses.

For more than five minutes he did not move as he contemplated what he had just been told. Had his son not been so sure in what he was saying, Carmichael would have just laughed it off and thought no more about it, but he had been sure and it was clearly something that Carmichael could see was troubling young Robbie.

As he sat there, Carmichael then recalled the comment Watson had made to him the day before when he'd suggested that something was the matter with Penny. He speculated whether his sergeant actually knew something and it was his way of checking to see if Carmichael was aware. Then, the even more alarming thought raced through his head that maybe everyone knew and it was just him that was still in the dark.

There is no way of telling how long Steve Carmichael would have sat alone in his car pondering his son's words. However, his thoughts were diverted when he received a call from the station to tell him that a body had just been discovered in the car park of the offices of Ogilvy, Cave and Kenyon.

'Bugger!' cursed Carmichael aloud. His instinct told him that it would be Kenyon, the very man he was planning to talk to once he'd dropped off his son.

Chapter 12

It took Carmichael little more than ten minutes to reach the crime scene, where he joined Cooper, Watson and Rachel Dalton who had all arrived together a few minutes earlier. Dr Stock was also there, bent over in his white overalls, carefully scrutinising the deep hole in the side of Ruben Kenyon's head.

'Morning, everyone,' announced Carmichael abruptly. 'So what's the story here?'

'It's Ruben Kenyon, one of the senior partners at the solicitors' practice,' replied Rachel, who as she spoke, pointed towards the offices of Ogilvy, Cave and Kenyon. 'He was found this morning by Mrs Osborne, his secretary. It looks like he was bludgeoned to death last night.'

'Young lady,' retorted Stock condescendingly. 'I think you should leave it to me to conduct the forensic analysis. After all, it's what I'm paid to do.' As he spoke, Stock turned his head in her direction and gave Rachel a disapproving look, which made the young DC's face redden.

'And what might your initial diagnosis be?' enquired Carmichael as calmly as he could.

'I won't know for certain until I get him back to the lab, but I think it's reasonable to say that he died from a single blow to his left temple with a hard implement, and before you ask, I'd hazard a guess that he died between seven and eleven last night.'

'So Rachel's totally unscientific assumption was about right,' muttered Watson to Cooper.

Carmichael took a close look at the wound on the side of the dead man's head. 'It must have taken some force to do that,' he observed.

Stock nodded. 'Yes, a considerable force I'd say. Whoever did this was very strong,' replied Stock. 'Although I suppose they could have done it as they sat next to him in the car, I would postulate that he was struck by a heavy, hard object through the open passenger window. Maybe a metal pole of some description.'

Carmichael walked around to the other side of the Bentley, where he could see that the passenger window was open.

'So he parked here, with the window down and the killer lunged at him through the open window with a metal bar that struck him on the side of the head. Is that what you think happened, Dr Stock?' enquired Carmichael.

'It's a possibility,' replied Stock. 'I'll hopefully be able to give you more information once I've got the body back to the pathology lab and I can take a better look at the angle of the blow.'

Carmichael nodded and wandered back to where his three officers were standing. 'With Kenyon being Marcus Ardleigh's solicitor I think it's a safe bet to say that the two deaths are linked,' he said. 'Rachel and Cooper, I want you to take Mrs Osborne's statement and then spend the rest of the morning going through Kenyon's filing cabinets and also anything he had on his laptop. I particularly want to find Ardleigh's will and anything that relates to the meeting that Ardleigh had set up this evening at The Lindley Hotel.'

DC Dalton and Sergeant Cooper nodded.

'Watson and I will pay a visit to The Lindley Hotel, but first I think we need to go and see Mr Napier again,' continued Carmichael. 'I'd like to see what sort of alibi he has for last night.'

Having been given their instructions, Rachel and Cooper walked over to the corner of the car park where Mrs Osborne was sitting on a wall, being comforted by a WPC.

'We'll meet at the station for a debrief at one thirty,' Carmichael shouted over to the two officers.

'Do you think you'll have any results from the rope and letter we dropped into you last night?' Carmichael asked Stock. 'Also, I'd like to see the full autopsy report from you on Marcus Ardleigh and your preliminary findings for this murder. Is there any chance of getting these both done by one thirty this afternoon?'

Stock gazed across at Carmichael with a look of incredulity. 'I'll have Ardleigh's autopsy report to you by then, but I'm not prepared to commit to anything over and above that,' he replied sternly. 'I'll do my best, but my priority is accuracy, not meeting your unattainable targets, Carmichael.'

'I understand,' replied Carmichael with a smile as he started to walk away towards his car. 'But I'm sure you can understand the importance of this information. We have a killer out there, so it's no time to be dithering.'

'Inspector,' replied Stock in a calm but clear voice, 'I can assure you that we will be as expeditious as we can and, having worked with you on many other cases in the last few years, I'm fully aware that for some inexplicable reason your murderers more often than not are serial killers, so for the wellbeing of the poor residents of Moulton Bank I'll be as quick as I can.'

Carmichael's smile widened on hearing Stock's words. He liked the old pathologist and, although he knew he would never get Stock to give him a firm guarantee to meet his timing plans, he was pretty certain that the information he wanted would be with him by one thirty that afternoon.

* * * *

As soon as Watson and Carmichael had climbed into Carmichael's BMW, the mobile started to ring over the car's sound system.

'Hello, sir,' said the voice at the other end. 'It's WPC Greening here. I've got back the trace on that licence plate you called in earlier. It belongs to a lady by the name of Miranda Coyle. She lives in Salford Quays in Manchester. Do you want the address?'

'Can you send it to me by email, please,' replied Carmichael. 'I'll follow it up later when I'm back in the office.'

'I'll do it now, sir,' replied the WPC before ending the call.

'Miranda Coyle,' remarked Watson as soon as the call had ended. 'Is that the same Miranda Coyle who works in the fashion industry?'

'I've no idea,' replied Carmichael. 'All I know is she drives a flash Lotus car and was nearly responsible for the death of me and my son this morning. She's a menace.'

Watson nodded but didn't reply.

'Anyway,' continued Carmichael. 'How come you've heard of her? I didn't know you were a big fashion expert.'

Watson laughed. 'No, it's the wife,' he replied. 'She's a big fan of Miranda Coyle – she does have a couple of her dresses. They are bloody expensive, I can tell you.'

*   *   *   *

Geraldine Ramsey was enjoying her vacation in her five-star luxury hotel situated on the banks of Lake Garda. She loved Italy and had holidayed there many times, although this was the first time she had been to that particular part of the country. As she lay back on her lounger and basked in the warm morning sun, the young, ever attentive waiter crept up on her. 'I have yesterday's *Guardian*, madam,' he said in his strong Italian accent.

'Oh thank you, Lucio,' replied Geraldine, her appreciation quite apparent in her voice. 'That's really ever so kind of you.'

She took the newspaper from the waiter with a generous smile, rested it on the small wrought-iron table next to her and resumed her relaxed pose.

* * * *

To get to Gordon Napier's antiques shop Carmichael had to drive past The Railway Tavern. As he did so, Carmichael slowed down slightly and took a quick sideways look through the large window into the lounge bar, the room he always frequented when he fancied a drink.

'Did you see that?' Watson blurted out abruptly.

'What?' replied Carmichael, whose eyes were still focused on the pub and his mind preoccupied with rerunning the conversation he had that morning with his son.

'Isn't that Lazarus?' replied Watson, pointing down the street where a furtive-looking Hugo Lazarus was making his exit from Napier's drive, on an old black bicycle. 'He looks very suspicious, like he's not keen to be seen.'

Carmichael turned his attention to the vision of Hugo Lazarus who was slowly and very awkwardly cycling off down the High Street. 'He's certainly no cyclist,' he replied. 'And that boneshaker has seen better days.'

Watson chortled. 'I wonder what he was doing there?' he said.

'Probably bringing Napier the news of Ruben Kenyon's untimely death,' replied Carmichael, 'although my guess is that our Mr Napier may have been all too aware of it already.'

'Shall we stop him and talk to him?' enquired Watson.

'No, he can wait,' replied Carmichael. 'It's Napier I want to talk to.'

Carmichael did not see his wife surreptitiously slip down the narrow passageway next to The Railway Tavern and sneakily enter the pub through the side door. However, unbeknown to Penny, her covert entrance into the pub didn't pass totally unnoticed. Helen Parkes, the owner of the village hairdresser's, spied Penny and, by the way Penny was acting, had instantly concluded that the police inspector's wife was trying hard to conceal her movements that morning.

* * * *

Cooper had left Rachel to take Mrs Osborne's statement and had started poring through the hundreds of files in Kenyon's office.

'This will take for ever,' he muttered to himself.

* * * *

Napier's van wasn't on the drive when Carmichael and Watson arrived, and although, according to the opening times listed in the shop window, the shop should have been open, it was abundantly clear that Napier was out.

'What now?' enquired Watson after having spent a good few minutes hammering on the door to no avail. 'Shall I break in?'

'No,' replied Carmichael. 'His van isn't here, so my guess is he is genuinely out this time. Let's get off to The Lindley Hotel. Our meeting with Mr Napier will just have to be put on hold for a wee while.'

The two officers sauntered back to the car and sped off down the road in the direction of The Lindley Hotel.

*　*　*　*

Within half an hour of Penny entering The Railway Tavern, Helen Parkes had mentioned what she had seen to all her staff and her three customers. By the end of the day her salacious observation would be common knowledge throughout the village.

Chapter 13

The Lindley Hotel and Spa was the premier hotel in the area, and because of its status, every function of any note was invariably held at The Lindley.

Carmichael knew the hotel well, having had cause to interview the staff, and take a look at its CCTV tapes in an earlier murder case. He was greeted by Sarah Pennington, the receptionist he'd met previously.

'Oh good morning, Inspector,' said Sarah in her familiar soft voice. 'It's so nice to see you again. I do hope your visit today is under better circumstances than our last meeting?'

'Regrettably no,' replied Carmichael, who held out his hand. 'Sergeant Watson and I need to talk to someone about a meeting that was arranged for this evening at eight o'clock.'

'Which meeting would that be?' enquired Sarah.

'It will probably have been booked either in the name of Marcus Ardleigh or Ruben Kenyon,' replied Carmichael.

'We certainly have nothing booked under Mr Ardleigh's name,' replied Sarah, without any need to refer to the computer in front of her. 'It was awful news about his suicide and since he was such a well-known person it would have been all over the hotel if he had booked a meeting room. I'll check for the other gentleman, though.'

Sarah Pennington's eyes studied the screen in front of her for a few moments.

'Ah here it is,' she announced after a short period of

searching. 'Mr Kenyon booked the Sefton Suite from seven until midnight. It looks like it's just the room; there's no food or drinks booked, which is quite unusual.'

Carmichael glanced across at Watson before returning his attention to the tall and imposing receptionist.

'Do you have a guest list for the meeting?' he asked.

Sarah Pennington shook her head. 'I'm afraid not,' she replied. 'The Sefton is our smallest meeting room. It can only comfortably accommodate ten people, so it must have been a fairly small party. Is there anything that the hotel should know about this booking, Inspector Carmichael?'

Carmichael elected to ignore Sarah's question. 'And to your knowledge has anyone booked into the hotel specifically to attend the meeting?' he enquired.

Again Sarah shook her head. 'Not that I am aware of,' she replied.

'Do you think I could take a look at the room?' Carmichael asked. 'And while I am doing that, do you think my sergeant here could just make a note of the guests who have checked in during the last twenty-four hours, and those who are booked to check in today?'

'Of course,' replied Sarah, who was now getting quite curious as to the reason for Carmichael's requests.

She picked up the telephone, dialled one number and summoned the porter to the desk. Within a matter of seconds a thin elderly man in a smart purple uniform arrived.

'Matthew, can you please take this gentleman to the Sefton Suite,' she instructed.

Matthew nodded dutifully and held his right arm out in the direction of the far end of the corridor. 'If you would care to follow me, sir,' he said humbly. 'It's this way.'

As soon as Carmichael was halfway down the long corridor, Sarah Pennington started to type instructions frantically into her computer. 'I assume that this has something to do with

Mr Ardleigh's death?' she probed, without taking her eyes off the computer screen.

'I'm afraid I can't tell you,' replied Watson tactfully. 'I'm sure you can understand.'

Sarah nodded and wandered over to the printer to retrieve the results of her request for information. 'Here you are, Sergeant,' she announced as she handed over two A4 sheets of paper. 'These are the names and addresses of the people who have checked in during the last twenty-four hours or who are due to book in today.'

Watson glanced through the twenty or so names. One stuck out like a sore thumb – it was the name Miranda Coyle.

Within the space of ten minutes Carmichael had returned to the reception desk.

'Do I take it that there is a problem with Mr Kenyon's booking?' she enquired.

Carmichael glanced across at Watson before answering. 'Unfortunately, Mr Kenyon was found dead this morning,' he replied. 'So with him and Mr Ardleigh no longer with us, it's unlikely that the meeting will proceed. However, I'd appreciate the hotel keeping this quiet from the guests as a couple of officers and I will be here just in case one or more of their party arrive.'

'As you know, Inspector,' replied Sarah with a wry grin, 'discretion is our mantra here at The Lindley.'

As the two officers made their way across the gravel drive to Carmichael's black BMW, Watson showed his boss the guest list and drew his attention to the name of Miranda Coyle.

'So that is where she was coming from this morning,' he remarked. 'It would be ironic if she were one of the three people Ardleigh's invited to the meeting.'

'If she was, she certainly knew by 8 a.m. this morning that Ruben Kenyon was dead,' replied Watson, 'because that's when she checked out.'

Carmichael pondered what his sergeant had just said for a

few seconds and took a quick look at his watch. 'Maybe I'll pay a visit to the famous Ms Coyle,' he replied. 'But it will take the best part of an hour to get to Salford Quays, so that will have to wait until after we've had the debrief.'

* * * *

Penny slipped out of the back door of The Railway Tavern just before lunchtime. She planned her exit carefully, trying hard to ensure that her departure was well before anyone she might know arrived for a lunchtime drink. She was also particularly keen to avoid being observed by any of the more sharp-eyed locals, who would no doubt enquire why she was visiting the pub at such an unusual time, and more specifically why she was doing so alone.

Penny was therefore horrified when she emerged out of the narrow side passage beside the pub to find herself confronted by one of the village's most renowned gossips.

'Oh hello, Mrs Carmichael,' said Mrs Hunter, her greeting delivered with an air of apparent astonishment.

Penny tried to appear calm and unruffled by this surprising and unwanted encounter. 'Good morning, Mrs Hunter,' she replied as she quickly walked past the old busybody and headed towards home.

'Is everything OK with Mr Robertson?' enquired Mrs Hunter, who was not about to allow Penny an easy escape.

'Fine,' replied Penny, who could sense that Mrs Hunter smelt a scandal. 'I'm sorry I have to dash; I'm late for an important appointment,' Penny lied.

With an unbridled sense of glee, Mrs Hunter watched as Penny walked with haste into the distance. The story that Helen Parkes had recounted to her that morning in the salon clearly had some substance.

As soon as Penny Carmichael was out of sight, Mrs Hunter looked at her watch and smiled. Then, complete with her new purple rinse, she marched off in the direction of the village hall, where she expected to find a host of people who she knew would be eager recipients of this juicy red-hot piece of village news.

Chapter 14

The debrief at Kirkwood Police Station started at precisely 1:30 p.m.

'So who wants to go first?' Carmichael asked as he sat back in his chair, his arms clasped behind his head in a display that said quite clearly, 'I'm the boss.'

The three officers gazed briefly at each other before Cooper decided to break the silence. 'I've got Stock's autopsy report on Ardleigh,' he announced. 'It's as Marc told us yesterday: Ardleigh was riddled with cancer, but the cause of death was from hanging and, apart from the rope burns to his wrists, there are no other marks on his body.'

'And what about the letter and the rope we found in Napier's van?' enquired Carmichael. 'Was the rope used to bind his hands?'

'There were no prints on the letter,' replied Cooper, 'but according to Stock there were clear traces of Ardleigh's skin and blood on the rope, so much so that Stock is certain that the rope was used to tie his hands.'

'Certain!' exclaimed Carmichael. 'That will be a first for Stock.'

'Shall we pick up Napier?' asked Watson who was already convinced that the antiques dealer was the killer.

Carmichael considered the question for a few moments. 'Yes, that's got to be our next move, but let's finish the debrief first.'

The perplexed look on Watson's face indicated that he disagreed with his boss.

'So what else do we know?' enquired Carmichael calmly.

'I've managed to find out a little more about Geraldine Ramsey,' announced Rachel. 'She's an old friend of Ardleigh's and lives a few streets away. I went round there earlier but there was no reply. The neighbours say she went away to Italy on holiday on Saturday so I couldn't speak with her.'

'That gives her a pretty good alibi,' interjected Watson sarcastically.

Carmichael nodded. 'So what else do we have?'

The three police officers' expressions showed that they hadn't much more to reveal. 'What about his cancer?' said Cooper hesitantly. 'Remember, Stock did say he was riddled with it.'

'Do you think that's relevant?' enquired Watson with an air of bewilderment.

'Personally I doubt it,' asserted Carmichael. 'Let's focus our time elsewhere for now.'

Cooper, Watson and Rachel Dalton all nodded their agreement.

'He didn't leave a note,' blurted Rachel almost randomly. 'Doesn't that suggest it was murder rather than suicide?'

'Not necessarily,' said Watson. 'It's true that suicides do tend to leave some sort of note, but not always.'

'You know, even if we found a note, I'd find it hard to believe this was a suicide,' Carmichael announced. 'Who would post three letters on Friday inviting people to attend a meeting the following Tuesday, then kill themselves? It makes no sense at all.' Carmichael puffed out his cheeks and thought for a moment. 'Did the great doctor reveal any other gems?'

'Not about Ardleigh,' Cooper replied. 'However, Stock

79

called about twenty minutes ago. He hasn't quite finished the autopsy on Kenyon, but he says the cause of death was one massive blow to the side of his head. Stock's now narrowed down the time of death to between eight and ten last night.'

Carmichael nodded. 'And has anyone spoken to Kenyon's wife?'

'I did,' replied Cooper. 'She's in a really bad way. She was so distraught that she wasn't that easy to follow but, from what I could gather, he called her at about seven thirty last night and told her he would be late home as he had to work on Ardleigh's affairs. When he wasn't home by the time she went to bed, she didn't think anything of it and it was only when she woke up at eight this morning that she realised he had not come home.'

'It all seems quite clear to me,' interjected Watson, who was by now totally frustrated that they had not already set off to arrest Napier, who he was sure would be their killer. 'Napier tied up Ardleigh on Sunday evening, killed him but tried to make it look like he hanged himself and once he was dead, he untied him. He then takes the rope away, hides it in his van, but we find it before he has a chance to dump it somewhere.'

'Your hypothesis does sound plausible,' agreed Cooper. 'And if Ardleigh had some nasty secret about Napier that he was planning to expose, that would give him a motive.'

'And I suspect', exclaimed Watson, who was now totally convinced that Napier was their murderer, 'if Kenyon also knew about this terrible secret that would also be a good reason for Napier to kill him, too.'

Carmichael nodded. 'What you are saying does make sense,' he replied. 'And certainly Gordon Napier has a lot of questions to answer but, if he was the killer, why leave the message on Ardleigh's answer machine?'

'Perhaps it's a ploy to throw us off the scent,' remarked Rachel.

'Let's keep our minds open on this until we know more,' continued Carmichael.

'I agree but shouldn't we pick him up now?' insisted Watson. 'Before he kills again or does a runner.'

'OK,' replied Carmichael, 'you and Cooper can go and do that. Rachel and I will stay here and consider the other alternatives.'

'Which are?' enquired Watson, his vexation clear for all to see.

'Well, there were three letters sent out,' replied Carmichael. 'So we also need to find out who the other two recipients were. You never know, Marc – they may have an even more compelling reason to kill.'

* * * *

Susan Watson and Penny Carmichael had become good friends. Despite the fact their respective husbands were different ranks in the police force, the two ladies had managed to form a strong relationship that was as good as any Penny enjoyed since returning to the village.

So when Susan heard Mrs Hunter gleefully spreading her poisonous story about Penny and the landlord of The Railway Tavern, she did what any good friend would do and invited herself round for coffee.

'So is there any truth in all this gossip about you and Robbie Robertson?' Susan asked with frankness only a true friend could get away with.

Penny's back stiffened at the bluntness of the question. 'And what are the gossipmongers saying?' she replied, trying hard to appear as calm as she could.

'That you have been spotted coming out of the pub at strange times of the day and that you looked as though you were trying your best not to be noticed,' replied Susan, picking her words as carefully as she could.

'I see,' responded Penny, who then took a small sip from her coffee mug. 'And it's all over the neighbourhood, you say?' she enquired.

'I'm afraid so,' replied Susan with a faint shrug of her shoulders. 'Mrs Hunter and Mrs Parkes are in full swing on this one.'

'Bugger,' replied Penny. 'That's all we need. I really didn't expect us to be found out quite so soon.'

'Found out!' exclaimed Susan who then proceeded to spill half the contents of her coffee over the kitchen table. 'You're not telling me it's true?' she said, her eyes now bulging with horror and disbelief at what she was hearing.

* * * *

'You're not convinced it's Napier, are you, sir?' Rachel enquired as soon as the two sergeants had left the room.

'I'm not sure,' replied Carmichael. 'I think Marc is probably right, but it all seems too easy. Finding the rope in Napier's car like that. It may be he's just careless, but if I had killed someone and there was evidence like that, I'm damn sure I wouldn't leave it in the back of my unlocked van on my drive. Napier went to Oxford; surely he's not that stupid.'

'It does seem a strange mistake to make, but if it's not him who else can it be?' Rachel asked.

'I don't know,' replied Carmichael pensively. 'But we shouldn't just focus on Napier. Hugo Lazarus has got to be a suspect and also the other two people who received the letters. We need to find them, too, before we jump to any conclusions.'

Rachel did not want to believe the dapper Hugo Lazarus was a murderer, but wisely said nothing.

'We also need to interview Miranda Coyle,' continued Carmichael. 'She stayed at The Lindley last night and she also ran me off the road this morning. I want to know what she was doing in Moulton Bank.'

'*The* Miranda Coyle?' remarked Rachel, who was a great admirer of the fashion icon.

'Yes, *the* Miranda Coyle,' replied Carmichael sarcastically. 'However, she will have to wait until tomorrow. I want to be here when they bring in Napier, and tonight we're all going to The Lindley. I want to see if anyone turns up to the meeting that the late Mr Ardleigh and the late Mr Kenyon arranged.'

'Surely they won't turn up now,' remarked Rachel in amazement.

'You never know,' replied Carmichael. 'You never know.'

Chapter 15

Watson and Cooper apprehended Gordon Napier at just after 3 p.m. By 3:40 p.m. they were back at the station, elated that they had managed to detain their prime suspect so soon.

At 4:35 p.m., having been formally charged and with the duty solicitor by his side, the forlorn and decidedly anxious Gordon Napier waited patiently in the main interview room at Kirkwood Police Station.

Rachel Dalton and Cooper watched intently through the two-way mirror as Carmichael and Watson entered the room.

With all the hallmarks of one of the great TV detectives, and much to the annoyance of his boss, Marc Watson theatrically pulled back his shirt sleeve to reveal his wristwatch, which he raised to within less than one foot from his face. 'The time is now four thirty-six on Tuesday, 17th August,' he announced as clearly as he could. 'This interview is taking place at Kirkwood Police Station with Gordon Napier of Station Road, Moulton Bank, in connection with the death of Marcus Ardleigh and the death of Ruben Kenyon. In attendance and acting for Mr Napier is Mr Vaughan, the duty solicitor. Also in attendance are PC Jamieson, Sergeant Marc Watson and Inspector Steve Carmichael.'

Carmichael looked directly into the eyes of Gordon Napier, who was clearly nervous. 'Mr Napier, we have had the lab report back on the rope that we found in the back of your van yesterday and it has confirmed that it was used to bind

Marcus Ardleigh's hands. As you can imagine, we are interested to know how the rope came to be in the back of your van. Can you please help us understand how it got there, Mr Napier?'

Beads of sweat were already starting to appear on Napier's brow and he shuffled nervously forward and back in his chair.

'I have no idea,' he replied feebly. 'My van is always open. Anyone could have put it there.'

Carmichael maintained his stare directly at Napier.

'And can you please remind us what you were doing on the evening of Sunday 15th August?' he asked.

'As I told you yesterday, Inspector,' replied Napier, 'I was at home on my own all evening.'

'What about yesterday evening?' Carmichael asked. 'Where were you between eight and ten last night?'

Napier scratched his head. 'I was at home.'

'Alone?' interjected Watson.

'Yes alone,' replied Napier. 'I ordered an Indian takeaway and watched TV.'

'What time did you order the takeaway?' asked Carmichael.

'It would have been about seven thirty, maybe seven forty-five,' replied Napier. 'It was delivered at about eight thirty.'

Watson lent over towards Carmichael. 'Even if what he is saying is true,' he said in a whisper, 'he would still have enough time to get to the solicitors' practice and murder Kenyon.

Carmichael nodded. 'And, Mr Napier, have you had a chance to think about what it was that Ardleigh and Kenyon were due to reveal to you tonight at The Lindley Hotel?'

Napier shook his head. 'To be honest, Inspector, I have absolutely no idea what it was that Marcus was talking about. I've been wracking my brain but I cannot imagine what he was referring to.'

Although the evidence against Napier was compelling and he was by far their most likely candidate for the murders, until that moment Carmichael could have accepted that Napier was telling the truth. However, there was no way he was prepared to accept that Napier didn't know what Ardleigh had been talking about.

'You're in big trouble here, Mr Napier,' he said firmly. 'We have more than enough evidence to hold you for the murders of Ardleigh and Kenyon, so I strongly suggest you spend some time with Mr Vaughan and you start to tell us the truth. I can assure you that you will help yourself enormously if you are completely honest with us.'

Napier continued to look troubled. 'Mr Carmichael,' he said, his voice trembling, 'I have done nothing wrong. I am innocent of both murders.'

'That maybe so, Mr Napier,' replied Carmichael, 'but you are guilty of something and Ardleigh knew it. You know what that letter was talking about, don't you? I can see it in your eyes. Is it really so bad?'

Napier gazed down at the table. 'I'm not saying anymore,' he replied.

'Very well,' replied Carmichael, who stood up as he was talking. 'We'll call it a day for now, but we will be interviewing you again in the morning, so I suggest you think hard about being more forthcoming with us.'

'Interview ended at four forty-eight,' said Watson as he switched off the sound recording.

*   *   *   *

Robbie Carmichael arrived home just before 5 p.m. He was hot and tired after a long day at the farm and was desperate for a shower.

Neither Penny nor Susan Watson heard the front door open or his footsteps as he made his way down the hallway.

Robbie was about to enter the kitchen when he realised his mother and her friend were inside. He liked Susan Watson and he instantly recognised that she was who his mother was talking to. The kitchen door was slightly ajar and through it he could hear the two ladies talking in hushed tones and without the customary laughter.

'No, Penny, it's not fair on either Steve or the children,' he heard Susan say with a real sense of urgency in her voice. 'You have to come clean with them. I know you care for Robbie and I understand you're in a real dilemma here, but you simply cannot pretend that nothing's going on. It's just a matter of time before Steve or one of the kids hears something. Now old mother Hunter has smelt a scandal, there's no way you can keep this quiet.'

'I know you are right but I promised Robbie I'd not tell anyone until he was ready,' replied Penny, much to the growing horror of her eavesdropping son.

'Look, I'm going to have to go,' said Susan, 'but please, please tell Steve. Do it tonight!'

Realising his mother's friend would very soon appear through the doorway, Robbie scampered down the hallway and silently opened the front door. Just as Susan and Penny emerged from the kitchen, Robbie slammed the door shut to give the impression he had just arrived.

'Oh hi, Robbie,' said Penny as if nothing was wrong. 'You're back early.'

Robbie stared back at his mother who was smiling at him from the end of the corridor.

'I'm going for a shower,' he mumbled as he quickly clambered up the stairs.

'Tell them tonight!' whispered Susan as she walked out through the front door. 'If you don't, you'll regret it.'

Chapter 16

'I don't understand,' said Watson as he and Carmichael walked down the corridor. 'Why did you end the interview like that? Surely we've enough evidence to nail him? Why didn't you give him a hard time?'

Carmichael carried on walking. 'Let him stew overnight,' he replied. 'He may well be our killer but I'm not convinced. I think he's been framed. I reckon someone else put that rope in his van. But if I'm wrong, he's not going anywhere tonight so he'll keep until the morning.'

On hearing these words, Watson stopped in his tracks and raised his eyes to the ceiling. He was certain his boss was wrong, but knew him well enough to know it would take more than his persuasive skills to get him to change his mind.

'So what now?' he asked in desperation as his boss got ever further down the corridor.

'We do three things,' replied Carmichael. 'We find the other two people who received those letters; we find out who benefits from Ardleigh's will – both of which we will need to get on to tomorrow – but first we get ourselves off to The Lindley to see if anyone turns up at tonight's meeting.'

Watson stood in complete disbelief as Carmichael disappeared from view.

'Bloody man,' he muttered to himself. 'He's definitely lost the plot this time.'

* * * *

Penny thought long and hard about what her friend had said. She did not want to break her word to Robbie Robertson but, thanks to Mrs Hunter, she knew the village jungle drums would already be sounding and she did not want Steve or the children to learn about her clandestine meetings with Robbie from anyone else. She knew deep down that she had to come clean with the family and decided she would tell them together that evening.

*   *   *   *

His interview over, Gordon Napier was allowed by the duty sergeant to make one short telephone call. He chose to call his old friend Hugo Lazarus.

'It's me, Gordon,' he whispered down the mouthpiece, hoping that he was not being overheard by the PC at the other side of the office. 'I'm at Kirkwood Police Station. They've arrested me for Marcus's murder and for the murder of Kenyon, too.'

'What!' exclaimed Lazarus. 'Why on earth do they think you did it?'

'It's that rope they found in my van,' replied Napier. 'They reckon it was used to tie up Marcus before he was hanged.'

'Don't panic,' replied Lazarus calmly. 'They'll never make it stick. Even an average lawyer would get you off if that's all they have.'

'They're really pushing me about what Marcus meant in that letter he sent me,' continued Napier. 'I'm scared they'll find out about the Quintet.'

'Say nothing about the Quintet, Gordon!' said Lazarus firmly. 'Hold your nerve. Now Marcus has gone, there's only you and I that know anything about the Quintet and I'm not going to say anything. So stay calm, hold your nerve and keep quiet.'

*　　*　　*　　*

'Oh hi, darling,' said Carmichael when his wife picked up the phone. 'I'm going to be a bit late this evening. The team and I are going over to The Lindley to see if anyone turns up. It's almost certainly going to be a wild goose chase, but we have to be there just in case.'

'So what time will you be back?' enquired Penny, who, having made up her mind to unburden her secret to the family, was now eager to get the whole thing over with as quickly as possible.

'Shouldn't be much after ten,' replied Carmichael. 'That's unless someone really does turn up.'

'OK,' replied Penny despondently. 'But try not to be too late.'

As Penny replaced the receiver, her son came thundering down the stairs and headed straight for the front door.

'Where are you going, Robbie?' Penny asked.

'I'm off out to see Brooke,' he replied without once giving his mother the pleasure of even the slightest of glances.

'But you haven't eaten anything,' remarked his mother anxiously.

'I'll get some chips,' replied Robbie as he headed out of the front door.

'Don't be too ...'

The door slammed shut before Penny could finish her sentence, leaving her alone to ponder whether she would be able to tell the whole family that evening after all.

Chapter 17

Dr Ernest Walker had made his considerable fortune from an assortment of diverse business ventures. He was now in his early fifties and, although his hair was starting to thin and turn decidedly grey, and in spite of the fact that he had more than a few deep lines on his forehead and around his eyes, he struck a dashing figure. He had broad shoulders, a toned body and bright blue eyes that shone out like searchlights from his cheery round face. He was not the tallest of men, but what he lacked in size he certainly more than made up for in charisma and personality.

What heightened his appeal even more was his sense of dress, which was impeccable. So much so that whenever he entered a room he had the knack of immediately being noticed, particularly by any ladies that happened to be there.

It was precisely 8:00 p.m. when Dr Walker strode confidently up to the reception desk at The Lindley Hotel.

'I'm here for the meeting in the Sefton Suite,' he said in a loud voice. 'Can you please direct me there?'

His request immediately grabbed the attention of the two individuals who had been loitering in the foyer for the past forty minutes.

'My God, one of them has turned up!' exclaimed Watson in whispered excitement. 'I would have bet a lot of money that Carmichael was wrong. Just goes to show.'

'Shh,' replied Rachel. 'Let's just do as we agreed and let him go up to the room.'

The receptionist, as instructed, gave no indication to Dr Walker that anything was amiss and with great self-assurance gave her guest directions to the room in question.

'Thank you so much,' replied Dr Walker with a broad smile as he made his way down the corridor.

Rachel Dalton and Watson followed slowly at a safe distance behind, but close enough not to let their quarry get out of sight.

Once inside the Sefton Suite, Dr Walker appeared a little shocked to see only two other people there.

'I take it one of you must be Marcus Ardleigh's solicitor?' he asked, holding out his right hand to cement his greeting.

'Actually no,' came back the reply. 'My name is Inspector Carmichael. I'm from the Lancashire Police Force and this is Sergeant Cooper.'

*   *   *   *

Robbie Carmichael was relieved when he saw his pretty girlfriend walking towards him as he sat on one of the wooden benches that the council had recently erected along the perimeter of The Common.

'Hi,' said Brooke cheerily as she planted a kiss on his cheek. 'You been here long?'

'Just a short while,' replied Robbie gloomily, although in truth he had been sitting there alone for well over an hour.

The young girl put her arm around his shoulders. 'Are you OK?' she asked.

'I think my mum's having an affair,' announced Robbie sullenly, his despair evident in his voice. 'I think she's seeing that fat landlord from The Railway.'

Until that moment he had hardly looked at his girlfriend, but when Brooke didn't say anything to allay his fears or disagree with what he had said, Robbie turned and looked directly into her eyes. 'Bloody hell,' he said angrily as he saw the expression on her face. 'You knew about this all the time, didn't you?'

Brooke was not sure how to respond. 'Well,' she said nervously. 'I didn't want to say anything, but I'm afraid I think it may be true. I heard Mum talking with Mrs Savage this afternoon on the phone. When I asked her about it, she told me and apparently it's common knowledge in the village.'

Robbie stared at her in horror. 'So you, your mum and the whole bloody village are talking about my mum, are they?' he snapped.

Brooke could see the hurt in Robbie's eyes. 'I'm sorry,' she said as she wrapped her arms around his neck. 'Mum doesn't normally get these things wrong but maybe it's not true. Let's face it, your dad's much nicer than Robbie Robertson – he's old and he's fat.'

*　*　*　*

'So they're both dead?' said Walker with genuine surprise in his voice. 'My wife told me that Marcus had committed suicide, but I had no idea his solicitor was dead, too.'

'So what made you still come here?' Carmichael enquired. 'If you knew Ardleigh was dead, why did you not assume the meeting he had arranged would be cancelled, too?'

'That did cross my mind,' replied Walker. 'However, I was so incensed when I read Ardleigh's nasty letter that I wanted to find out from his solicitor what the hell they were on about.'

At that point Walker extracted a letter from his pocket which he handed to Carmichael.

Carmichael studied the letter carefully. Apart from it being addressed to Dr Walker, it was identical to the letter Napier had received.

'So what is the secret he mentions in the letter?' enquired Carmichael.

'I have absolutely no idea,' replied Walker without any hesitation. 'I hardly knew Ardleigh, so I have no idea what he's referring to.'

'So when did you first meet Ardleigh?' Carmichael asked.

'We met about five years ago at a mutual friend's party and after that I would occasionally see him in the village and at various socials, but we weren't friends. We shared a love of art, so he has visited my house a few times to see some of my pictures and sculptures, but he knew nothing about me really, so I have no idea why he felt I had some shady secret.'

'Can I ask what your movements were on Sunday evening and also yesterday evening?' continued Carmichael.

'Of course,' replied Walker. 'On Sunday, at about eight in the evening, I travelled down to Birmingham. I gave a lecture at 9 a.m. on Monday, so I travelled down on Sunday to make sure I was there on time.'

'And when did you return?' enquired Carmichael.

'I decided to stay over a further night,' replied Walker. 'I met some old colleagues at the conference and we all went out for dinner last night. I got back at about two this afternoon.'

'I'm sure you can understand that we will need to check this out,' said Carmichael, although he fully expected that Dr Walker's story would prove to be true. 'If you can give a full statement to my sergeant here, that would be very helpful.'

'Of course,' replied Walker. 'I'll do everything I can to help you.'

With a small movement of his head, Carmichael indicated to Cooper that he wanted him to take Dr Walker's statement. Rising up from his chair, Carmichael made his way slowly and pensively towards the doorway.

As he reached his destination, he turned back to face Dr Walker.

'You say you have a doctorate,' he said. 'Is that in medicine?'

'No,' replied Walker with a laugh. 'I'm not that clever. My doctorate is in Astrophysics. I lecture on the subject all over the world.'

'And you said you shared a love of art with Ardleigh,' continued Carmichael. 'Whose art in particular?'

'I have varied tastes,' responded Dr Walker. 'And I'm very fortunate to also have an income that allows me to buy certain pieces. My favourite artists are Russell Flint and Douglas Hoffmann. I have quite a few of their works. I also have a few sculptures by Sir Antony Caro. I'm quite proud of those, and as I recall, Marcus was a fan of Caro and Hoffmann, too.'

'Is that right,' replied Carmichael, who hadn't heard of any of the three artists. 'Thank you for your time, Dr Walker.'

Carmichael left the Sefton Suite even more perplexed than he had been when he entered it a little under two hours earlier.

*   *   *   *

It was just before 10 p.m. when the doorbell rang. Intrigued to find out who would be paying her a visit at that late hour, Penny walked briskly down the hallway and opened up the front door.

'Good evening, Mrs Carmichael,' said the tall, well-built police officer who stood in front of her. 'We've brought your son home. I'm afraid he's a little worse for wear.'

The officer then moved aside to reveal Robbie, who was being held up by a second officer.

'What's happened?' Penny shrieked, at first thinking her son had been set upon.

'He's OK, I think,' replied the second officer as reassuringly as he could. 'But he's as drunk as a lord and we thought it may be a good idea to get him home before he got himself into any further mischief.'

Penny could feel her pulse rising but did not want to show her feelings in front of her husband's colleagues.

'You'd better bring him in,' she said as she stood aside.

Chapter 18

'So what now, boss?' Watson asked as he, Rachel Dalton and Carmichael ambled slowly down the marble staircase that led to the sumptuous and ornate reception of The Lindley Hotel.

Carmichael pondered a few moments before responding. 'God knows,' he replied, with a frankness that took his two colleagues by surprise.

'Let's go and have a drink in the bar while Cooper takes Walker's statement,' he continued. 'While we wait for him it will give us a chance to have a quick review of where we are with this bizarre case.'

Although neither Rachel nor Watson relished the thought of spending what still remained of the evening discussing the case, they didn't offer any resistance and meekly followed their illustrious leader into the bar.

* * * *

Penny was totally disgusted with the state her son was in. As soon as the two officers had bid her goodnight and the door was shut, she turned on her heels and fixed her son with her laser-sharp glare. 'What the hell do you think you're playing at?' she yelled.

'What am *I* playing at?' replied her son with no attempt to hide his slurred speech. 'I'm not the one bonking the landlord of the bloody Railway,' he replied.

97

Penny froze to the spot as she heard her son's cutting words. Even in his drunken state, Robbie could see the hurt in his mother's eyes, which wounded him just as much. 'Well, why don't you deny it?' he continued, but now with a much more calm and insightful tone. 'Even Brooke knows; that's how discreet you've been.'

Penny's mouth went dry and her eyes filled with salty tears that blurred her vision of the young man she loved so much. For once Penny was unsure what to say; Robbie's outburst had been such an unexpected bombshell.

'Just go to bed,' she said before wandering off to the kitchen, leaving her inebriated son to make his own way up the stairs, as confused as he had been at any stage during a long and painful evening.

With tears pouring uncontrollably down her face, Penny sat alone on a hard wooden stool trying to take in what had just happened. She looked up at the clock through her moist red eyes. It was now 10:15.

'Where the hell are you, Steve?' she mumbled to herself. 'I need to talk to you.'

* * * *

Carmichael took a sip from his pint of Boddingtons. 'So what do we know?' he enquired.

'Well, we know that Ardleigh invited Napier, Walker and someone else to a meeting,' Rachel said.

'He was then murdered,' continued Watson. 'And whoever killed him tried to hide his death as a suicide and either put the rope that bound his hands in Napier's van to try and make it look like Napier, or more likely it was actually Napier and he's just not good at covering up his tracks.'

'So what about Kenyon?' asked Carmichael. 'Why was he killed?'

'Because he knew the secret?' replied Watson. 'It's got to be Napier. He's no alibi for either evening, he got one of the letters, he knew where Ardleigh kept his key and the rope was in his van. He has to be our man.'

'I think Marc's right,' interjected Rachel. 'When you look at it like that, he's got to be our prime suspect.'

Carmichael took another sip of his beer. 'Maybe,' he muttered. 'But until we've found out who the number three recipient was and what each of the three people who received letters is hiding, we continue to investigate other avenues.'

In total unison the three tired officers all took a sip from their respective glasses, albeit that Watson's and Dalton's were filled with soft drinks unlike their boss's more alcoholic libation. As their glasses came back to rest on the table, they were joined by Cooper, who having completed taking Ernest Walker's statement had come to find his colleagues.

'I think Dr Walker's innocent,' announced Cooper. 'He seems quite genuine and if his story holds water he couldn't have killed either of them as he was away both nights.'

'Both?' questioned Carmichael. 'I thought he said he went to Birmingham at eight. If that's the case, he could have killed Ardleigh before he left.'

'But I thought Dr Stock said the time of death was about nine thirty,' Rachel correctly recalled.

'Well, he could be lying about the time he left,' replied Carmichael, who felt like he was clutching at straws. 'Maybe he left home at eight but killed Ardleigh at around nine thirty and then dumped the rope in Napier's van on his way to Birmingham.'

'It's possible, I suppose,' said Cooper. 'But if his friends back up his story for Monday evening, he's certainly in the clear on that one.'

Carmichael nodded. 'True,' he mumbled.

'So what's the game plan?' enquired Watson after a brief pause.

Carmichael took his time before answering.

'I'd like you to check out Dr Walker's story in the morning,' he said, looking at Rachel. 'Then if you have time, try and locate that woman who posted the letters.'

'Geraldine Ramsey,' responded Rachel.

'Yes, that's her,' he replied.

'What do you want me to do?' asked Cooper.

'I want you to interview Napier once more,' replied Carmichael. 'If he's still not going to tell us his nasty little secret, we'll have to release him. Then go and see Hugo Lazarus. Find out what he knows. He's Ardleigh's old chum from Cambridge so he probably knows quite a bit more than he's saying. He found the body, too!'

'It was Oxford, sir,' interjected Rachel.

'Isn't that what I said?' snapped Carmichael, who was by now getting tired.

'And what are we going to do tomorrow?' enquired Watson

'I want you to pick me up at my house at eight and we'll drive over and pay a visit to that famous fashion icon and crazy motorist, Miranda Coyle,' announced Carmichael, before draining his glass. 'I want to find out what she was doing here on Monday and why she checked out so early this morning. My bet is she's got letter three, so she's up there with Napier on my list of prime suspects.'

* * * *

It was nearly 11 p.m. when Carmichael eventually arrived home. Exhausted and ready for his bed, he hung up his jacket and wandered down the unlit hallway to the kitchen where his wife was still sitting quietly alone in the half-gloom.

'I've had a bugger of a day,' he said before seeing her

distressed expression and puffed-up cheeks from an hour of constant tears.

'I have to talk to you,' Penny said in a trembling voice. 'Can you sit down, please?'

Chapter 19

Wednesday 18th August

'Morning, sir,' chirped Watson, who had arrived at Carmichael's house at 8 a.m. prompt as instructed. Had the poor sergeant seen the dark expression on Carmichael's face as he had approached the car, or had he known that his superior had only managed a few hours' sleep, he would certainly have been less cheery. However, Marc Watson did not see Carmichael's expression and he had no idea that the boss had spent most of the night mulling over what his tearful wife had told him. But this soon became clear to Watson. It took only a few short words to make him realise all was not well with the inspector that morning.

'Do me a favour, Marc?' announced Carmichael, as he clambered into the passenger seat. 'Cut the small talk this morning – I've a lot on my mind.'

Watson knew immediately that his superior wasn't joking. 'No problem, sir,' he replied. 'I'll just drive!'

* * * *

As soon as she heard her husband leave the house, Penny clambered out from under the covers, put on her dressing gown and walked slowly down the hall to her son's bedroom. She gingerly pushed open the door only to find her son dead to the world. There would be no chance of him getting to work today, she thought.

After quietly closing the door, Penny tiptoed down the stairs to the hallway, where she picked up the telephone receiver, and keyed in six digits.

After only three rings Robbie Robertson picked up the phone.

'I've told Steve,' Penny announced. 'I know what I promised but I had to. The rumour mill in this place has spun out of control, so I had to tell him. And you need to know that I'll be telling the children, too, this morning.'

* * * *

The forty-five-minute journey to Miranda Coyle's luxury apartment was spent in total silence. Not one word was uttered by either Watson or Carmichael until they pulled up outside Miranda's opulent residence in Salford Quays.

'I'll do the talking,' Carmichael announced as he clambered out of the car.

'That's fine with me, sir,' replied Watson, who had no desire to cross Carmichael in the mood that he was in.

The two officers walked briskly up the neatly laid brick pathway to the entrance lobby. Carmichael studied the dozen or so names that were each written next to a corresponding shiny brass button, until he spotted the name of Miranda Coyle. He pressed it and held his finger on the button for ten to fifteen seconds.

'Yes,' came the clear but slightly irritated voice out of the speaker. 'Who is it?'

'My name is Inspector Carmichael from Lancashire Police,' he replied. 'My sergeant and I would like to talk to you, please, if you can spare us a few moments of your time.'

Suddenly the release on the door clicked and Miranda's

voice crackled out through the speaker once more. 'Come up – I'm on the top floor, Apartment 12.'

Carmichael and Watson pushed open the glass door and marched inside.

* * * *

Geraldine Ramsey stretched out on her poolside recliner to take in the warm morning sun. As she did, she spied from under her straw sunhat the unmistakeable figure of the handsome young waiter walking towards her.

'Good morning, madam,' he said in his thick Italian accent. 'I have Tuesday's newspaper for you, the *Guardian*.'

'Thank you so much, Lucio,' she said as she took it out of his hands. 'I'll read that now, I think.'

The smile of appreciation remained on her face as she unravelled the newspaper and started to examine the front page. However, it took just a few seconds for that smile to turn to a look of horror as she read the headline:

'Marcus Ardleigh, advisor to two prime ministers, is found hanged at his home.'

* * * *

Miranda Coyle flung open the door to her apartment and, cigarette in hand, stood menacingly in front of the two plainclothes officers. On any other day Carmichael would almost certainly have managed her aggressive posture with more tact. Unfortunately for Ms Coyle, Carmichael was in no mood to spend time with diplomacy. His large right hand shot out from his jacket pocket clutching his identity card, which he thrust under Miranda Coyle's nose.

'Inspector Carmichael,' he announced. 'May we come in?'

Miranda Coyle was not used to being spoken to so briskly and was so taken aback that she was momentarily lost for words. By the time she had gathered her thoughts the two officers were already inside the apartment.

'May I ask what this is all about?' Miranda enquired as soon as she had regained her poise.

'May we sit down?' replied Carmichael, who by now was already in the living room.

'Be my guest,' responded Miranda with a theatrical wave of her arm in the direction of one of the three large sofas which occupied the expensively furnished room.

Carmichael and Watson sat down in sync.

Miranda stubbed out her cigarette in the ashtray on the round glass table that separated the sofa taken by her unwanted visitors and the sofa she elected to use. 'So again, Inspector, I ask you, what on earth is this all about?'

Carmichael fixed Miranda in his gaze. 'I suspect you are fully aware of the reason for our visit. However, to make sure there are no misunderstandings, I'll spell it out to you.'

* * * *

Geraldine Ramsey, tears streaming down her cheeks, rushed back into the foyer of the hotel.

'Is there anything wrong, madam?' shouted Lucio, the very concerned waiter, just as he saw her disappear out of sight.

Geraldine did not hear his call. She was trembling and clearly in shock from the headline she had just read. She grabbed her room key which was still on the desk where she had placed it five minutes earlier and rushed upstairs.

Once inside her bedroom, Geraldine riffled through her handbag to find her diary, giving no regard whatsoever to the fact that most of its contents were being recklessly jettisoned onto the bedroom floor. Then, as soon as she had located the little red book, she threw the now unwanted bag heedlessly onto the bed.

Having found the number she desired, she picked up the telephone, dialled 9 for an outside line and, replacing the first 0 in the number with 0044, proceeded to make her call.

* * * *

To Watson's utter amazement, the no-nonsense, brusque approach adopted by his boss seemed to work perfectly. No sooner had Carmichael finished explaining to Miranda that they knew she had been staying at The Lindley on Monday evening, that they suspected this was due to her receiving a letter from Marcus Ardleigh and that it was he, Carmichael, who had been run off the road the morning before as a result of her dangerous driving, the demeanour of the normally confident, self-important, fashion connoisseur dramatically changed.

No longer did she have the air of a woman in control.

Nervously, Miranda lit another cigarette.

'I see,' she said almost meekly, the smoke bellowing out of her nose. 'You are correct, Inspector. I did receive a letter from Marcus. I did go to Moulton Bank. I did stay at The Lindley as you have said and in my haste to get away from that hideous little village I did drive a little carelessly. I'm so sorry about that. I hope you and your vehicle are OK. I will pay for any damage, of course.'

'The car is not why we are here, Ms Coyle,' interjected Carmichael, who was also amazed at the ease with which he had been able to get Miranda to cooperate. 'It's the deaths of Ardleigh and his solicitor we are so keen to know more about and also the reason behind Ardleigh sending you the letter in the first place.'

'Is Kenyon dead, too?' enquired Miranda, her face indicating that this was news to her.

'Yes,' replied Carmichael. 'He was murdered on Monday evening. Did you know Mr Kenyon?'

Miranda looked uncomfortable. 'Briefly,' she replied. 'Marcus introduced him to me once many years ago. I know he was Marcus's solicitor.'

'You have a good memory, Ms Coyle,' interjected Watson, who had forgotten his instructions to remain quiet, a point that he quickly remembered after receiving an icy look from his boss.

'May we see the letter you received from Marcus?' Carmichael asked, his attention now firmly back with Miranda Coyle.

'Of course,' replied Miranda, who stood up and walked slowly over to the sideboard and opened the top drawer.

* * * *

Geraldine Ramsey struggled to fully comprehend what she was being told.

She grasped the telephone receiver tightly in her hand as she listened intently to the faint, highly emotional voice of Lyn Osborne, who explained to her the distressing details of the previous two days.

A little over half an hour earlier, Geraldine had been totally relaxed and was thoroughly enjoying her holiday in Italy, but now, with the harrowing knowledge of the death of her old friend Marcus Ardleigh and also the news that his trusty solicitor Ruben Kenyon had been murdered, too, her state of mind was one of traumatised incredulity.

'I just cannot believe it,' she mumbled down the phone. 'Marcus would never take his own life, and who would want to kill poor Ruben?'

At the other end of the line, Lyn Osborne, who had known Geraldine Ramsey for a number of years through various women's social events they had both attended in the village, was herself in floods of tears. Trying hard to maintain her composure, she felt comfortable enough in her relationship with Geraldine to feel able to share her considered opinion on the deaths. 'The police and their forensic people are still here,' she replied, trying hard to prevent the two police officers who were in the adjoining room from hearing what she was saying. 'They have been here pretty much ever since I found poor Mr Kenyon's body yesterday morning. As you'd expect, they're keeping very tight-lipped about Marcus's death, but the impression I get is that they think it may not have been suicide.'

'Well, I agree with that conclusion,' remarked Geraldine. 'I simply cannot accept that Marcus would commit suicide. It's true that he did always say he believed in euthanasia and that in certain circumstances it should be legalised, but he had everything to live for, so I cannot believe he'd take his own life.'

'I think that's what they think,' concurred Mrs Osborne.

'This must have been a terrible couple of days for you too, Lyn,' said Geraldine, with true compassion in her trembling voice. 'With it being you who actually found the body and now having to cope with police in the office all the time, it must be very hard.'

'It is,' replied a tearful Mrs Osborne. 'However, I've decided I need to be strong and do whatever I can to help the police find whoever it was that killed them both.'

'That's very public-spirited of you, Lyn,' remarked Geraldine, who was genuinely concerned about the wellbeing of the solicitors' receptionist. 'So do you know exactly what the police are looking for?'

Lyn Osborne looked around the room to make sure she would not be overheard. 'They appear to be trying to find a copy of Mr Ardleigh's last will, but it's gone missing. I also overheard them talking about finding copies of some letters that either Mr Ardleigh or Mr Kenyon had recently posted.'

Not for the first time in the last hour, Geraldine was taken aback at what she was hearing. 'If that's the case,' she said timidly, 'you had better put one of them on the phone, as I

108

think I can help them to some extent in both of those matters.'

* * * *

Carmichael took his time reading the letter that Miranda Coyle had given him. Apart from her name at the top, it was identical to the letters received by Gordon Napier and Dr Walker. He handed it to Watson, before turning his attention to Miranda.

'How long have you known Marcus Ardleigh?' he asked.

Miranda, who was once again seated on the sofa opposite the two officers, raised her eyes skyward. 'Donkey's years, Inspector,' she said nonchalantly. 'We met in Oxford. He was a student there; I worked in a dress hire shop.'

For the first time that day a hint of a smile appeared on Carmichael's face. 'So what is your guilty secret, Ms Coyle?' he asked.

Miranda took a huge drag on her cigarette and fired out two strong jets of smoke from her nostrils. 'That's the mystery,' she announced with a calmness she had not demonstrated before. 'I have absolutely no idea what he is referring to. When you find out, please do tell me.'

Chapter 20

Cooper had not had the most successful of mornings. Gordon Napier had stuck firmly to his story, maintaining stoically that he had no idea what secret Ardleigh had been referring to in his letter; and was adamant he'd played no part in either of the deaths.

As a result, he had no alternative but to release Napier. As Cooper watched the suspect and his solicitor make their way through the ranks of newspaper reporters and photographers who had been waiting outside, the duty sergeant ambled up beside him and handed him a small scrap of paper.

'The officers at Kenyon's office have just spoken to this lady on the phone,' he said. 'She maintains she has some information about Ardleigh's will and also about some letters he sent out recently.'

Cooper studied the details on the scrap of paper.

'This phone number,' he enquired, 'I don't recognise the dialling code. Where is it?'

'It's a hotel in Italy, I believe,' replied the duty sergeant. 'I understand Ms Ramsey is holidaying there.'

Cooper spent a few more minutes looking out of the window, until Napier and his brief had managed to finish running the gauntlet of the press and clamber into the waiting car. Once they were safely away, he read again the contents of the note he had been given before making off to his desk to make the call.

*   *   *   *

Rachel's morning was spent at her desk checking Ernest Walker's alibi. He had claimed to have left home on Sunday at about eight in the evening, travelled down to Birmingham, given a lecture at 9 a.m. on Monday, stayed over another night at the hotel and only returned to Moulton Bank at about 2 p.m. on Tuesday afternoon.

Three short telephone calls, one to the hotel and then one to each of the two friends, corroborated Dr Walker's story exactly.

'How are you doing?' Cooper enquired as he entered the room.

'You're right,' replied Rachel, 'Dr Walker couldn't have killed either of them. His story has been totally supported by the hotel and by his chums. It has to be Napier.'

'Whether it is or not,' replied Cooper with a scowl, 'he is sticking to his story so I have had to let him go.'

'So what now?' enquired Rachel with more than a hint of frustration in her voice.

'Well,' replied Cooper, whose frown had now been replaced with a wry smile, 'it looks like we've found Geraldine Ramsey.'

He passed over the scrap of paper with her details to his surprised-looking colleague. 'Let's go into the boss's office and call her together on his squawk box. Then I suggest we both go over to have another chat with Hugo Lazarus. If we're lucky, we can be back here by mid-afternoon, for the debriefing with Carmichael.'

'Sounds a great plan,' replied Rachel with a broad grin. 'But I lead the conversation with Geraldine Ramsey. After all, it was me the boss assigned to find Ms Ramsey.'

'It's a deal,' replied Cooper, with a chuckle. 'I'll just listen.'

*   *   *   *

'So what did you make of Miranda Coyle?' enquired Carmichael as he and Watson descended the white-tiled staircase that took them down towards the exit.

'She smokes a lot,' replied Watson. 'She lit up at least three times and we were only in there about forty minutes.'

'Maybe she was nervous,' commented Carmichael.

'I'd say she probably has good reason to be,' replied Watson. 'She may not be the killer but she's got to be up there.'

'I agree,' Carmichael concurred. 'I certainly don't buy that she doesn't know what the letter was referring to. If she didn't, she wouldn't have bothered travelling over to Moulton Bank and booking into The Lindley. I think she knows exactly what Ardleigh was on about.'

Watson nodded. 'She could have easily killed Kenyon, too,' he remarked. 'Not sure about Ardleigh though, especially if the toy boy she mentioned verifies her story that he spent the night at her apartment.'

'Graham Calvin,' remarked Carmichael. 'You need to check that out, Marc, but I'd wager he'll back her up, whether he was there or not. I fancy Ms Coyle will be briefing him even now.'

*   *   *   *

It took the hotel almost ten minutes to locate Geraldine Ramsey and connect her to the two officers from Lancashire Police who were waiting patiently at the other end of the line.

'Hello, Geraldine Ramsey here,' she said when she eventually picked up the receiver. 'Thank you for calling me back.'

With a look of relief on her face Rachel Dalton leaned across the desk and spoke loudly into the speaker. 'Good morning, Ms Ramsey, my name's DC Dalton and I'm here with my colleague, DS Cooper. We understand you might have some information that could help us in our enquiries into the deaths of Marcus Ardleigh and Ruben Kenyon?'

*   *   *   *

'You can drop me off here, Marc,' announced Carmichael suddenly as his car neared the level crossing in Moulton Bank. 'You get back to the station and see how the others are doing. Check out Miranda Coyle's alibi for Sunday night, too, and, if you've time, see if you can get Stock's post-mortem report on Kenyon. I've a few things to do here. I'll meet you back at the station. Remind the others we have a debrief at two thirty.'

Watson dutifully stopped the car, right outside The Railway Tavern. Carmichael waited until the car was out of sight before he made his way down the narrow alleyway that led to the back door of the public house.

He knocked loudly three times and waited.

The door opened slowly and Carmichael looked up into the eyes of Robbie Robertson.

'Can I come in?' Carmichael asked calmly. 'I know everything and I think we need to talk.'

Chapter 21

It was nearly lunchtime when Robbie Carmichael finally stirred. Although he was still only seventeen, he was taller than most boys of his age and looked much older. As a result, he had been getting into pubs for long enough to be able to handle a few pints. On the previous evening, however, he had consumed far more than he had ever drunk before and it was also the first time he'd been foolish enough to mix pints of lager, vodka shots and black Sambuca during the space of one evening.

He sat delicately on the edge of his bed, feeling sick and empty. His head ached like it had never ached before. So much so that if at that moment he had been offered a fifty–fifty chance of either death or an instant miraculous cure, he would have almost certainly risked all and taken his chances just to escape the pain and misery of his suffering.

'So how are you feeling?' he heard his mother say, as a steaming mug of tea was thrust in his direction.

'I feel crap, if you must know,' he announced abruptly, his sentence punctuated with a couple of loud burps. 'I just want to die.'

'I'm not surprised,' Penny replied with a kindly smile. 'I suspect you drank the pub dry last night by the state you were in.'

Robbie took a sip from the mug, which helped mask the terrible taste in his mouth. 'I hope you aren't here to give me a lecture?' he continued disrespectfully. 'If it had not been for you I wouldn't have got into that state. It's actually your fault. Well, you and that fat publican you named me after.'

Penny remained calm although his words hurt her deeply. 'You're right,' she replied.

This was not what Robbie expected or wanted to hear. He lifted his head and stared in disbelief at his mother. 'So it's all true then, is it?'

'That depends on what you've been told,' she replied, trying hard to pick her words carefully. 'It's true that I did think of your name when you were born, because I liked the name. And, as I only ever knew one person who was actually called Robbie, I guess you could say I named you after Robbie Robertson, although as you know Robbie is just his nickname. It's also true that I've been spending a lot of time with Robbie in the last few weeks and we've tried to keep our meetings a secret.'

'So are you saying that it's true what they say and you've been sleeping with him?' Robbie shouted, his anger clearly palpable in his bloodshot eyes.

Penny sat down next to her son and placed her hand on his shoulder. 'I truly regret that I was not more honest with your dad and the three of you,' she said in a trembling voice. 'Please let me explain.'

*   *   *   *

At 2:30 p.m. exactly, Carmichael started the debrief in the main incident room at Kirkwood Police Station.

'OK, team,' he announced. 'Let's follow our standard procedure and go over what we know to be fact first before we start to look at what our next steps should be.'

The three officers around the table nodded to indicate they understood the instruction.

'Marc, did you get Stock's autopsy report on Kenyon?' Carmichael asked.

Watson held up a file that had previously been resting on the desk in front of him. 'Yes, boss,' he said with excitement. 'I've got it here.'

'So what does the good Dr Stock say about the demise of Mr Kenyon?' he asked with eager anticipation. 'He's normally pretty adept in uncovering some juicy revelation or throwing in a curve ball.'

Watson smiled broadly. 'Well, he's not let you down this time either,' he remarked with an air of smugness, knowing that it was he who would have the pleasure of enlightening the rest of the team.

'Go on then!' Carmichael urged. 'Put us out of our misery. What's good old Harry Stock uncovered?'

'Well,' continued Watson, trying hard to make his announcement as dramatic as he could. 'As Stock has already told us, Kenyon was killed between eight and ten on Monday evening. The cause of death was a single violent and heavy blow to his left temple. He was subsequently struck a number of times afterwards but Stock believes the first blow would have killed him.'

'Did Stock indicate what sort of weapon was used by the murderer?' Rachel asked.

'No,' replied Watson, who took Rachel's question as his cue to hold up an enlarged photograph of the indentation on the side of Kenyon's head. 'As you can see, it's almost circular in shape and about an inch in diameter.'

Carmichael, Cooper and Rachel, looked intently at the photograph.

'It looks like the end of a hollow tube,' remarked Cooper.

'Yes, like the end of a scaffolding pipe, but a lot smaller,' Rachel observed.

'I assume so far the SOCOs have not found anything at the scene that resembles the weapon?' Carmichael enquired.

'Not yet, sir,' replied Watson. 'But they are still looking.'

Carmichael gazed blankly at the wall beyond his three officers.

'So is that everything from Stock's report worth noting?' he asked with more than a hint of disappointment in his voice.

'Oh no,' continued Watson who could barely contain his excitement at the prospect of revealing the most interesting find of the forensic team. 'Cigarette ash was found on the floor by the front passenger seat,' he eagerly announced. 'Which they are certain was left there on the evening Kenyon was killed and they have established that the ash came from Marlboro cigarettes.'

'Isn't that the brand Miranda Coyle smokes?' enquired Carmichael, even though he knew full well that it was.

'Yes,' replied Watson, who had already made the link himself.

'But thousands of people smoke Marlboro cigarettes,' remarked Cooper. 'Maybe Kenyon or even his wife was a Marlboro smoker.'

'I've checked that already,' replied Watson, with no attempt to hide his self-righteousness. 'Kenyon smoked cigars and his wife has never smoked; she positively hates smoking.'

'Good work, Dr Stock,' muttered Carmichael. 'And you, too, Marc,' he quickly added when he saw the look on Watson's face change from unbounded elation to bemusement. 'You've both done a great job,' he reiterated to drive the point home. 'Miranda Coyle made no mention of meeting Kenyon when we spoke to her this morning. So she's now got to be high up there on our suspect list, that's for sure.'

Watson nodded, although in truth he was still fairly certain that Napier had killed Ardleigh and Kenyon.

'So what have you two uncovered?' enquired Carmichael, turning his attention to Rachel Dalton and Paul Cooper.

'We've not had time to speak with Hugo Lazarus yet,' remarked Cooper. 'But I spoke with Gordon Napier again this morning, as you instructed. He was still adamant that he had no idea what Ardleigh was talking about in his letter. He flatly denies any involvement in the two deaths and reluctantly I had to release him.'

'I'm not surprised you couldn't get him to come clean,' replied Carmichael. 'He's certainly hiding something but whether he's the murderer is still not easy to say and, despite us finding the rope in his van, it will not be easy to prove anything without more evidence. For what it's worth, my money's probably on Miranda Coyle now,' he continued. 'She certainly has got to be our prime suspect for Kenyon's death.'

'Maybe,' replied Watson, who was still sure it was Napier. 'The only problem with that theory is that her alibi for Sunday night was backed up by her young toy boy, Graham Calvin. I spoke to him just before and he is saying he was with her from 8 p.m. on Sunday evening until Monday morning. Mind you he could be lying.'

'But if he's telling the truth, she's in the clear,' replied Rachel.

'Unless of course there were two murderers,' remarked Cooper.

Carmichael sighed. 'Marc, you need to see if the apartment Miranda lives in has any security tapes. An apartment that fancy almost certainly will. If it does, check them out for Sunday night and Monday morning. Once you've done that, we need to talk to Miranda again about her story, but check out the tapes first.'

Watson nodded. 'Will get on to it straight after the debrief.'

'What progress have you made, Rachel?' Carmichael enquired.

'I checked out Dr Walker's alibi,' she replied with a shrug of her shoulders. 'It's watertight. There is no way he could have killed Kenyon and it would have been pretty difficult for him to have killed Ardleigh, unless he did it in about ten minutes and drove like a madman down to his conference in Birmingham. I think he's in the clear.'

'Maybe so,' replied Carmichael. 'But until we find out his secret he stays on the list, albeit I agree as an outsider.'

'Agreed,' replied Rachel.

'So did you uncover anything else?' Carmichael asked.

'Well,' replied Rachel who now saw this as her turn at being the excited bringer of good news. 'We've located Geraldine Ramsey. She's on holiday in Italy at the moment, but we managed to talk with her earlier. She's saying that she only learned of Ardleigh's death from the newspaper this morning.'

'But it was in Tuesday's papers and all over the news on TV,' remarked Watson.

'Yes but she's in Italy,' replied Rachel abruptly. 'She's not been watching TV and they get the English newspapers a day later there, so she only got Tuesday's paper this morning.'

Realizing he had spoken before thinking – a trait that he was more than occasionally guilty of displaying – Watson did not take the conversation further, preferring to let his embarrassed expression tell its own story.

'So what else did she say?' Carmichael asked eagerly.

'She maintains it was she who posted the three letters for Ardleigh. She says he had wanted to get them into the last post on Friday but they missed the last collection and they would have only been collected on Saturday.'

'So it sounds like Ardleigh had wanted the three recipients to get them on Saturday not Monday,' Carmichael commented.

'Yes, that's what I think,' replied Rachel.

'What else did she say?' continued Carmichael. 'Did she know what was in the three letters she posted?'

'I didn't ask,' replied Rachel sheepishly. 'She said she is going to try and get a flight back to UK either today or tomorrow. She sounded really distressed. She also said she had a copy of Ardleigh's will. She said it's at her house.'

'What's in it?' enquired Carmichael impatiently.

'She doesn't know,' replied Rachel. 'She says it's sealed and she's never opened it. She maintains that Ardleigh gave it to her a matter of only two or three weeks ago so it has to be his current will. She also says that Ardleigh told her he'd given another copy to Hugo Lazarus.'

'Really,' remarked Carmichael who was now sensing that the team were starting to make some headway. 'We absolutely have to speak with him today then. I wonder if he's opened his copy. We'll do that together, Paul,' he continued whilst gazing in Cooper's direction.

'That's fine with me, boss,' replied Cooper.

'So to be clear, Ms Ramsey confirmed that the three letters she posted were the ones sent to Napier, Miranda Coyle and Dr Walker, but you're not sure if she knew their contents?' Carmichael enquired.

'That's correct, sir,' replied Rachel.

'OK,' Carmichael said after giving all he'd heard some moments to sink in. 'It seems to me that we have four potential suspects. Any of them may have singlehandedly or with one of the others or even someone we have yet to uncover, been responsible for the two deaths. We, of course, have Napier, but until we discover his secret I'm not sure we will get much further with him. We have Miranda Coyle, who you are going to investigate, Marc. We have Hugo Lazarus, whom you and I will follow up on, Paul, and we have Dr Walker. In his case, we will need to find out his secret, too, before we can make any more progress because his alibi is the strongest of the lot.'

The team nodded.

'What do you want me to do?' enquired Rachel, who was starting to feel a little left out.

'I want you to do a few things,' replied Carmichael. 'Firstly, check out exactly when Geraldine Ramsey is coming home. If it's today, make sure you meet her at the airport and bring her back here. I'd like to talk with her. But also find out as much as you can about Ardleigh, particularly from his time at university in Oxford. I want to know what sort of man he was, whether he was liked, what enemies he had, and in particular anything murky from his past in Oxford. Other than Dr Walker, he met the other three suspects at Oxford when he was an undergraduate. I want to know what they got up to back then. It's possible these nasty little secrets stem from his days in Oxford.'

'Will do, sir,' replied Rachel as enthusiastically as she could, albeit that inside she had no idea where to start.

Chapter 22

Hugo Lazarus lived in Fiddlesticks Cottage, a neat rose-clad dwelling on the outskirts of Moulton Bank. It was one of the best kept houses in the village and its gardens were the envy of most of the amateur horticulturists in the surrounding area.

As Carmichael's BMW glided to a standstill on the gravel path he glanced at the clock on the dashboard. It was precisely four o'clock.

'Here we are,' he announced. 'Quite a pad isn't it, Sergeant?'

'Absolutely,' replied Cooper. 'I would fancy Mrs Cooper would love us to live in a place like this. Mind you, I suspect it's worth a pretty penny. More than a mere sergeant like me could afford.'

'Yes,' agreed Carmichael. 'Probably well out of my league, too.'

It had been another bright, warm summer's day and, even though the sun was already quite low in the sky, its reflection off the gleaming whitewashed walls of Fiddlesticks Cottage still made Carmichael and Cooper narrow their eyes and bow their heads to evade its dazzling glare. 'So let's see what Mr Lazarus has to say for himself,' Carmichael remarked as the two officers lumbered over to the front door.

Before either of them had time to knock on the stout wooden door they were joined by the owner, who appeared unexpectedly from behind a gigantic bush to the right of the cottage. The shrub, which stood over six feet tall and at its base seemed even wider, was bejewelled with masses of tiny yellow flowers that gave off a stunning perfume.

'Good afternoon, Inspector,' Lazarus announced as he strode confidently towards them.

'Oh, good afternoon, Mr Lazarus,' replied Carmichael. 'I'd like a few minutes of your time if I may to ask you some questions.'

'Of course,' Lazarus responded, who by now was close enough to the two officers to offer his mud-caked hand as a greeting. 'Why don't we sit in the garden? It's such a lovely afternoon it would be such a shame to waste it by sitting indoors.'

'That's fine with me,' replied Carmichael, who firmly shook Lazarus's hand. 'Lead on.'

Hugo Lazarus had impeccable manners and made sure he also shook Sergeant Cooper's hand before he led the two officers round the side of the cottage and into the beautifully tended rear garden.

Although Lazarus was now in his sixties and was dressed in his gardening clothes, he still cut a dash, with his piercing dark eyes, wavy silvery black hair and well-tended moustache.

As they followed, Carmichael recalled how young Rachel Dalton, who was less than half his age, had appeared to be quite smitten by this handsome well-spoken gentleman when she first met him at Ardleigh's house just a few days earlier. To a degree, he could understand how such a sophisticated and courteous old gentleman like Hugo Lazarus could have this effect on the opposite sex.

'Do you live alone, Mr Lazarus?' Carmichael enquired as they eventually arrived at the large, circular, wrought-iron garden table.

'Yes,' replied Lazarus. 'But please do call me Hugo. I've never married and to be honest I have always enjoyed my own company. It may surprise you to hear but living alone is a luxury I cherish.'

'I see,' remarked Cooper in a tone that Lazarus took as a question mark regarding his orientation.

Lazarus smiled broadly. 'I do have lady friends, Sergeant, but I've never found the right lady. Well, maybe not one that would have me.'

'You have a lovely house, Hugo,' interjected Carmichael. 'You must be doing very well in your work to afford a place like this. What is your occupation?'

Lazarus smiled again. 'I wish I could say that I had been successful, but alas I cannot, Inspector. I was, as they say, born into money and, in spite of a few minor flirtations into the world of industry many years ago, I've been, I suppose pretty idle for most of my life in that respect. My father died when I was at university at Oxford and his estate was worth a considerable sum. He and my mother had been divorced since I was about three and as I was his only child I was left with more than enough to keep me ticking over quite nicely for the past, almost forty years.'

'I see,' replied Carmichael, who found this piece of news quite infuriating, especially given that when his own father had died some ten years earlier his inheritance had been a very modest sum. 'Can we please go over your statement that you gave DC Dalton?'

'Of course,' countered Lazarus. 'But before I do, can I offer you gentlemen some refreshment. Some tea, or maybe a soft drink?'

'I'd love a cold drink,' replied Cooper without hesitating. His seat at the table was the only one that the large parasol was not fully shading and as such he was feeling quite warm in his suit and tie.

Carmichael shot his junior officer a withering look. He was keen to get the discussions under way and to get off home. 'Well, we can't linger too long, Hugo,' he said through gritted teeth, 'but I suppose a cold drink would be nice given that it's such a hot day.'

'I fully understand,' replied Lazarus as he rose from the table. 'I know that others are still working even if I'm not. I'll be as quick as I can.'

'Lucky sod,' remarked Cooper as soon as their genial host was out of earshot. 'It's amazing how the other half live.'

Carmichael gazed at the spritely figure of Hugo Lazarus walking away across the carefully manicured lawn. 'Something tells me his life's not as perfect as he'd like us to believe,' he muttered sagely. 'Mind you, he does look pretty good for his age. Not unlike either Miranda Coyle or Dr Walker in many ways.'

'How do you mean?' enquired Cooper.

'They all look for the world like people who are confident, clearly not short of a few bob and in full control of their lives,' he replied as Lazarus disappeared into the house. 'My guess is that, once we start peeling away at their carefully polished exteriors, we'll find with all of them the truth paints a totally different picture.'

*   *   *   *

Robbie Robertson's appointment with the specialist was at 4:20 p.m. This was the third time he had been to Princess Margaret's Hospital since his GP had referred him just under a month earlier. During his previous two visits – the first an initial consultation and the second a full body scan and a barium meal – he had been accompanied only by Penny, the one person he could bring himself to confide in since his doctor hinted that he might have cancer. On this occasion, however, he was not just supported by Penny, but also by his daughter Katie.

Had Penny not called him that morning to tell him she was going to share their secret with the rest of her family, it is unlikely the publican would have had the courage to tell his daughter. But with his hand having been forced by Penny, Robbie had reluctantly spoken with Katie and, as a result, was now relieved that his situation was at last known to his only daughter. In total silence, the three of them patiently sat on the hard, uncomfortable chairs that had been scattered randomly around the drab empty waiting room. It took twenty minutes before the doctor eventually arrived. He was the same doctor Penny had seen on the previous occasions – late forties, smartly dressed with a cheery open round face.

'Mr Robertson, would you care to come through?' said the doctor as if Robbie's attendance was more or less optional.

Robbie Robertson gingerly got to his feet but, with a brace of positive supportive smiles supplied by his two female companions, he found the courage to amble tentatively towards the open door of the doctor's small consulting room. The door closed firmly behind them leaving his anxious friend and an even more concerned daughter to wait for him to re-emerge.

'Why didn't he tell me sooner?' Katie whispered angrily through gritted teeth. 'What did he think I'd say?'

'He was worried how you'd react,' replied Penny. 'I told him he was wrong to hide it from you, but he was concerned not to worry you.'

'Silly old fool,' responded Katie. 'I'm twenty-five for pity's sake. It's not like I'm a twelve-year-old.'

'I know,' replied Penny, who put her arm around Katie's shoulders, 'With your mum dying of cancer he found it hard to talk to you about it. Anyway he's told you now, that's the main thing.'

'So today's the day he gets his test results?' remarked Katie apprehensively. 'I hope they're not positive. Or do I mean I hope they are positive. I'm not sure how you say it.'

Penny smiled. 'Me neither, but I know what you mean.'

It would be a further fifteen minutes before Robbie Robertson re-appeared from out of the doctor's consulting room. During that long agonising wait Penny did her best to keep up Katie's spirits by focusing the conversation on the young woman's plans for her upcoming marriage to Barnaby Green, the handsome local cleric; a subject that Katie was more than happy to discuss at great length.

*　*　*　*

Carmichael took a sip from his glass of home-made lemonade. 'In your statement, Mr Lazarus, you said you arrived at Marcus Ardleigh's house at eight o'clock.'

'That's correct,' replied Lazarus in his softly spoken Home Counties accent. 'But, Inspector, do call me Hugo. I still think of Mr Lazarus as my father.'

'OK, Hugo,' continued Carmichael. 'You also said that there were several people who knew where Marcus left his spare key, including Geraldine Ramsey and Gordon Napier.'

'That's also correct,' replied Lazarus. 'There could even be more.'

'So in your opinion there could be a number of people who could have let themselves into Marcus's house on Sunday evening?'

'Well,' replied Lazarus nervously. 'It couldn't have been Geraldine; she's on holiday. I cannot believe it would be Gordon and it certainly wasn't me. So if he was murdered, it's possible that someone else knew about the key. Of course, he could have just let someone in, I suppose.'

'Why are you so sure it wasn't Mr Napier?' enquired Carmichael.

'Gordon!' exclaimed Lazarus, who almost choked on his lemonade at the notion. 'Gordon couldn't hurt a fly. He was one of Marcus's oldest friends and the very thought of him having anything to do with Marcus's death is just unthinkable.'

'Maybe not,' replied Carmichael. 'He received a letter from Marcus advising him that he was about to reveal a nasty secret about his old friend. You know that don't you, sir?'

'Well yes, I am aware of the letter,' replied Lazarus timidly. 'I was there when Gordon's call came through to Marcus's phone on Monday. But Gordon has since told me about the letter and that another two people received letters, too. So it could just as easily be one of them.'

'It could,' responded Carmichael calmly. 'But Mr Napier has no alibi for the evening Ardleigh died; he received one of the three letters; the rope used to bind Marcus's hands was found in his van, and if that was not enough, Mr Napier hasn't got an alibi for the murder of Ruben Kenyon. So, as you can see, it's actually not looking good for your friend Gordon Napier.'

Carmichael took a deep breath before picking up his lemonade glass once more; his eyes, however, remained fixed on Hugo Lazarus.

'I see,' replied Lazarus after a short pause.

'Can I ask you, sir, whether Mr Napier is a keen yachtsman?' Cooper enquired.

'Good God, no,' replied Lazarus with a smile. 'Actually we always tease him about his hatred of water. He gets terrible seasickness even when the sea is calm. No, Gordon hates boats, Sergeant.'

'So do you like boats?' enquired Carmichael.

'In my youth, yes,' replied Lazarus. 'In fact, it was Marcus who introduced me to sailing when we first met at Oxford. He was a very keen sailor. I haven't sailed in years, though. Is that relevant to Marcus's death?'

'It may be,' replied Carmichael. 'The knots used to tie Marcus's noose to the banisters were sailing knots.'

'So that definitely lets Gordon off the hook,' announced Lazarus with enthusiasm. 'He wouldn't know a reef-knot from a bowline.'

'Maybe not,' replied Carmichael. 'But you certainly do, sir.'

'So am I your prime suspect number two?' remarked Lazarus with a hint of sarcasm in his voice.

'At this moment, sir, we have no prime suspects,' replied Carmichael. 'Just a list of questions we need answers to.'

Lazarus nodded. 'Of course, Inspector,' he remarked. 'I fully understand. Do you have any more that I can answer?'

'Yes,' replied Carmichael. 'I still have several more questions if that's all right with you?'

'Of course,' repeated Lazarus.

'Let's start with the call you got from Marcus to invite you to the pub,' said Carmichael. 'Exactly when was that call and what did Marcus say?'

'It must have been at about seven thirty on Saturday evening,' replied Lazarus, who looked as if he was trying hard to recall everything as accurately as he could. 'He sounded very agitated. He said he wanted to discuss something important with me and asked me to meet him in the pub the following day.'

'Did he give any indication as to what he wanted to talk to you about?' enquired Cooper.

'No,' replied Lazarus. 'He merely said he would tell me when we met.'

'And why the pub?' enquired Carmichael. 'Surely a meeting at his house would have been more appropriate.'

Lazarus shrugged his shoulders. 'I really don't know,' he replied.

'Maybe it was to discuss his will?' suggested Carmichael, who studied Lazarus's facial expressions to see if this remark would catch him off guard.

'He didn't say,' replied Lazarus.

'But you do have a copy of Marcus's will, don't you, Hugo?' enquired Carmichael.

'Actually I do,' replied Lazarus, who was now becoming patently uncomfortable, as he shuffled from side to side in his chair. 'Marcus was good enough to give me a copy of his will a short time ago.'

'Would you please get the will for us, Hugo?' Carmichael asked.

'You want it now?' enquired Lazarus, his discomfort evident in his voice.

'If that's not too much trouble, sir,' replied Carmichael sarcastically.

Reluctantly, Lazarus rose slowly from his chair, and for the second time that afternoon walked across his carefully clipped lawn and back into his chocolate-box cottage.

'He's not so cocksure now,' remarked Carmichael with a wry grin.

'No, sir,' concurred Cooper, 'but do you think he's got anything to do with the murders?'

'That's a good question, Paul,' replied Carmichael, his smile now totally vanished. 'He may have, and even if not, he's certainly still hiding something, I'm sure of that.'

* * * *

As soon as the debrief finished, Watson had sped off to Miranda Coyle's apartment. Having established that Carmichael was correct and the luxury complex did have security tapes, he headed off home for an evening's viewing.

Rachel Dalton, meanwhile, as instructed by Carmichael, had spoken again with Geraldine Ramsey, who had informed her that her flight back from Italy would touch down at Manchester Airport at 6:30 p.m. the following evening. Having decided she could do no more with that part of her assignment, Rachel was diligently trying to find out anything she could about Ardleigh's time at Oxford.

It took her less than an hour to make a breakthrough so interesting that she felt compelled to let her boss know.

*　　*　　*　　*

Lazarus was still in the house when Rachel's call came through.

'Sorry to disturb you, sir,' she said, the excitement in her voice palpable. 'I just thought I should give you an update.'

'That's perfectly fine, Rachel,' replied Carmichael as he took a sip of his cold lemonade. 'Cooper and I are very busy, but I have a few moments to talk.'

Cooper got the joke and smiled back at his boss to register this acknowledgement.

'I've spoken to the local police,' continued Rachel. 'They've been very helpful. When I mentioned that Ardleigh, Napier and Lazarus all went to Oriel College in the 70s they suggested we speak to a Mr Constantine; he was a maths tutor at the college back then. I've spoken to him on the phone and he says he remembers them all very well, especially Ardleigh.'

'Great work, Rachel,' replied Carmichael. 'We need to get down there and speak to him.'

'The only thing, though, is that he's about to fly to Australia on Saturday to see his daughter for two months,' continued Rachel. 'I was wondering whether I should go down there tomorrow.'

Carmichael thought for a moment. 'What about Geraldine Ramsey?' he asked. 'When does she get back?'

'Her flight gets into Manchester tomorrow evening,' replied Rachel, 'at about six thirty.'

'I'll tell you what,' continued Carmichael. 'You stay here tomorrow. During the day you can help Cooper interview Dr

131

Walker again. I want to know why he got a letter. Then in the evening meet Geraldine Ramsey off the plane. I'll go to Oxford.'

'Right you are, sir,' replied Rachel, who could not hide her disappointment.

'Call Mr Constantine back,' continued Carmichael. 'Get all his details and tell him I'll be with him in the morning at ten o'clock.'

'Will do, sir,' said Rachel.

'Look, I'm going to have to go,' Carmichael announced, as he saw Lazarus reappear from the cottage. 'I'll call you later.'

Carmichael rested his mobile phone on the table. 'Have you ever been to Oxford, Paul?' he asked.

Cooper shook his head. 'No, I can't say I have, sir,' he replied.

'Me neither,' continued Carmichael.

Lazarus arrived at the table and handed Carmichael a long rectangular envelope. 'This is Marcus's will,' he said.

'I see the envelope has been opened,' remarked Carmichael. 'Did Mr Ardleigh tell you that you could read it?'

'Of course,' replied Lazarus indignantly. 'Do you think I'd open it if he wanted it kept private?'

Carmichael did not reply. He was far too preoccupied with extracting the will from its envelope.

'So, in brief, what does it say?' Cooper asked.

'He left everything to Geraldine Ramsey and me,' replied Lazarus. 'But with a caveat that should either of us die before him then their half of the estate would go to our old college in Oxford.'

'Oriel College,' remarked Carmichael.

'That's quite correct,' replied Lazarus, who looked genuinely surprised that Carmichael knew which college they had attended.

'That's very generous,' observed Cooper. 'Did you discuss the will with Marcus?'

'No,' responded Lazarus sharply. 'I only opened the will on Monday after he was dead.'

'Why do you think he chose you two and not Gordon Napier?' Carmichael asked.

'I'm absolutely baffled as to why he left Gordon out of his will,' replied Lazarus. 'Honestly I am.'

'So what sort of man was Marcus Ardleigh?' enquired Carmichael. 'He seems quite complicated to me.'

'Yes, he was a very unique person,' replied Lazarus without any hesitation. 'He was a confident, logical, pragmatic person. He was highly intelligent and, for as long as I can remember, he liked to be in control of his own life.'

'A control freak?' remarked Carmichael indelicately.

'Well, in the nicest possible way I suppose he was!' replied Lazarus, who had clearly never considered his friend in that way before. 'Actually,' he continued with a wry smile, 'if you weren't careful, he'd organise yours, mine and everyone else's lives around him, too.'

'Did he talk to you about the three letters he sent out?' Carmichael asked.

'Absolutely not,' responded Lazarus without hesitating. 'I only found out about them from Gordon after I went to see him on Monday.'

'That would be after you heard Napier's answerphone message?' added Carmichael.

'That's correct,' replied Lazarus nervously.

'He doesn't seem to have trusted you very much?' continued Carmichael.

'Why do you say that?' replied Lazarus.

'Well, he sends Ernest Walker, Miranda Coyle and his old friend Gordon Napier some quite nasty letters, but doesn't tell you anything about them. What sort of person does that?'

Lazarus shrugged his shoulders. 'I can't give you an answer to that question, Inspector,' he replied tamely.

Carmichael rose from the table. 'We've taken enough of

your time, Mr Lazarus,' he said. 'If you can think of anything more that will help us, I'd appreciate it if you could contact us right away.'

'Of course,' replied Lazarus, who was noticeably relieved that the interview was at an end. 'If I think of anything, I'll call you straight away.'

The three men walked back across the lawn towards the tidy country cottage.

'You have a lovely garden, Mr Lazarus,' remarked Cooper. 'It's clearly a passion of yours.'

'Yes, Sergeant, I adore my garden,' replied Lazarus. 'It's here I feel the most at ease.'

As they reached the house Carmichael stretched out his hand. 'There's just one more question I'd like to ask you,' he said, as Lazarus shook it warmly. 'What was Gordon Napier's reaction when you told him that Marcus was dead?'

Lazarus hesitated. 'I don't understand.'

'Well,' continued Carmichael, 'I understood from DC Dalton that after you finished your statement with her on Monday, you heard Napier's phone message to Ardleigh and you then went to see him. So I assume it was you who broke the sad news to Mr Napier. All I would like to know is how he took the news of Ardleigh's death?'

'Yes, it was me that told him about Marcus's death,' replied Lazarus, trying hard to regain some poise. 'He was devastated, of course, like all of us. Yes, he was terribly shocked and very distressed.'

Carmichael nodded. 'Well, thank you for your time today, sir,' he said as he and Cooper clambered back into his black BMW.

'What do you think, Paul?' enquired Carmichael as he carefully manoeuvred the car out onto the main road.

'I'm not sure he was telling us the truth when he said he had only opened the will after Ardleigh had died,' replied Cooper. 'And getting your hands on half of Ardleigh's estate

134

would be a good enough reason for many people to think about killing him.'

Carmichael nodded. 'I agree he's keeping something from us and maybe my visit to Oxford tomorrow may help me understand what. I'm certain that most of what we have yet to learn about this case is to be found in Oxford.'

Hugo Lazarus watched as the car drove away. As soon as it had disappeared completely out of sight, he collected the glasses from the table and walked back towards his chocolate-box cottage.

Chapter 23

Carmichael decided not return to the office after the meeting with Hugo Lazarus. Having given Cooper specific instructions for the entire team to follow the next day, Carmichael elected to make his way home. He figured that if he was to be in Oxford for 10 a.m. the following morning he would have to leave home at around 6 a.m., so he wanted to be able to spend some time at home that evening with the family.

As Carmichael drove down the quiet, sunlit Lancashire country lanes, he pondered on the afternoon's meeting with Hugo Lazarus and, having exhausted his brain on that subject, then went on to analyse the other main suspects. His immediate conclusion was that, with the exception of Dr Ernest Walker, on whom he had yet to form any real opinion, the other people in the frame were more than capable of murder. Napier, Coyle and Lazarus all had a motive, whether it was to prevent an embarrassing secret from coming out in the case of Napier and Coyle or, in the case of Lazarus, to benefit financially from Ardleigh's will. However, something deep down in his gut told him that none of them was the killer.

'The answer to all this is back in Oxford,' Carmichael muttered to himself as at last he arrived at his house in Moulton Bank.

He locked the car and strode confidently up the driveway that led to his front door. Carmichael couldn't help smiling to himself as he imagined what Marc Watson would make of his instructions for the next day. He knew Watson hated anything laborious, so it tickled Carmichael's sadistic humour to think of poor Marc not only going through the security tapes from Miranda Coyle's apartment, but also then going to The Lindley Hotel and studying its tapes too. Carmichael liked Watson and saw him as a valuable team member, but at times he found the cocky sergeant a bit too much to bear and felt no guilt at all about occasionally bringing him down a peg or two. In fact, he quite enjoyed the experience. Carmichael did not expect Marc to be finished with his tape-watching duties until at least lunchtime tomorrow, which is precisely when he intended to call his troops again to get an update on their progress.

Before he had a chance to push his key into the lock, the front door opened abruptly and Penny, with tears streaming down her face and a smile as wide as any of Mr Hayley's barn doors, burst out of the house and gave her husband an almighty squeeze.

'He's got the all-clear,' she announced in an irrepressible high pitched shriek. 'Robbie's tests were all negative.'

'Fantastic,' replied Carmichael. 'That's great news. I expect he's really relieved.'

'Yes,' said Penny, 'so much so that he's invited us all to a celebration tonight at The Railway.'

'Will the beer be on the house then?' he enquired.

'Hold your horses, Steve; he's only been told that he hasn't got cancer,' replied Penny. 'Knowing Robbie as we do, I think he'd need to have been raised from the dead before he went that far.'

Carmichael smiled down at his wife's delighted expression. 'Let's go inside, I'm starving.'

*　*　*　*

Carmichael could not remember The Railway Tavern being so full on a Wednesday evening. By the time he and Penny arrived it was only 7:30, but already the lounge and the snug were both packed with locals celebrating Robbie's good news.

'I thought this was supposed to be a big secret until earlier today?' enquired Carmichael.

'It was,' replied Penny, who had to shout to be heard over the noise, 'but you know how things are in small villages – word soon gets around.'

'First drink is on the house,' announced Katie as Carmichael eventually made it to the bar.

'All their drinks are on the house tonight, Katie,' corrected her father, who was stood behind her. 'After all Penny did for me that's the least I can do.'

'That's very kind,' replied Carmichael, with a true look of delight on his face. 'I'll have a pint of best bitter and Penny will have a dry white wine.'

'Coming up, Steve,' replied Katie.

'Hey, you'll never guess, Penny,' boomed Robbie Robertson from the other end of the bar, 'I've just heard that the gossip around the village was that we were having an affair. How ridiculous is that?'

Carmichael looked at Penny, who gazed back at her husband with a quizzical expression on her face. 'Plain ludicrous, I'd say.'

'Let's try and find a seat,' said Carmichael, once their drinks had arrived. 'I think there are a few empty tables over in the corner.'

Penny nodded her agreement and followed her husband as he barged his way through the packed drinkers standing close to the bar.

Having found their way to a free table, the Carmichaels sat down and took a sip of their drinks.

'So how was your day?' Penny asked.

'Busy,' replied Carmichael. 'I interviewed Miranda Coyle this morning and Hugo Lazarus this afternoon.'

'And are either likely to be the murderer?' Penny asked.

'They could be,' replied Carmichael, 'but I'm not sure. I am sure they are both lying to me, though.'

'So where do you go now?' Penny enquired.

'Well, actually, Oxford,' replied Carmichael. 'I'm going down there early tomorrow to meet an old man who used to be a lecturer when Ardleigh, Napier and Lazarus were undergraduates.'

'He must be cracking on a bit then,' replied Penny. 'They are all in their late fifties and sixties, so he must be almost ninety.'

'I guess so,' replied Carmichael. 'I better get down there soon before he expires.'

Penny elbowed him hard in the ribs. 'That's not nice,' she said, although she was smiling from ear to ear.

'Anyway, what was your day like?' Carmichael enquired.

'Well, I had a frank conversation with your children this morning, particularly your son,' she replied. 'I think they're happy that I'm not the village strumpet. Then of course I went with Robbie and Katie to see the consultant. That was about it.'

Carmichael laughed. 'And how is our Robbie now? He seemed very quiet at dinner.'

'He's fine,' replied Penny. 'He's embarrassed, he's feeling a bit of a fool and he's still hung over, too.'

'He's probably relieved,' said Carmichael with a grin.

'I can't believe he thought I was having an affair,' said Penny indignantly. 'But what's even more galling is that Brooke and her damn mother appear to have been active in spreading this appalling lie about me.'

'I don't know her mother,' said Carmichael as calmly as he could. 'But surely Brooke would not have done anything so malicious. She seems such a sweet little thing.'

'Maybe,' replied Penny. 'But just wait until I meet her bloody mother – I'll give her a right mauling over this.'

Carmichael could tell how angry his wife was, by the way she had used 'damn' and 'bloody' in the space of a few sentences. Penny hardly ever swore, so a 'damn' and a 'bloody' in such close proximity meant she was really mad.

Much to his relief, they were joined at that moment by Robbie Robertson, who plonked himself and his large pewter tankard at their table. 'Weird, isn't it?' the landlord remarked. 'Who would have thought a few weeks ago that I'd be buying drinks in my own pub with a load of the regulars to celebrate being told I have a twisted bowel and gallstones?'

Carmichael laughed. 'You must be very relieved, Robbie. I'm glad it wasn't what you feared.'

'I am,' he replied. 'I was so worried I can tell you.' The larger-than-life landlord took a deep gulp from his tankard. 'And I'm really grateful to you, Penny,' he said sincerely. 'I'll not forget your support these last few weeks.'

Penny smiled. 'It was nothing. That's what friends are for.'

Robbie smiled and turned to face Carmichael. 'So how's the murder investigation going?' he asked. 'Do you know who killed Ardleigh and Kenyon yet?'

Carmichael sighed. 'Not yet, Robbie, but you'll be the first to know when I do.'

Robbie stood up. 'I know,' he mumbled, 'you cannot talk about your cases to the likes of me. But if you ask my opinion, it will be something to do with his work with either Thatcher or Blair. From what everyone is saying, it looks like a professional hit.'

The possibility that Ardleigh and Kenyon had been assassinated by a hit man had never entered Carmichael's mind. He pondered the prospect for a few seconds before replying. 'I think you should stick to pulling pints, Robbie, and let me be the village Hercule Poirot.'

Robbie gave out a huge laugh which seemed to emanate

from the depths of his substantial frame. 'Maybe you're right. Anyway, I must get back to help Katie; the pub's manic tonight. If I don't get a chance to talk to you again later, I'll see both on Saturday at the Prom.'

On that note, the publican marched back towards the bar.

'What's he talking about?' Carmichael whispered to Penny.

'Oh,' interrupted Penny uneasily. 'I forgot to tell you. I bought us all tickets to attend the Prom Evening at Rivingham Hall on Saturday.'

'What!' exclaimed Carmichael. 'What's that all about?'

'It's a bit like the Proms at the Albert Hall,' replied Penny enthusiastically, 'but outdoors, with a re-enactment of Napoleonic battles and a flypast from some Spitfires. It will be great!'

'What on earth possessed you to do that?' remarked Carmichael, slowly shaking his head from left to right and screwing up his brow with incredulity.

'It's all in a good cause,' replied Penny. 'It's in aid of local cancer charities. I bought them at the hospital this afternoon. It will be fun!'

'Fun!' exclaimed Carmichael. 'I can think of other words that would better describe it.'

Chapter 24

Thursday, 19th August

The alarm clock's piercing ring brought Carmichael's deep slumber to an abrupt conclusion at precisely 5:25 a.m.

'Bugger!' he exclaimed through gritted teeth. 'It can't be time to get up already.'

Clumsily, Carmichael rolled out of bed and made his way to the bathroom, cursing the fact that he'd only had four and a half hours' sleep. This was a direct result of his reluctance to leave The Railway Tavern at a more sensible hour, compounded by his inability to get to sleep, the latter due to a mixture of his mind racing as it continually analysed the complex case he was working on and his beloved wife's thunderous snoring.

'Sorry, Pen, I'm going to have to turn on the light,' he said when he returned fifteen minutes later. 'God, I feel dreadful!'

'I'm not surprised,' replied Penny, who, even before Carmichael had flicked on the bedside light, had already submerged herself below the duvet. 'You certainly made use of Robbie's generosity with the drink last night.'

'What do you mean?' replied Carmichael, his proclamation of innocence as plausible as an Italian striker taking a dive in the penalty box and crying foul to the referee. 'I could only have had three or four.'

'Pints, yes,' agreed Penny. 'Then there were the three

double whiskies you had with Robbie and the large one you poured yourself before we went to bed.'

With his memory having now been jolted, Carmichael thoroughly regretted being so stupid and getting so little sleep, but he couldn't do anything about that now, so he decided to get dressed and leave without any further conversation.

'Drive carefully!' Penny mumbled as her husband gracelessly exited the bedroom and awkwardly clumped his way down the stairs and out of the front door into the cool morning air.

'Just my bloody luck to get stopped this morning,' he muttered to himself, fully aware that he was probably still over the limit.

*   *   *   *

Marc Watson's reaction to his latest instruction was precisely as Carmichael had forecast. He'd spent three hours watching the tapes from the apartment, and with the end almost in sight, to be told that he now had to collect similar tapes from The Lindley and go through those before he could interview Miranda Coyle, made him irritable and angry.

'This is a job for a wooden top!' he announced after being told by Cooper. 'It will take me all bloody morning to get through these tapes. Sometimes I think Carmichael does it on purpose. He never gives you or bloody golden girl such crap jobs!'

Cooper shrugged his shoulders. 'Sorry, mate,' he replied calmly. 'They were his orders and he was quite specific.'

At that moment Rachel Dalton entered the office. 'Morning!' she said brightly, not realising that one of her colleagues was in a foul mood.

'So what assignments do you two get today?' continued Watson who was so incensed that he was visibly trembling.

143

Cooper tried his hardest to make their latest tasks seem as tedious as he could.

'Well, Rachel and I have to re-interview Dr Walker today and this evening Rachel is going to meet Geraldine Ramsey off the plane when she touches down in Manchester.'

'Typical!' shouted Watson. 'That's bloody typical of Carmichael. What happened to seniority? I was the first one made sergeant so I should be interviewing Walker while one of you two watch these tedious bloody CCTV tapes.'

'If you want to swap assignments, that's fine with me,' replied Cooper, who was quite shocked by his colleague's outburst.

'No way!' interrupted Rachel. 'If anyone swaps, it's me. There's no way I'm going out today with him while he's in such a wretched mood. I'll watch the tapes, you two go and do the Walker interview.'

'That's sorted then,' announced Watson with no shame. 'The natural order is re-established!'

After spending no more than two minutes updating DC Dalton where he was with the tapes from the apartment, Watson grabbed his jacket from behind his chair and, now in a much more joyful frame of mind, indicated to Cooper that he was ready to go.

'Are you OK with this, Rachel?' Cooper asked the young DC. 'I'll stay and watch the tapes if you want.'

'No, I'm fine,' replied Rachel. 'Call me when you've finished with Dr Walker. Hopefully I'll have seen all the CCTV tapes from the apartment and from The Lindley by then and we can decide how we proceed from there.'

'Sounds a good plan,' said Cooper with a comforting smile. 'I better catch up with Mr Grumpy. See you later.'

Cooper left the office and quickly made his way down the corridor after his colleague, leaving Rachel to decide whether she should complete the laborious task of watching the tapes from the apartment before she went to The Lindley to get their tapes from Monday evening, or get herself over to The Lindley, retrieve their tapes and watch them all together. She was desperate for a coffee and, figuring that the traffic would still be quite bad for the next hour or so, she decided on the former option as the best alternative.

*   *   *   *

Carmichael's estimate of the time it would take him to get from Moulton Bank to Oxford was three hours and fifteen minutes. Allowing for a thirty-minute break for breakfast and fifteen minutes to find the house and park his car, he was confident that having started the engine of his BMW at 5:50 a.m. he could easily get to Constantine's house in Mansfield Road, Oxford just before his appointment at 10 a.m. With a smug air of confidence he had headed south.

The journey went exactly to plan until he reached the outskirts of Oxford, when for some reason the traffic slowed down and after a few miles ground to a complete standstill. 'Bugger!' he exclaimed out loud.

For the next twenty minutes he remained motionless in his car. Carmichael looked at the satellite navigation system which indicated that he was just three miles from his destination, but with the time on the clock already saying 9:57 a.m. he knew that he was now going to be late. Carmichael hated being late for anything and could feel his blood pressure rising. He dialled the number Rachel had given him the day before. After ten seconds his call was answered.

'Good morning, Francis Constantine speaking,' announced the well-spoken but rather frail voice at the end of the line.

'Oh good morning, Mr Constantine,' Carmichael said in as loud a voice as he could. 'It's Inspector Carmichael here. I just wanted to let you know that I may be a few minutes late. I'm about three miles away but I'm stuck in traffic.'

'Oh dear,' he replied. 'Neither Erasmus nor I were intending to go anywhere else this morning. We'll see you when you eventually arrive, Inspector.'

At that point the traffic suddenly started to move.

'I expect to be with you in the next thirty minutes,' shouted Carmichael, although in truth he was not exactly sure. 'Is it easy to park near your house?'

'Oh yes,' replied the old man. 'However, make sure you buy a ticket as the traffic wardens in Oxford are assiduous fellows. They will have you if they can. I'll see you presently.'

On that note the phone went dead, which Carmichael took to be Mr Constantine having decided to end the call.

Carmichael's mood lightened immeasurably as soon as he had come off the phone as the traffic started to move much more freely.

'Erasmus,' he muttered to himself. 'I wonder who he is.'

* * * *

'I reckon Carmichael fancies Rachel,' announced Watson glibly as he and Cooper drove down the winding country roads that led to Dr Ernest Walker's house.

'I don't think so,' replied Cooper with a look of total bewilderment. 'I really think you've got that wrong, Marc.'

'Maybe you're right,' replied Watson. 'But he does give her some cushy numbers. Actually, come to think of it, he was like that with Lucy Clark. Remember how it was her that went with him to the US that time. She was just a rookie DC, too. I reckon he fancies his chances with the young female DCs; either that or he has an issue with women and they take advantage of him.'

'You do, do you?' remarked Cooper, who tried to make the tone of his response as disdainful as he could.

'Come on, Paul,' persisted Watson. 'You must have noticed

how we get the crap mundane tasks all the time while the pretty young DCs get all the interesting jobs.'

Cooper pondered the question for a few moments. He didn't want to give Watson any encouragement but he did have some sympathy with what he was saying.

'Maybe you need to look at it differently, Marc,' he said somewhat sagely.

'Oh yes,' replied Watson, who was keen to gain the benefit of his colleague's opinion. 'And how would you advise I do that?'

'Well, firstly I hear that Lucy Clark, that young rookie DC of four years ago, is doing really well in London and stands a good chance of making Inspector soon,' remarked Cooper. 'So maybe the boss saw something in her. What's more I don't seem to get really bad assignments from Carmichael. Have you considered that it's just you he has a downer on?'

Watson considered carefully what his companion had just told him.

'No,' he said firmly. 'I reckon I'm right and he's got a problem managing women; that's what I think. And, as for Lucy, I can only see one way she'll make Inspector so bloody quickly!'

*　　*　　*　　*

It was 10:20 a.m. when Carmichael managed to park his car in a cul-de-sac called Savile Road, located behind Mansfield College.

From there it was a short walk to flat 7a, Constantine's 1920s ground-floor apartment.

Carmichael knocked loudly three times on the green wooden door.

He did not have to wait too long before the door opened and a wiry wrinkled old man in an open shirt and corduroy trousers greeted him with a welcoming smile.

147

'You must be Inspector Carmichael,' he proclaimed. 'Please do come in.'

Without answering, Carmichael entered the tiny hallway and followed his host into a small living room.

Despite his obvious advanced age and failing hearing, Professor Constantine was in fine health. He stood almost six foot tall and had no hint of a stoop. His handshake was firm and, although his face was a mass of lines and wrinkles, his piercing blue eyes were bright. As soon as the two men started to converse it was clear to Carmichael that he was in the presence of a man with immense intellect and a mind that was probably as razor sharp and agile as it would have been in his prime, many decades before.

'We were saddened to hear of young Ardleigh's death,' Constantine pronounced from the comfort of the voluminous cushioned armchair which appeared to have engulfed him. 'He was a clever boy, one of the brightest I taught in over thirty-five years here at Oxford.'

The portrayal of Marcus Ardleigh as a young man tickled Carmichael, but he tried not to show his amusement.

'Yes,' he replied with a straight face. 'His death has been a shock to many people.'

'It was not a surprise to me,' announced Constantine. 'To be honest I'm surprised he made it beyond his thirties.'

'Why was that, sir?' enquired Carmichael, who could not believe what he had heard.

'Well, in their youth, Marcus and his chums were a little wild – alcohol, fast cars and drugs I suspect. Then, when he graduated and entered that murky world of politics, I'm sure he made some heavyweight enemies. I'm sure you understand where I'm coming from.'

'I'm not sure I do,' replied Carmichael. 'Can you elaborate a little?'

Constantine leaned forward and scooped up a mass of ginger and white fur and plonked the purring blob on his lap.

'Well, Erasmus,' he said as he gently stroked his fierce-looking cat. 'It looks like we need to share our memories with the inspector.'

Carmichael didn't like cats, but he tried not to let his mild phobia show as he was keen to learn more about Marcus Ardleigh's past from a man who clearly saw him in a different light from all the other people he had come across so far that week.

'Well, where do I start?' Constantine asked himself. 'I guess I should start with the Quintet. Has anyone mentioned the gang of five to you already, Inspector?'

Carmichael shook his head. 'No, what was the Quintet?'

Chapter 25

Ernest Walker's house was one of three impressive residences situated at the end of a private gravel drive. It had been built five years earlier in the style of a converted barn. Walker's house was number 6a, which was situated to the left of the other two. To the side of the house were a pair of gleaming white garage doors, and parked outside of these was a top-of-the-range Jaguar XF and a bright red two-door Mercedes sports car.

'Nice gaff,' remarked Watson, in a deliberately derisive tone.

'Forget the house,' replied Cooper. 'Just look at those cars. You wouldn't get much change from a hundred grand for those two beauties.'

Cooper's battered dirt-spattered old Volvo looked sad and forlorn compared to them. However, that did not bother the detective sergeant, who had a great interest in cars but would never dream of spending more than a few thousand on one for himself.

'Right, let's see what we can find out from Dr Walker,' remarked Watson as they crunched their way across the gravel to the front door.

Before they had a chance to knock on the door, it flew open and an attractive well-groomed lady in her mid-forties appeared. She looked startled to see the two men on her driveway.

'Good morning, Madam,' Cooper said as if he were

addressing royalty. 'My name is DS Cooper and this is my colleague DS Watson. We are here to speak to Dr Ernest Walker.'

'That's my husband,' replied the lady briskly. 'I'll fetch him for you.'

With that she turned around and shouted back into the house.

'Darling, there are some gentlemen here from the police.'

From deep in the house they heard a faint reply of, 'OK, my dear, I'll be down in a second.'

Turning back to the two officers, Mrs Walker smiled. 'Would you be so kind as to move your car as I'm late for work and you appear to be blocking me in.'

Cooper carefully reversed his car and, as soon as it was out of the way, Mrs Walker tiptoed awkwardly across the gravel drive and very gently eased herself into her red Mercedes. With a friendly wave, she glided passed Cooper's Volvo and slowly drove out onto the main road. Once on the road the car was hidden from their eye line; however, from the roar of its engine it was clear that Mrs Walker was not frightened to put her foot down. When the two officers turned back towards the front door they could see the unmistakable figure of Dr Ernest Walker who, despite the early hour, was dressed as immaculately as he had been when they first met on Tuesday evening at The Lindley.

'I imagine that car's pretty quick?' Cooper remarked.

'Yes,' replied Walker apprehensively. 'And my wife loves speed. I've begged her to slow down but she won't have it and I'm fearful that her damn car will be the death of her one day. You wouldn't believe that she's only just come off crutches following a very nasty skiing accident in January.' The three men remained stationary as they listened to the car's engine as it sped down the quiet country road.

'Anyway, please come in,' Dr Walker said as he took a pace

backwards and, with a sweep of his left arm, ushered the two officers into his house.

Walker remained at the entrance until the sound of the engine had disappeared completely. Only then did he shut the door behind them.

*   *   *   *

Having missed work the day before, Robbie Carmichael was eager to return to Mr Hayley's farm. His motives were partially financially driven; however, his main desire was to have a word with Spot On. He could not wait to tell him the real reason why his mother had been seeing so much of Robbie Robertson and he was determined to extract an apology from the loud-mouthed farm labourer.

As soon as Robbie Carmichael arrived at the farm he asked where he might find Spot On and was annoyed and frustrated to discover that he had been given the morning off by Mr Hayley and would not be turning in until around twelve.

For the next three hours Robbie could feel himself getting more and more angry with the farmhand who had so recklessly insulted his mother. The night before as he had lain in his bed, Robbie had practised in his mind how he was going to approach the subject with Spot On and how, if he could not extract an acceptable apology, he might even have to clout the ignorant lout. Of course, in his imagination the fact that Spot On was ten years older than him, was over three stone heavier and had rippling muscles from the many years he had grafted at the farm had never featured that heavily in the enactment of their confrontation.

By the time Robbie spied Spot On ambling, almost gorilla-like up the road, his blood was boiling and the meticulous plan he had constructed with his carefully rehearsed words had vanished from his head. He put down the tray of eggs he had been holding and without any hesitation shot out of the outbuilding where he was working and hurriedly made his way towards Spot On.

Spot On had been drinking in his local, The Tavern Inn in nearby Newbridge, the evening before and there he had been made aware of the real reason for Penny Carmichael's secret assignations with the publican from The Railway. He felt really bad about what he'd said a few days earlier and had made up his mind he would apologise to Robbie as soon as he saw him.

Spot On did not notice Robbie until he was almost upon him. He certainly did not anticipate the painful thud of his fist as it smashed into his jaw and sent him sprawling backwards onto the ground.

From his prone position, Spot On checked the damage to his mouth by rubbing the fingers of his right hand over the blood-stained area where the blow had connected. 'I suppose I deserved that,' he said as he sat up. 'I shouldn't have been so gobby the other day. I know the rumours were all lies; I'm sorry, lad.'

Robbie had not expected this outcome and, given that his foe seemed genuinely contrite, and also given that it had suddenly dawned on him that, should the battle continue, Spot On would probably kill him without too much trouble, he decided to accept the apology. In any case, his right hand was in real pain. Robbie had never hit anybody that hard before and he was quite certain that at least one and maybe two of his fingers had been broken.

'Just make sure you don't say anything more about my mum,' he shouted before offering his left hand to Spot On to help him to his feet.

Spot On took hold of Robbie's arm and hauled himself up on his feet. 'You've loosened two of my bloody teeth,' he muttered in his thick Cumbrian accent.

'You think you've got problems,' replied Robbie, his left hand now gently cradling his right. 'I can't move any of my blasted fingers.'

Chapter 26

For over two hours Steve Carmichael had listened intently to every word uttered by Professor Constantine. The old man's memory of events over thirty years earlier was impressive and, although Carmichael was still not able to say for certain who had been responsible for the deaths of Ardleigh and Kenyon, he felt he now knew much more about the three men who had studied at Oxford in the '70s. And more crucially he had been given a few good leads to follow in his quest to discover the deadly secrets of certainly one, and if he was lucky, two of his suspects. Carmichael now felt that he knew Ardleigh a little better than he had just a few hours earlier and, whilst it was clear Ardleigh was highly intellectual, Carmichael could not help feeling that the man he had first seen dangling at the end of a rope that Monday morning was not as upright and respectable as people might have thought. Certainly, Professor Constantine's opinion of him as a young man was none too flattering.

Carmichael rose up from his chair and stretched out his hand to thank his host. 'I really appreciate your time today, Professor,' he said warmly. 'You have been a great help to me.'

'I do hope so,' replied the old man. 'Far be it from me to tell you how to do your job, Inspector, but I'd most certainly check out the full details of the accident, and a trip to the public records office might be wise, too.'

Carmichael's smile became a wide beam. 'I wish I had

people in my team with minds as sharp as yours, Professor,' he replied. 'We'd cut down our unsolved crime figures significantly if we did.'

That was the cue for Constantine to grin, which was accompanied by a slight blushing of his cheek. 'My father would have liked to have heard you say that,' he said. 'He was a policeman from Bromsgrove, where I grew up. He never really saw being an academic as having a proper job. I think he'd have preferred it if I had joined the police, too.'

Carmichael made his way out of the house and across the sunny street to his parked car. He was in a triumphant mood and felt that at last he had made a breakthrough in the case. As he arrived at his car, his frame of mind took an instant nosedive as he noticed the familiar black and yellow tape attaching a notice to his windscreen.

'I don't bloody believe it!' he mumbled to himself as he ripped the notice off his car and started to tear open the envelope.

'£50!' he exclaimed quite loudly. 'I bloody well paid the right parking fee. So what's this all about?'

Now very angry, Carmichael strode briskly down the road in the direction of the traffic warden, who was merrily attaching tickets to scores of cars down Mansfield Road.

'Excuse me,' announced Carmichael when he eventually reached the traffic warden. 'You've just put this on my car, but I've paid the £4.50 for the three hours I was parked. Why have you given me a ticket?'

The traffic warden was clearly well used to being accosted in this manner. He calmly took the ticket from Carmichael's hand, read the details and, with a mildly sympathetic smile, said, 'I see from this that you are parked in Savile Road.'

'Yes,' retorted Carmichael in an agitated tone. 'I'm a police officer from Lancashire down here to interview someone. I parked, as you can see, less than three hours ago, I paid the correct fare of £4.50 for three hours and, although

I'm still a few minutes inside the time, you've given me a ticket. It's clearly a mistake.'

The traffic warden, as cool as you like, passed the notice back to Carmichael.

'You can of course write to us at the address in the notice to protest about the fine, but I'm afraid where you parked is a residents-only area. The paid parking zones do not extend into Savile Road. I post about ten of these every day down there. If you go back and check carefully, I'm afraid you'll see that I'm right.'

Without waiting for a response, the traffic warden turned away from Carmichael and, using the attention-grabbing black and yellow tape, fixed a notice on the car windscreen of a blue Ford Fiesta. Another fixed penalty notice to some unsuspecting poor soul.

* * * *

Dr Walker's drawing room measured about six metres square and was tastefully decorated with a dark red carpet and dark green wallpaper, not that much of the wallpaper was visible given the size and number of oil paintings and watercolours that bedecked the walls.

Watson and Cooper sank down into the depths of a luxurious leather sofa, one of three that graced the opulent room.

Dr Walker followed them through and, glancing at his watch, smiled at his guests. 'I dare say it's late enough to offer you gentlemen a glass of sherry,' he said, patently wanting them to accept so that he too could enjoy a glass of his favourite tipple.

'Not while we are on duty,' replied Cooper.

'A coffee would be good, though,' remarked Watson.

Dr Walker was clearly disappointed that he hadn't been given an excuse to open up his drinks cabinet, but smiled kindly at the pair of officers. 'Of course,' he replied. 'Is it coffee for both of you?'

Cooper nodded vigorously. 'Yes, coffee would be great, thank you.'

Dr Walker exited the room, closing the door behind him.

'My goodness,' said Cooper under his breath. 'These paintings must be worth a fortune.'

Watson rose from the sofa and wandered over to look more closely at a stunning painting of two young girls in ballet outfits patiently waiting, presumably, for a performance to begin. 'I'm no expert, Paul,' he replied, 'but I'd say these are worth thousands of pounds, maybe tens of thousands.'

As he turned back he noticed that Dr Walker was again in the room.

'Tatiana will bring our refreshments in a moment,' he said. 'You like the Hoffmanns, Sergeant?'

Watson stepped back and turned his reddened face towards Dr Walker. 'Are these all originals?' he asked nervously.

'Yes,' replied Dr Walker. 'Paintings are my passion; and Douglas Hoffmann is one of my favourite artists. I have about a dozen of his works scattered around the house.'

'Your collection must be extremely valuable,' observed Cooper.

'To me they are priceless,' responded Dr Walker with a glint in his eyes. 'In total, my entire collection, including the sculptures, is valued for insurance purposes at around two million pounds, but the works I've amassed here and throughout the house represent a lifetime's search for only the best that these artists produce. I've only originals in my collection and they are all the very finest from my favourite artists, so for me that price tag of two million is far too low.'

The two officers exchanged a glance as they each tried to absorb the magnitude of the value of Dr Walker's collection.

'It is a very impressive collection, sir,' remarked Cooper.

158

'Anyway,' continued Dr Walker as he sat himself down on one of the leather sofas. 'I'm certain you are not here to admire my artworks. How can I help you?'

Watson returned to his seat. 'No, sir,' he said. 'We're here to ask you a few questions about the letter you received from Marcus Ardleigh and about your relationship with him in general.'

'Well, I think I told Sergeant Cooper everything at The Lindley on Tuesday evening,' replied Dr Walker with more than a hint of irritation in his voice.

'We realise that you hardly knew Mr Ardleigh,' continued Cooper. 'And we know that you could not have murdered either Ardleigh or Kenyon, as your alibi checks out completely. However, we would like you to think long and hard about the secret that Ardleigh talked about in his letter. We would like you to think very carefully about that, as we do feel this information may prove to be key to our investigation.'

At that juncture a pale-faced women, with a sour-looking expression, entered the room carrying a tray of hot drinks.

'Oh that's excellent, Tatiana,' said Dr Walker. 'Just put them down on the table; we can help ourselves.'

The three men temporarily abandoned their conversation while they watched the young, po-faced woman walk slowly across the room, place the tray on the glass coffee table and then, without uttering a single word, depart.

Dr Walker handed the two officers their coffee cups.

'Help yourselves to sugar,' he said as he offered the sugar bowl first to Cooper and then to Watson. 'I've been wracking my brain now for two days,' he continued. 'But I can assure you I have absolutely no idea what Ardleigh is referring to in his letter. As I said before, I hardly knew him. He admired my collection, but honestly, gentlemen, he was not a great friend of mine, and believe me when I say that the content of the letter he sent is as baffling to me as it is to you.'

*   *   *   *

Knowing that it was unlikely his car would receive two tickets for the same offence on the same day, Carmichael figured it made sense for him to replace the ticket back on his windscreen while he concluded his business in Oxford. Constantine had told him that the police station was just a matter of fifteen minutes' walk and, with the traffic policy in Oxford being clearly one that victimised the motorist, Carmichael felt his best course of action was to leave the car where it was.

Having regained his poise, Carmichael dialled Watson's mobile; he was eager to find out what the CCTV tapes had revealed.

*   *   *   *

Ernest Walker was sticking steadfastly to his story. 'I can assure you, officers, that I do not have the slightest idea as to what Ardleigh was on about!' he had said for the third or fourth time in the last twenty minutes. 'If I did, I would tell you, but I don't. And yes, of course I do know how serious a charge it is to pervert the course of justice.'

Cooper and Watson were getting nowhere, so the sudden ringing of Watson's phone was a welcome break from their fruitless questioning.

'Oh hello, sir,' said Watson when he realised it was Carmichael. 'Just give me a moment while I find somewhere private to talk.'

Watson stood up and walked towards the door. 'Do you mind if I take this in the hall?' he asked Dr Walker.

'Not at all,' replied Dr Walker.

Once out of the room, Watson put the phone back to his ear. 'I can talk now, sir!'

'How are you getting on with those CCTV tapes?' Carmichael asked.

160

'Err, we had a change of plan,' replied Watson. 'Rachel is looking at those. Cooper and I are at Dr Walker's at the moment, but he's not being very cooperative. He just keeps saying that he has no idea why he received the letter or what it was about.'

Carmichael was not particularly interested in Dr Walker anymore. 'He's probably telling you the truth,' he said. 'I've had a very productive morning down here and, based upon what I've been told, I think we need to put our main focus on Napier, Lazarus and Miranda Coyle. I've a few things I need to check out which might take me a few more hours, but I want you all to focus on those three for now.'

Watson listened intently. He had already made his mind up that either Miranda Coyle or Gordon Napier was the killer, so this latest news from Carmichael only served to reinforce this belief. 'What did you find out, sir?' he asked.

'I've no time to tell you now,' replied Carmichael. 'But I want you and Cooper to bring in Lazarus and Napier. Put them in separate rooms and ask them to tell you everything they know about the Quintet.'

'The what?' enquired Watson.

'The Quintet,' repeated Carmichael. 'It's a group that they were part of in Oxford in the 70s.'

Carmichael looked at his watch. 'I'll try and get back for around seven. I'll meet you, Cooper and Rachel at the station then and we can have our next debrief.'

'Remember that Rachel is meeting Geraldine Ramsey at Manchester airport at six thirty, sir,' replied Watson.

Carmichael thought for a few seconds. 'I'll call Rachel now,' he replied. 'She's going to have to send a PC to collect Miss Ramsey. We can talk to her tomorrow. I need us to focus all our energies on Coyle, Napier and Lazarus. I'm convinced that the answer to all of this is buried here in Oxford and involves one, two or maybe all three of them.'

Chapter 27

For the second time in two days Penny found herself sitting in the waiting room of Kirkwood Hospital. Whereas before she was accompanying her friend who feared he had cancer, this time it was her son she was escorting.

'I can't understand why you got into a fight!' she whispered angrily to her son, who was clearly in real discomfort. 'I thought I'd brought you up better than that. Fighting doesn't solve anything. I hate to think what your dad will say when he finds out.'

At that particular moment Robbie Carmichael was not overly concerned about how his father would react when he found out he had been fighting and, as a result, had broken three of his fingers. He was more concerned about having been sacked by Mr Hayley and feared, if he did not get any treatment soon, he would pass out with the tremendous pain he was feeling. 'How long do we have to wait?' he groaned. 'This is agony.'

*   *   *   *

It was almost 1:30 p.m. when Carmichael called Rachel Dalton.

'I hear you and Watson decided to swap assignments,' he remarked sarcastically. 'And I bet I can guess whose idea that was.'

'Actually I didn't mind,' replied Rachel diplomatically. 'I've just finished now as it happens.'

'And?' enquired Carmichael.

'Well, unless Miranda Coyle is spider-woman and can climb down the side of her apartment building, she's totally in the clear for the night of Sunday 15th. Graham Calvin, her very attractive young man, arrived at her apartment at about seven thirty and he didn't depart until nine fifteen the following morning. In the interim neither of them left the building, I'm certain.'

'So neither could have killed Ardleigh?' Carmichael asked.

'That's correct, sir; they're both in the clear.'

'What about Kenyon?' enquired Carmichael. 'Could she have killed him?'

Flushed with excitement, Rachel Dalton took a deep breath. 'I think she could have,' she replied enthusiastically. 'The Lindley CCTV tapes clearly show her getting into her tangerine sports car at six fifty-five on Monday evening and she doesn't return to the hotel until eight thirteen. That would give her just enough time to get to Kenyon's office, kill him and then to get back to the hotel.'

'Great work, Rachel,' replied Carmichael.

'Do you want me to pick her up?' enquired Rachel.

'Not yet,' replied Carmichael. 'I need you to do a few more things for me this afternoon before we bring her in.'

After Carmichael had given Rachel her instructions, he finished the call by telling her to make sure she was available for the debriefing at 7 p.m.

'What about Geraldine Ramsey?' replied Rachel 'I'm due to meet her at the airport at six thirty?'

'I know,' continued Carmichael. 'You need to get a PC to do that. We know about the will and we know who were sent the letters, so she can wait for us to interview her another day. The priority for us now is Miranda Coyle, Gordon Napier and Hugo Lazarus.'

*   *   *   *

After receiving Carmichael's call, Watson curtailed the interview with Dr Walker as quickly as he could, and he and Cooper made a hasty exit. On the way out of the house Cooper noticed a large space on the hall wall, which was unusual, given that other than this space, both walls were packed tight with paintings. Also, as the wallpaper in the empty space looked much newer and brighter, Cooper deduced that a painting must have been recently removed.

'Did you sell one of your pieces?' he asked.

'My God, no!' responded Dr Walker. 'I buy, I don't sell. It's gone to be reframed. My wife accidently knocked it the other week and it fell. Fortunately, the painting itself was undamaged. A mighty relief really as it is one of my favourites, another masterpiece by Hoffman as it happens. However, alas, the frame was badly split in the fall so it's with the restorers at the moment.'

'And how much would that cost to reframe?' enquired Watson.

'About five hundred pounds,' replied Walker in a tone that suggested to him five hundred pounds was nothing.

As Watson and Cooper's car disappeared down the drive, Dr Walker was joined at the door by Tatiana, the maid.

'Did you manage to overhear what the officer was saying on the phone earlier?' he asked her.

'Yes,' she replied obediently. 'He was listening mainly, but he did mention a lady called Geraldine Ramsey and that she was being met at the airport tonight at six thirty.'

Dr Walker nodded gently. 'I was wondering when his faithful little poodle would reappear,' he said before closing the door.

Chapter 28

The traffic heading north on the M6 had been extremely heavy that afternoon and as a result it was 7:20 p.m. by the time Carmichael eventually walked into Kirkwood Police Station.

Being late for appointments normally made him irritable, but on this occasion Carmichael's mood when he arrived was still one of elation. His long day in Oxford had provided him with a sense that progress was being made and he now felt sure he knew what sort of person Marcus Ardleigh really was, and, more importantly, he was now certain that he was getting close to discovering at least two of the three secrets.

'Evening, team,' he announced cheerily as he entered the room. 'What a day this has been!'

All three of his trusted squad had completed the various tasks they had been set, but as yet had not had enough time to share their findings with each other in any great detail. As such, they were all eager to learn what the others had to say, but at the same time were keen to share their own findings with the group.

'Marc and Paul,' Carmichael said, 'since you decided to deviate from my explicit instructions, why don't you kick off by sharing how you both got on this morning?'

'With Dr Walker?' enquired Watson.

'I understood it was Dr Walker you both interviewed,' replied Carmichael scornfully, 'leaving poor Rachel to watch the CCTV footage.'

'Well, we learned very little,' replied Cooper. 'Dr Walker continues to maintain he is innocent and insists he has absolutely no knowledge of what Ardleigh was on about in his letter.'

'Anything else?' enquired Carmichael.

'No, not really, sir,' replied Cooper.

'He's loaded,' announced Watson. 'He's got a very expensive house, he and his wife have very expensive cars, and his art collection must be worth millions.'

'So he's rich,' confirmed Carmichael.

'Undeniably,' replied Cooper. 'He's wealthy and there's no mistaking that.'

'Unfortunately,' interjected Carmichael, 'unless I've missed some recent landmark legislation, being loaded, as you so tactfully put it, Marc, is not an offence.'

Watson didn't respond, but looked decidedly sheepish.

'So he's not a prime suspect in your opinion?' Carmichael asked.

'I believe his story,' said Cooper. 'And he's a cast-iron alibi for Kenyon's murder and would have been really hard-pushed to kill Marcus Ardleigh so, even though he received one of the letters, I'd say he's a real long shot.'

'I agree,' added Watson. 'It's not him.'

'OK,' continued Carmichael calmly. 'So were your assignments this afternoon of more help in getting this case solved?'

'Not sure,' replied Cooper, 'but my interview with Napier this afternoon was very different to the interviews we've had with him before. As soon as I mentioned the Quintet, he became very agitated. Then as he started to talk about it, he became surprisingly cooperative. So much so that by the end of the interview I got the impression he was almost on the point of making a clean breast of it and telling me what his guilty secret was.'

'*Almost?*' remarked Carmichael with a smile. 'Is he still here?'

'Yes,' replied Cooper. 'You said not to release them.'

'What about Lazarus?' Carmichael enquired of Watson.

'Pretty much the same,' he replied. 'At first he had kept to the same story, but when I told him we had Napier in as well and that we were asking them both to tell us about the Quintet, I think he realised that he couldn't keep to his story any longer and he was very candid indeed.'

'Quintet?' said Rachel, who was feeling excluded by her male colleagues. 'What on earth is the Quintet?'

Carmichael grinned. 'Sorry, Rachel, let me explain, and feel free to chip in, guys, if you've information from Napier or Lazarus that is additional to what Professor Constantine has told me.'

Rachel sat back in her chair, eager to learn more.

* * * *

Penny had spent nearly six hours in Accident and Emergency before she was finally able to take her son home. With three fingers in splints and a dressing that had been bound tightly from his wrist to the fingertips, Robbie looked decidedly forlorn.

'This is still killing me, Mum,' he said as they eventually parked up outside their house.

'It's no use moaning to me,' replied Penny with zero compassion in her voice. 'It's self-inflicted so you are just going to have to suffer.'

Having been kept up to speed on the afternoon's proceedings by regular text messages sent by Robbie using his left hand, Brooke Taylor, his pretty young girlfriend, arrived at the house no more than half a minute after Penny and Robbie had scrambled out of the car.

'Hello, Mrs Carmichael,' she said in a light and breezy voice. 'I thought I'd come and see how Robbie's doing. Isn't it brave of him to be fighting over you?'

Robbie shot a look at his girlfriend to try and stop her from continuing, but she didn't see.

'What do you mean?' Penny asked

'She's got it wrong,' interrupted Robbie. 'It was nothing to do with you.'

'Come inside, Brooke,' continued Penny as she ushered the poor young girl into the house. 'Let's make a cup of tea and you can tell me everything.'

Brooke suddenly realised that she had spoken out of turn but, being a well-mannered girl, was not about to lie to her boyfriend's mother.

Robbie followed a few steps behind, trying hard to think how he could prevent his mother from knowing that she had been the subject of salacious tittle-tattle at Hayley's farm, and the reason for his brawl with Spot On.

* * * *

Realising his officers were desperate to learn more about his discoveries in Oxford, Carmichael made himself comfortable and prepared himself for the task of enlightening the team.

'The Quintet, Rachel,' he stated in a self-important manner, 'was a group of Oxford undergraduates in the early 70s who formed an exclusive club at Oriel College when they were in their first term.'

'Presumably it's called The Quintet because there were five of them?' suggested Rachel.

'That's correct, Rachel,' replied Carmichael as he placed his hands behind his head in a pose clearly designed to confirm his authority.

'I suppose you'd have expected a bunch of Oxford students to have thought up something less obvious,' he remarked. 'But they didn't. However, the rationale of their little club was much more interesting than their name.'

Carmichael then turned his attention to Cooper and Watson. 'Did Napier or Lazarus explain the club's main *raison d'être?*' he enquired.

'No,' replied Watson. 'Lazarus didn't.'

'Napier did,' added Cooper. 'In fact, he was very forthcoming on that issue.'

'And what did he tell you?' Carmichael asked.

'Well, the club had two rules apparently,' continued Cooper. 'The first was that the five members would pool a third of their salaries for the first five years after they graduated into one account and the funds would be held in suspense until one of them achieved greatness.'

'And how did they define greatness?' enquired Watson.

'According to Professor Constantine,' interrupted Carmichael, 'it was to be based upon a minimum of two other members agreeing that the said greatness had been achieved, plus it also had to be upheld by Constantine, who was the only person outside the five who knew about the pact.'

'And he agreed to it?' remarked Rachel. 'He doesn't sound like much of a role model to these young men.'

Carmichael shrugged his shoulders. 'You may be right, Rachel,' he said. 'But I suspect that at Oxford University what passes for normal may not be the same as we mere mortals from outside those cloistered surroundings would class as reasonable behaviour.'

'So what was the second rule?' enquired Watson.

'That if any of them uttered a word about the pact outside the group they would lose their money and lose their right to claim,' confirmed Cooper. 'Isn't that right, sir?'

'Quite right, Cooper,' confirmed Carmichael.

Rachel and Watson looked sideways at each other.

'So who were the five people in the Quintet?' Rachel enquired enthusiastically.

Carmichael resumed his superior pose, with his hands

169

behind his head. 'Well, three you can guess. There's Marcus Ardleigh, a grammar school boy and the son of a small-town bank clerk. Then there's Hugo Lazarus, the son of a very wealthy landowner who went to Charterhouse. And then there's Gordon Napier who also went to public school, but from what I was told, his family were also wealthy but nowhere near as well off as his friend Hugo Lazarus.'

'And who were the other two?' Rachel asked.

'One was called Adrian Dent,' interrupted Watson, who wanted to demonstrate some of his newly acquired knowledge from his discussions with Lazarus. 'According to Lazarus, he was a brilliant sportsman. He was a keen rugby player and was a strong candidate to become a blue and take part in the university boat race.'

'So what happened to him?' Rachel asked.

'He was killed in a car accident,' continued Cooper, not wanting to be outdone by his colleagues. 'It was a nasty accident by all accounts and one that left him dead at the scene and one of his passengers with a broken leg.'

'The passenger being Marcus Ardleigh,' Carmichael announced.

'So who was the fifth person of this Quintet?' asked Rachel, her eagerness to be brought up to speed clear for all to hear.

'His name was Alain "Boots" Boutilier,' replied Carmichael. 'He was a French Canadian and, according to Professor Constantine, the cleverest of them all. He described him as having the greatest mind of any undergraduate that he'd come across in the thirty-five years he was a lecturer at Oxford. He was also apparently the group's leader and, according to Constantine, was also dating a local girl in Oxford.'

'So what happened to him?' enquired Rachel.

The room lay silent as the three male officers glanced at each other.

'Nobody seems to know,' replied Carmichael. 'About six

months after Dent was killed, Boutilier disappeared. It sounds like he almost vanished into thin air. He didn't leave a note, he never went home to Canada because his passport was found in his room, and he never tried to access his money from his bank account. The inference was that he was killed, but the local police could not find anyone who could give them any information about where he went or how he died. It's now over thirty years since his disappearance and it's still a mystery in Oxford.' Carmichael turned his gaze to Cooper and Watson. 'Did Lazarus or Napier say anything more to either of you?'

The two officers both shook their heads.

'No, nothing,' replied Watson.

'Same with Napier,' added Cooper.

Rachel Dalton thought for a while before asking, 'What happened to the girlfriend?'

'Good question,' remarked Carmichael, who was very impressed that Rachel had picked up on that point. 'The lady in question was called Miranda Merchant. And not long after Boutilier vanished she then started to date none other than Marcus Ardleigh.'

'And I assume that the young lady in question is Miranda Coyle?' enquired Watson with the excitement palpable in his voice.

'The very same,' replied Carmichael, 'Although before she became Mrs Coyle she was actually Miranda Ardleigh for a short while.'

'Ardleigh and Coyle were married!' exclaimed Cooper.

'Oh yes,' replied Carmichael. 'I've a copy of their marriage certificate here to prove it.' With that, he pulled out a copy of the marriage certificate of Marcus Ardleigh and Miranda Merchant dated 30th June 1976.

'So where does all this new information lead us?' enquired Cooper.

'Another good question,' remarked Carmichael. 'Not a

171

great deal in isolation. It establishes a connection between Ardleigh and Coyle. It provides some background on Ardleigh as a man, but on its own, not too much. However, after I left Constantine I did some poking around in the files at Oxford Police Station and I also asked Rachel to check up on a few things for me. I'm hoping the combination of our research will tell us even more. From my investigations I managed to unearth something interesting about the car Dent was driving.'

The three junior officers looked on with great interest as their boss enthusiastically shared his new found knowledge.

'It was actually Napier's much-loved red sports car, which he had a few weeks earlier been banned from driving for six months,' continued Carmichael. 'I also discovered something fascinating when I was searching for the marriage certificate of Marcus Ardleigh and Miranda.'

'What was that, sir?' enquired Cooper.

'That they were never divorced,' replied Carmichael with a grin.

'So that makes Miranda a bigamist,' concluded Watson.

'Correct,' replied Carmichael. 'And that is what I suspect is her nasty little secret.'

'Bugger me!' exclaimed Watson. 'She's definitely the murderer in my view.'

Rachel shook her head. 'She may have killed Kenyon but she most definitely did not kill Ardleigh. The CCTV tapes at her apartment confirm she never left that evening. She's one hundred per cent innocent of Ardleigh's death.'

'Before we start making any further assumptions I think we need to hear what Rachel found out this afternoon,' announced Carmichael. 'That may change your view, Marc.'

The three officers then turned their gaze to Rachel Dalton whose smile indicated she had indeed discovered something of value to the investigation.

Chapter 29

Within ten minutes Penny had managed to extract the full story out of Robbie's obligingly cooperative girlfriend.

'So you were fighting over me!' she exclaimed. 'Well, I'm flattered, but to be honest it still doesn't excuse you from punching someone.'

Robbie said nothing. Instead, he gestured to Brooke with a movement of his head that he wished them both to vacate the kitchen.

Brooke quietly but obediently obeyed.

'Why did you go blabbing to my mum?' he said grumpily as they made their way down the hallway.

Penny did not hear poor Brooke's reply as within seconds they had clambered noisily up the staircase to Robbie's bedroom.

As soon as they were safely out of sight, Penny allowed herself a small smile of smug satisfaction. Secretly, she was really chuffed with the way her son had gallantly sprung to her defence, although she was also still a little embarrassed at being so foolish and giving the villagers reason to believe she was having an affair. She was just relieved that Steve did not appear to have been unduly bothered about all the frivolous scandalmongering.

* * * *

At Kirkwood Police Station, Rachel Dalton excitedly began to share what she had uncovered. 'Well, I was asked to check out the bank accounts of Marcus Ardleigh, which I did this afternoon. And what I found was very interesting.'

'And what was that?' Watson enquired.

'Well, as far back as I could go, Marcus Ardleigh was receiving a regular monthly payment of one thousand pounds from Miranda Coyle.'

'Really?' interceded Carmichael. 'I was not expecting that. I thought he may have been getting a payment but I thought it would be from Napier.'

'And you were right about that, sir,' Rachel replied. 'He was getting seven hundred and fifty pounds a month from him.'

The three male officers remained silent for a moment.

'Blackmail money,' said Cooper, 'but what about?'

'Well, for Miranda Coyle that's obvious,' remarked Watson. 'It would be to stop him reporting her as a bigamist.'

'I think you're right,' remarked Cooper. 'And if she hadn't got such a solid alibi, it would be a strong motive for her to have killed Ardleigh.'

'But she could easily have killed Kenyon,' added Watson. 'She's no alibi for his murder. In fact, as she's almost certainly the owner of that cigarette ash we found in Kenyon's car, I'm certain she's involved. She may not be Ardleigh's killer but Miranda Coyle may well be Kenyon's.'

'Hang on, Marc,' interjected Cooper. 'Napier's an even stronger candidate. He's obviously being blackmailed by Ardleigh about something; he's no alibi at all for either death; the rope used to bind Ardleigh's hands was found in his car, and he knew where Ardleigh kept his front-door key.' If anyone's our man, surely it's Napier.'

'It could also be Hugo Lazarus,' announced Rachel.

'You've changed your tune,' Watson teased. 'The other day you were saying he was definitely innocent. What makes you now less certain?'

'Because up until three months ago, Marcus Ardleigh was paying five hundred pounds into Hugo Lazarus's account a month, and had been doing so for years.'

The interview room lay quiet as the four officers contemplated what they had just learned.

'Unless you've any more bombshells to drop, Rachel,' said Carmichael with a smile, 'I suggest we have another chat with Mr Lazarus and Mr Napier this evening as they've been so good as to remain here.'

'What about Miranda Coyle?' Watson asked.

'She can wait until the morning,' replied Carmichael. 'I want to talk with those two this evening. And before I go home I want them to have finally stopped messing us about and tell us the truth – all of it!'

Chapter 30

It was Gordon Napier that Carmichael decided to interview first. As he and Cooper entered the interview room, Carmichael gazed briefly at the two-way mirror to his left, behind which the other members of the team were sitting, waiting to watch and listen to their boss in action.

Cooper turned on the tape. 'The time is eight thirty-seven on Thursday 19th August,' announced Cooper. 'Interview with Gordon Napier, conducted by Inspector Carmichael. Sergeant Cooper and PC Tyler in attendance. Mr Napier has declined the offer of a solicitor.'

Napier looked tired and agitated. 'How long do you intend to keep me here?' he enquired. 'Are you intending to charge me?'

'I'm sorry to have kept you here so late, Mr Napier,' Carmichael replied calmly. 'You are not currently being charged; however, since you were last spoken to some new evidence has come to light which I'd like you to comment upon.'

Napier slumped back in his chair. 'I told him earlier all I know.'

Carmichael stared at him but elected not to say anything. Years of interviewing had taught him to allow the suspects to do as much of the talking as possible. This tactic had worked for him in the past on countless occasions.

'OK,' continued Napier, 'I admit I could have told you about the Quintet before, but I did not see it being of any relevance. That was years ago.'

Carmichael, with an exaggerated frown etched across his forehead, leaned forward in his chair so that his face was little more than two feet away from Napier's. 'Tell me about Adrian Dent and Alain Boutilier?' he said without taking his eyes off Napier.

'They were friends of ours back at Oxford in the 70s,' replied Napier. 'The five of us – that's Dent, Boots, Ardleigh, Lazarus and I – were very close. We hung around together and we formed a club we called the Quintet. There's not much more to tell.'

'I think you should try a bit harder, Mr Napier,' continued Carmichael whose composed face was now no more than fifteen inches away from the heavily perspiring Napier. 'What about the pact where you were all going to pool a third of your salaries?'

'It was just a silly agreement we conjured up, no doubt fuelled by ego and testosterone,' replied Napier dismissively. 'We never actually implemented it.'

'But I assume the reason for that was simply because Dent died and Boots disappeared,' remarked Carmichael. 'Tell me more about how Dent died.'

'He died in a car crash,' replied Napier. 'It was all very tragic.'

'I bet it was,' continued Carmichael. 'Can you share a little bit more about the car crash?'

'What more is there to say?' responded Napier, who was clearly not keen to be more expansive.

'Then let me help you with what I know,' continued Carmichael. 'The accident was indeed tragic. He was a young man in the prime of his life, and for it to be taken away so suddenly must have been heart-breaking for his family and friends.'

'Yes, it was,' remarked Napier solemnly.

'Remind me, Mr Napier,' Carmichael continued. 'Who was in the car that day and whose car was it?'

Napier's nervous perspiration worsened. 'It was my car,' he replied meekly. 'And to be frank, I'm not sure I remember who was in it.'

Carmichael smiled. 'Well, the report that was made at the time says that there were three occupants. Dent, who was driving; Ardleigh, who sustained a broken leg, and Boutilier, who escaped unharmed.'

'If that is what the report said, that's obviously how it was,' said Napier. 'I had lent it to them as I recall, not sure what for.'

'I believe the car was a red sports car?' Carmichael added.

'Yes,' replied Napier. 'My father bought it for me as an eighteenth birthday present. It was my pride and joy at the time.'

Carmichael paused for a few seconds. 'You know, Mr Napier, that is what has been puzzling me.'

'What?' replied Napier.

'Why you would be willing to lend out your pride and joy like that. Why weren't you in it yourself? Can you answer that for me, Mr Napier.'

Napier shook his head. 'No, not really, I suspect they must have been very persuasive.'

'Then there's the secret that Ardleigh mentioned in the note he sent you,' continued Carmichael. 'That's also been nagging at me, too.'

Napier was now clearly so nervous that he could no longer stop himself from shaking. 'I don't know what you are getting at,' he shouted angrily. 'I've done nothing wrong.'

Carmichael paused for a few seconds before continuing. 'Let me tell you what I think happened.'

'I wish somebody bloody would,' Watson whispered to Rachel Dalton behind the darkened glass. 'I don't mind admitting that I'm a bit confused.'

'Shh,' said Rachel who was keen not to miss anything.

'I think,' continued Carmichael, 'that there were four

people in that car, maybe even five. I think you were in it, too. In fact, I think you were driving. I think that you crashed and Dent died. I think you all agreed you should say that Dent had been driving to save your skin, especially as at the time you had been banned from driving. Let's face it – it wouldn't hurt him as he was already dead.' Carmichael glared intently at Napier as he spoke. 'How am I doing so far?'

Napier's face became ashen grey and his eyes turned downwards and stared at the table, but he said nothing.

'I think that is your secret and Ardleigh was threatening to make it public,' continued Carmichael.

'It's certainly a strong motive for killing Marcus Ardleigh,' remarked Cooper.

Napier took a deep breath. 'For over thirty years that accident has haunted me,' he said quietly. 'You are right, Inspector Carmichael; I was also in the car. I was driving and in the moments after the accident happened, before anyone else was on the scene, Ardleigh suggested we make up the story that Dent was driving to save my miserable skin. Hugo Lazarus wasn't in the car, but Boots was and, although he wasn't keen on the plan, in the end he agreed and I scarpered before the police arrived.'

'Sounds like a kind gesture from good friends,' remarked Carmichael. 'But I sense that wasn't the case.'

'No, it wasn't,' replied Napier angrily. 'We all stuck to our stories and after a few weeks I thought I was out of the woods, but then it started to get complicated.'

'Complicated,' remarked Cooper. 'What do you mean?'

Napier laughed. 'Well, it was then I found out what sort of person Marcus really was. He'd broken his leg in the accident and was in hospital for a few weeks. When he came out he came to me one day and, as bold as anything, said that if I did not pay him five hundred pounds he would tell the police the real story and I would end up in jail. I could not believe it, but he was deadly serious.'

'So you paid?' confirmed Cooper.

'Yes,' replied Napier wearily. 'I paid him the five hundred and I hoped that would be the end of it, but I soon found out it wasn't going to be so easy.'

'So what happened?' Carmichael enquired.

'About six months later, Marcus wanted another five hundred,' continued Napier. 'It just went on and on.'

'And given that Ardleigh's bank statements indicate you are still making payments of seven hundred and fifty pounds a month to him,' interjected Carmichael. 'I assume you were paying right up to his death?'

Napier nodded his head. 'Yes, I've been paying ever since the accident. He even made me locate my business here in Moulton Bank just so he could keep an eye on me. Just imagine that, Inspector, having to live in this dump for over twenty years and having to work myself crazy just to pay him his blackmail money each month. It has been a nightmare.'

'It's certainly enough to drive anyone to murder,' remarked Cooper.

'It is,' replied Napier. 'And God knows how many times I thought about doing just that. But it wasn't me. I'm delighted that miserable excuse of a human being is dead, but it wasn't me who did it. I'm far too cowardly I'm ashamed to say.'

Carmichael considered what he had just heard. 'Tell me about Boutilier?' he asked. 'You say he agreed to go along with the story?'

The nervousness Napier had displayed before appeared to have totally evaporated. His guilty secret now in the open, he looked more relaxed than he had done all week.

'Boots was everything Marcus wasn't and everything Marcus wanted to be,' said Napier. 'He was from a wealthy respectable family, he was sociable, he was popular and what Marcus hated the most, I think, is that Boots was clearly going places. Everyone liked Boots.'

'So who was the most intelligent, Ardleigh or Boutilier?' Carmichael asked, remembering what Constantine had said that morning.

'Academically, Marcus was brilliant,' conceded Napier. 'He was a great mathematician, but Boots, in my view, was even brighter. It's difficult to compare two people with such great minds, especially when they specialised in totally different subjects, but for me Boots was the smarter, and I think deep down Marcus knew that, too.'

'So what did Boots study?' enquired Cooper.

'PPE,' replied Napier.

'Which stands for?' Cooper asked.

'Philosophy, Politics and Economics,' replied Napier. 'In my view he would have been Canada's First Minister, no problem.'

'But he agreed to the deception, too?' Carmichael said. 'If he was such a great honest person, why did he agree to lie to the police about Dent?'

Napier shrugged his shoulders. 'As I said before, he was not happy about it, but went along with it. Just after Marcus started to blackmail me, Boots had spoken to me about how troubled he was by what we had done and he was talking about going to the police.'

'Really?' remarked Carmichael eagerly. 'Roughly when was that?'

Napier looked Carmichael straight in the eye. 'About three days before he disappeared,' he replied. 'I will leave you to draw your own conclusions from that.'

Carmichael leaned back in his chair. 'So what about Lazarus?' he enquired. 'Was he in the car? Did he know about the lie you all told and did he know you were being blackmailed by Marcus?'

Napier continued to stare at Carmichael. 'He was definitely not in the car. To my knowledge, he knew nothing about me being the driver and he's never given me cause to believe he knew I was paying Marcus to keep him silent, but I don't honestly know. He and Geraldine Ramsey were both really close to Marcus, so it's possible one or both of them may have known.'

Carmichael looked at his watch; it was nine precisely. 'We will certainly be speaking to them both very soon,' he said.

'So what will happen to me?' asked Napier.

Carmichael stood up and started to walk to the door. 'We are going to release you, but I want you back here in the morning. You need to make a full statement, this time omitting nothing. You'll certainly be charged with offences relating to the car crash and your subsequent attempt to pervert the course of justice, but I'm happy to let you go for now.'

Cooper was shocked at what his boss had just said, and as soon as they were outside the interview room he challenged Carmichael about his decision. 'Are you sure, sir?' he enquired. 'Surely Napier is our prime suspect. He's got a strong motive; he has no real alibi and remember we found the rope in his van.'

'You may be right, Paul,' replied Carmichael. 'But Lazarus and Miranda Coyle are strong candidates, too. We can't arrest them all. Anyway, I doubt he will be going anywhere tonight. No, I'm fine about releasing him.'

Behind the smoked glass, Watson turned swiftly to face Rachel. 'I have a couple of observations from that interview. Firstly, I think Napier may well at last be telling the truth, which means the murderer has got to be Miranda Coyle. What do you think?'

'I can't see Napier being our killer, but I'm not convinced it's Miranda Coyle either. Let's wait to see how the interview with Lazarus goes,' she replied.

Watson slowly shook his head. It was clear to Rachel Dalton that in true Watson fashion he had already made his mind up. 'So what was your second observation?' she asked.

'I also think our friend Gordon Napier is wearing a hairpiece,' responded Watson with a wry smile.

Rachel chuckled. She'd also suspected as much but, unlike Watson, had not felt it appropriate to mention Napier's bad toupee.

* * * *

Robbie Carmichael sat sulkily on the corner of his bed. 'What the hell were you playing at telling Mum why I hit Spot On?' he grunted angrily.

'Why are you being so tetchy?' enquired his bemused girlfriend. 'She asked me and, anyway, it's the truth. I think she was very proud of you. So I think I did you a favour.'

'Oh do you?!' retorted Robbie angrily. 'Well, maybe I didn't want my mum to know what the lads at the farm were saying about her. Did that never occur to you?'

Brooke considered what Robbie had just told her. 'I didn't think of that,' she replied meekly, placing her arm around his shoulders. 'I'm sorry!'

Robbie shrugged off poor Brooke's attempt to patch up their differences. 'That's your problem, Brooke,' he spat out angrily. 'You never bloody think! In fact, you made things worse convincing me that your mum's malicious gossip was true. If you'd have said nothing, I'd probably never have hit Spot On and would still have a job.'

Brooke sprung up to her feet. 'If you're going to be like that, I may as well go home,' she snapped, while at the same time quickly wiping away a tiny teardrop that had begun to trickle down her cheek. 'I'll see you when you're not feeling so bitter and so sorry for yourself.'

Robbie made no attempt to persuade his girlfriend to stay. In fact, he didn't even lift his gaze from the floor as she stomped past him and out onto the landing. It was only when she was halfway down the stairs that he finally realised he needed to try and diffuse the situation. He hurriedly walked out after the now very upset young woman.

'I'm sorry,' he shouted down the stairs at her. 'Hang on a moment – I'll walk you home.'

Relieved that he was at last being friendlier, Brooke waited at the front door for Robbie to reach her. She only turned to face him after she had wiped away her tears. There was no way she wanted him to think she'd been crying.

'OK, I'll let you walk me home,' she conceded. 'But only because it's a twenty-minute walk and because my mum would kill you if she thought you'd let me walk home on my own when it's starting to get dark.'

* * * *

Carmichael and Watson entered the interview room at 9:35 p.m. Hugo Lazarus and his solicitor were sitting waiting for them.

'Inspector, I'm more than happy to help you as much as I can,' announced Lazarus before either officer had had an opportunity to say anything or take their seats. 'However, it's pretty late and I've been here hours.'

'Yes,' interjected the solicitor. 'My client and I would like to know when he can leave.'

Carmichael ignored their remonstrations until he and Watson had sat down.

'You are free to leave at any time, Mr Lazarus,' he remarked calmly. 'However, as a close friend of Marcus Ardleigh, I would have thought you'd be eager to do all you can to help find his killer?'

'Of course I am,' replied Lazarus forcefully. 'But I think I've told you everything I know.'

Carmichael stared into Lazarus's eyes. 'I think you should let us be the judge of that.'

Rachel Dalton and Paul Cooper made themselves comfortable behind the darkened window.

'Tell me about your friend Marcus Ardleigh?' Carmichael asked. 'What sort of man was he?'

'He was a wonderful chap,' replied Lazarus without any hesitation. 'He was a mathematics genius and a loyal friend, but above all, he was a kind and generous human being.'

'He was certainly generous,' remarked Carmichael flippantly. 'He was giving you five hundred pounds a month for years. What was that for?'

Lazarus looked a little shocked at this sudden disclosure. 'It's true that Marcus was taking care of my mortgage. It's something that he insisted on doing some fifteen years ago, when he found out that my money had all run out. He was that sort of man.'

'So why did it stop three months ago?' Watson enquired.

'Because', replied Lazarus haughtily, 'my mortgage was fully paid off in May of this year, so there was no need for any more financial help from Marcus.'

'And where did Ardleigh get this money from?' asked Carmichael.

Lazarus laughed. 'Marcus was a wealthy man, Inspector. He had accumulated a great deal of wealth over the years, from a number of ventures, primarily from his work with the government, but from lecturing, too.'

'What about blackmail and extortion?' continued Carmichael. 'Were they part of Ardleigh's many ventures?'

The expression of incredulity on Lazarus's face suggested that this was not something he knew, or, if he did, he hid it well. 'Blackmail!' he exclaimed. 'You must be mistaken, Inspector. Marcus was an academic and a gentleman. He was totally honest. He was no blackmailer.'

Carmichael took a moment to consider his next question. 'Tell me about the Quintet and about Dent and Boutilier?' he asked in a quiet and controlled manner.

'Dent and Boots were both good friends of ours,' replied Lazarus. 'They were with Marcus, Gordon and me at Oxford and we five were the founders of the Quintet.'

'We know that Dent was killed in a car accident,' continued Carmichael. 'But what happened to Boots?'

'It's a total mystery,' replied Lazarus. 'I have no idea what happened to him, but Marcus and I always felt that he'd probably had enough of Oxford and took off somewhere to start a new life.'

'What made you come to that conclusion?' asked Watson with amazement.

'He was very close to Adrian Dent,' replied Lazarus. 'We felt that Dent's death was too much for him to bear. We figured that he couldn't cope, so he absconded.'

'I'd say that was pretty unlikely,' remarked Carmichael without any attempt to hide his misgivings. 'What sort of person would leave a place at Oxford University, take no money with him and sever all contacts with his friends and his family. He would have to be very unhappy to do that!'

Lazarus shrugged his shoulders. 'Well, that is what we felt was the most likely reason for his disappearance.'

'I'd say the most likely reason he disappeared was that someone killed him,' interjected Carmichael. 'And the saintly Marcus Ardleigh is top of my list of potential murderers.'

Lazarus shook his head. 'Inspector, I am happy to help you trace the murderer of Marcus Ardleigh, but I'm not prepared to continue this conversation if you insist on making such wild, insulting and unfounded claims, defaming the character of my dear departed friend.'

Carmichael paused for a few moments. 'Thank you for your time, Mr Lazarus,' he said as calmly as he could. 'You're free to go.'

Hugo Lazarus wasted little time in getting up from his seat. 'Inspector Carmichael,' he said firmly. 'I'm not sure where you get these astounding assumptions about Marcus, but they are not correct. Marcus was a good friend and a generous and warm human being.'

Carmichael forced a small smile. 'Once again, Mr Lazarus, many thanks for your time.'

'That was quick,' remarked Cooper from behind the darkened glass. 'I think the boss is keen to get off home tonight.'

Rachel Dalton smiled. 'I think you might be right, but looking at Lazarus I'm convinced he knew nothing about Ardleigh being a blackmailer and I think that's what the boss thinks, too.'

* * * *

The mile journey to Brooke's house normally took about twenty minutes to walk. However, on this particular occasion, it took the young couple the best part of an hour, with frequent stops along the way for them to cuddle and kiss and generally demonstrate their re-found affection for one another.

By the time Robbie eventually left Brooke at her garden gate, it was 10:35 p.m.

Brooke rushed quickly into the house and ran upstairs. From her bedroom window she could see her boyfriend as he walked slowly home. She gazed lovingly at him as he disappeared down the half-lit road.

She was just about to close her curtains when she noticed someone she knew coming out of the small cottage across the road. 'That's weird,' she muttered to herself as the familiar figure made its way down the path and then vanished into the gloom.

Chapter 31

Before leaving the station that evening Carmichael gave the team clear instructions for the next day. The plan was for he and Watson to interview Miranda Coyle in the morning, Cooper was to find out as much as he could about Dent and Boutilier, while Rachel had been assigned the task of looking deeper into the private life and finances of Marcus Ardleigh.

Carmichael had also instructed both Rachel and Cooper to bring Geraldine Ramsey into the station at around lunchtime, which was when he expected to be back after interviewing Miranda Coyle. He wanted to question Geraldine Ramsey in person.

* * * *

It was almost 11 p.m. by the time Carmichael's black BMW glided to a halt in the drive. It had been a long and eventful day and Carmichael was exhausted and ready for his bed. As he clambered out of the car he noticed his son turning into the drive.

'Hello, Robbie,' he said cheerily. 'Been out with Brooke?'

'I've just walked her home,' replied Robbie. 'How was Cambridge?'

'Oxford,' announced his father with a look of derision. 'Anyway what have you done to your hand?'

'Oh, I've broken a few fingers,' replied Robbie nervously.

'Did you do it at work?' enquired Carmichael.

'Yes,' said Robbie, who by that time had already passed his father and was at the front door. 'I'm really tired. Mum will fill you in on the details.'

On that note, the young man turned his key in the lock, barged his way inside the house and headed up the stairs, leaving the door ajar and his father open-mouthed.

*　*　*　*

It took two large whiskies and over an hour for Carmichael and Penny to update each other on their respective day's activities, by which time they were both ready for bed.

'So who do you think murdered Ardleigh and Kenyon?' Penny asked as she lay in bed waiting for her husband to join her.

'I've no idea,' he replied as he discarded his screwed-up socks into the laundry basket. 'Tomorrow we are going to interview Miranda Coyle again and I want to speak to Geraldine Ramsey, too. I'd also like a talk with Dr Ernest Walker myself, if I can fit it in. I'm hoping that after I've spoken to the three of them I'll have a better idea. To be totally honest with you, it could be any one of a number of people. It could even be more than one of them working together.'

Carmichael finally got into bed at 12:35 a.m., over nineteen hours since his alarm had so rudely woken him. He kissed his wife gently on the cheek and turned off the bedside light. Tired as he was, it still took him over half an hour to eventually get to sleep. His mind was still actively trying to decipher the many facts he had gathered that day.

Chapter 32

Friday 20th August

Miranda Coyle's place of work was situated in the heart of Manchester's business district. Her fashion empire was centred in a large, well-equipped suite of offices on the tenth floor of one of the city's tallest buildings. The offices were primarily built of glass, which provided a modern feel and also enabled its occupants to enjoy spectacular views across the metropolis.

Dressed in one of her own designer power suits, Miranda leaned back in her leather swivel chair and considered carefully what Carmichael had just put to her. She took a massive drag on her cigarette, which was followed by two powerful jets of smoke shooting out of her nostrils before changing into small grey clouds, slowly rising into the upper atmosphere of her office.

'It's no use denying it, Inspector,' she said eventually, in a controlled manner. 'Technically, I am a bigamist. It's true, but only because that bastard Marcus refused to divorce me. He said it was on religious grounds. He was a Catholic you see, not that he ever went to bloody church. However, it was actually because he was a mean, malicious, controlling bastard.'

'So you admit that you knowingly married Mr Coyle without bothering to end your marriage to Marcus Ardleigh?' Carmichael asked calmly.

'Yes,' replied Miranda, 'although I can assure you that my marriage to Peter Coyle was ended legally, albeit also a tad acrimoniously.'

'*Technically*,' interrupted Watson, 'your union with Peter Coyle was never ever a lawful marriage. So I'm not sure technically that you could legally divorce Mr Coyle.'

'And when did the blackmail start?' enquired Carmichael, who was keen to stick to his line of attack and not allow Watson to side track the conversation.

'As soon as Marcus heard about my second marriage,' replied Miranda, who took another massive drag from her cigarette. 'Ironically, it was when Peter and I were divorcing … or should I say, parting,' Miranda said as she shot a scornful look in Watson's direction. 'We had a rather public row over my settlement, which Marcus read about and he agreed to keep quiet as long as I paid him fifty thousand up front and then a thousand a month thereafter.'

'That arrangement must have badly eaten into your settlement?' continued Carmichael.

'It was an inconvenience,' replied Miranda carefully. 'As we divorced almost ten years ago I've already paid him around one hundred and seventy thousand, but as my settlement was over a million I'm still in pocket.'

'But of course if this secret got out it would not only mean charges against you for bigamy, but also the strong likelihood that you'd have to pay back the settlement money to your ex-partner,' continued Carmichael, who also picked his words carefully.

'And that would be grounds for killing someone, too,' added Watson, less subtly.

Miranda Coyle shook her head. 'I didn't kill Marcus. I was with Graham Calvin all night; you can check with him. I may be in trouble for bigamy but I'm totally innocent of murder.'

'Your alibi for the night Marcus died is solid,' replied Carmichael. 'However, your alibi for the night Ruben

Kenyon died is less so. Also we have evidence that you met with him in his car on the night he died.'

Miranda Coyle looked shocked at this announcement and, in keeping with her previous behaviour, she took a large drag on her cigarette while she considered how she should respond.

* * * *

It was just after nine thirty when Penny heard a loud knock on the front door. This was unusual as most callers normally used the doorbell which was quite visible to visitors.

Penny opened the door to discover a tall muscular young man, probably in his mid-twenties with short black hair and piercing dark eyes.

'Is it Mrs Carmichael?' the young man asked in a thick Cumbrian accent.

'Yes,' replied Penny, who was trying hard to fathom out who this person was.

'That's champion,' came back the reply. 'I wasn't sure I was at the right place. I was wondering whether Robbie was about. Mr Hayley's sent us to tell him his job's safe.'

'And you are?' enquired Penny, although she was pretty sure she knew.

'My name's Chris Callow,' he replied. 'I work with Robbie. He may have mentioned me. My nickname's Spot On, although I'm not totally sure why.'

Penny thought for a second before opening the door wide. 'Come in, Chris,' she said. 'I'll get Robbie for you.'

The young man didn't need to be asked a second time. He strode confidently into the hallway.

'I suspect he's still in bed,' continued Penny. 'Why don't you go through into the kitchen and I'll check on him? And maybe I can make you a cup of tea while you're waiting.'

'That would be spot on,' said Spot On, as if to confirm without any doubt his identity.

192

*   *   *   *

'I did meet with Kenyon,' Miranda said. 'I called him when I was at the hotel and he suggested we met in the church car park on Ambient Hill.'

'At what time was this?' enquired Carmichael.

'I called him at about six thirty,' replied Miranda. 'And we arranged to meet at seven. I got a little waylaid, so it was about half past seven when I arrived. Kenyon was already there.'

'Why did you request a meeting?' Watson asked.

'To try and stop this bloody announcement going out and to try and stop the blackmail once and for all,' replied Miranda.

'And what happened at your meeting?' Carmichael asked.

Miranda thought hard before replying. 'I asked him to tell me what he was going to do now Marcus was dead. I wanted him to cancel the meeting the following night.'

'And what was his response?' Carmichael asked.

'He laughed and told me that he knew all about my arrangement with Marcus and he would consider not revealing my secret at The Lindley on the understanding that the financial payments would continue each month, but that they would be paid to him from now on and in cash.'

'And what was your reply?' enquired Carmichael eagerly.

'At first I told him to rot in hell! Which I hope is what he's doing right now,' replied Miranda angrily. 'But in the end I agreed. What alternative did I have? Apart from murdering him of course.'

Carmichael's eyebrows raised, but he declined to ask her the obvious next question. 'And what time did your meeting end?'

'It was over in minutes,' replied Miranda. 'I left him in his car in the car park and drove back to the hotel. I never saw or spoke to him after that. But I'm not sorry he's dead and when

193

you find out who killed that little wart please let me know as I'd like to shake his hand.'

* * * *

As soon as Robbie was aware that Spot On was in the house, he launched himself out of bed and quickly threw on whatever clothes he could grab. The less time Spot On was alone with his mother the better, he thought, as he knew she would wheedle all sorts of information out of him within minutes, much of which he suspected would be about him and as such potentially dangerous.

Within five minutes of his mother leaving his room, Robbie was entering the kitchen. 'Hi,' he said as he tucked his shirt into the top of his jeans. 'What are you doing here?'

'I've got some great news,' replied Spot On as he rested his mug of tea on the table. 'I told Mr Hayley what the fight was about and, given the circumstances and our previously un-blemished records, he's said we can both have our jobs back.'

Robbie's eyes lit up at the news. 'Really?' he said excitedly.

'Aye,' replied Spot On. 'He said you can come back on Monday. He even said that for the first few days you could be excused heavy duties while your hand got better.'

'And you're reinstated, too?' enquired Penny.

'Well yes,' replied Spot On somewhat nervously. 'That's based upon me promising to come here and apologise in person to you, Mrs Carmichael, for spreading those ridiculous rumours.'

'I see,' replied Penny in anticipation.

'Actually, to be honest, Mrs Carmichael,' continued Spot On, 'had I met you before, I'd never have believed what I heard in the pub. There's clearly no way an attractive woman such as you would give a fat old bloke like Robertson a second look. Whoever started the rumours must need their head seeing to.'

194

Penny smiled and took his words as a compliment, albeit a little crudely put. 'Apology accepted,' she said as she plucked two pieces of toast from the toaster. 'Are you sure two is enough?' she asked him.

'Two will be spot on,' replied Spot On.

'You do realise now why I was spending time with Robbie Robertson, don't you?' enquired Penny as she passed over the plate of toast.

'Oh aye, I do now,' replied Spot On, who started to spread a thick layer of butter on the first piece. 'I heard he'd been for tests for cancer and you were holding his hand, so to speak.'

'That's right,' replied Penny. 'Fortunately he's been given the all-clear, so we are all relieved.'

'I only hope they've got it right this time,' continued Spot On, much to the frustration of Robbie, who was eager to find a pause in the conversation so he could get Spot On out of his house.

'What do you mean?' asked Penny.

'Well, I overheard a woman in the pub the other night telling someone else that she was a nurse and that earlier in the year some local doctor had somehow mixed up two people's results and that they told one poor guy that he had cancer and he'd only a few months to live. He'd packed in his job and then gone out and spent all his money only to be told that there had been a mistake and that he was fine.'

'What happened to the poor fellow who did have cancer?' enquired Penny.

Spot On shrugged his shoulders. 'Dunno,' he replied before taking a massive bite out of his toast. 'I imagine he must have died by now.'

Robbie shook his head in disbelief at what he was hearing. 'This woman wasn't the same one that told you my mum was having an affair was it by any chance?' he asked despairingly.

'I tell you it's true,' exclaimed Spot On. 'The woman in the pub was really upset because the doctor had blamed the mix-up on her and had sacked her.'

Penny didn't know what to believe, other than it was clear Spot On was as much a gossip as any of the fishwives she knew in Moulton Bank, of which there were many.

'Actually, Mrs Carmichael,' continued Spot On, 'thinking about it, I would quite like another couple of pieces of toast, if it's not too much trouble?'

*　*　*　*

Having established that Miranda Coyle was a bigamist, that she was being blackmailed by Ardleigh, that she had met with Kenyon on the night he was murdered and she had little time for her ex-husband, Carmichael decided to try and gather some insight into the five young men whom she had met in the 70s in Oxford.

'I understand you are from Oxford,' said Carmichael, 'and you were initially Alain Boutilier's girlfriend. What do you remember of those days?'

Miranda Coyle stared dreamily past her inquisitors, as if in a trance. 'They were happy days,' she replied with sensitivity. 'Alain was a wonderful, handsome man. He was like nobody else I'd ever met. He was Canadian to start with. He was so clever, but never snobbish, not like most of the stuck-up misfits that go to Oxford. He was my first real love and probably my only true love.'

'And what about the others in the gang?' asked Watson.

'The Quintet, you mean?' responded Miranda. 'Dent and Napier were OK, quite a laugh as it happens. Lazarus was a bit aloof; he had pots of money as I recall. Then there was Marcus. He was also very clever, but not as clever as Boots. Looking back, I think Marcus was a little envious of Boots.'

'So why did you take up with Ardleigh after Boutilier disappeared?' enquired Carmichael.

'Why do young girls do foolish things?' she responded. 'After Boots went, Marcus was very attentive and seemed genuinely keen to help me get over him. He was also by far the one I was most attracted to and it seemed, at the time, the logical thing to do.'

'But it was a mistake?' prompted Carmichael.

'The biggest of my life,' retorted Miranda, who again dragged hard on her cigarette. 'And one I've been paying for one way or another ever since.'

'So what do you think happened to Boutilier?' Carmichael asked.

Miranda wistfully shrugged her shoulders. 'At the time I thought he'd just had enough and absconded.'

'And now?' enquired Carmichael.

'And now I think Marcus probably had him killed,' she replied with sadness in her voice. 'Don't ask me why but I'm sure he's dead and I'm certain Marcus will have had some involvement ... but now that he's dead, too, I guess we will never know.'

Chapter 33

'So what's your verdict on this morning's meeting with Miranda Coyle?' enquired Carmichael as the two officers sped back towards Kirkwood Police Station.

'If she had not got such a solid alibi for Sunday night, then I'd say she's got to be the killer,' replied Watson. 'It's clear she hated Ardleigh and there would be no way she would want the truth to come out about her bigamist marriage to husband number two, especially as she benefited so handsomely from the divorce settlement; so she certainly had a strong enough motive. Also, she admits meeting Kenyon on the night he died and, if he was going to blackmail her, that's reason enough to kill him.'

Carmichael nodded. 'If we were just looking at Kenyon's murder, she would be my prime suspect,' he conceded. 'But we aren't. We have two suspicious deaths to investigate, which makes it much trickier to unravel.'

Watson nodded. 'I agree,' he said with a frustrated sigh.

*   *   *   *

It was 11:35 a.m. by the time Cooper and Rachel arrived at Geraldine Ramsey's small bungalow.

Although only ten minutes' walk from the centre of Moulton Bank, Rose Bush Meadow, the private drive where Geraldine Ramsey lived, gave the impression of being completely detached from the relatively noisy village.

Surrounded on two sides by common land and on a third by a small copse, the small row of ten tiny bungalows was largely hidden from the rest of the village. And if it were not for the two large houses, one of which was where Robbie's girlfriend lived, that stood opposite the entrance to Rose Bush Meadow, the small private lane would have been totally shrouded by the gentle Lancashire countryside.

The two officers crunched their way up the small gravel path of number 6 and rang the doorbell. After several rings with no reply Cooper decided to take a quick peek through the large window adjacent to the front door. Inside, the small neat living room looked as it always did, fastidiously tidy with everything in its place. 'No sign of life here,' he reported back to Rachel who rang the bell for the fourth time.

'Maybe she's in the village?' suggested Rachel.

'Could be,' replied Cooper, who by this time was making his way down the small pathway that led to the back garden. 'I'll just have a quick look round the back.'

Within a few minutes Cooper came rushing to the front, his face grey and sombre and his breathing heavy. 'Rachel, you had better call an ambulance, and call Carmichael, too. She's lying in a pool of blood on the kitchen floor. I'm going back to break down the door.'

* * * *

By the time Carmichael's BMW screeched to a halt outside the bungalow, an ambulance, two police cars and several vehicles belonging to Stock's team were already at the scene.

'Why is it that your murders always come in clusters?' Stock asked as he saw Carmichael approaching along the hallway.

Carmichael glanced up at the clock on the kitchen wall. 'And a good afternoon to you, too, Harry,' he replied, having established that it was now ten past twelve. 'So what's your prognosis?'

'I think you mean hypothesis,' remarked Stock smugly. 'One should only use the term "prognosis" when talking about the cause of a disease.'

'I do enjoy our meetings,' Carmichael said with a wry smile. 'I always find them educational. Now, other than my vocabulary needing some attention, what else are you able to tell me, preferably relating to the death of this poor woman?'

Stock looked up at Carmichael from his crouched position beside the lifeless body of Geraldine Ramsey. 'This poor woman was struck with one massive blow to the back of her head,' he said. 'I would estimate that she died instantly and I would put her time of death at between 9 p.m. and midnight last night.'

Carmichael looked across at Cooper and Rachel Dalton. 'Have we found the murder weapon?' he asked.

'Yes,' replied Rachel. 'The SOCOs have already bagged up a cast-iron door stop. It's got hair and blood all over it.'

'Fingerprints, too, I hope,' added Stock.

'Thanks, Stock,' Carmichael said as he indicated to his three officers that he wanted them to join him outside the house. 'How soon can you carry out the autopsy? I'm keen to know your findings, particularly if you can be more specific with the time of death, that would be most helpful.'

'As always I'll be as quick and thorough as I can,' replied Stock. 'I should be able to carry out the autopsy this afternoon, so hopefully you should have my preliminary report this evening.'

'That would be appreciated,' Carmichael responded.

'Not a problem,' replied Stock without bothering to make eye contact with Carmichael. 'It's the least I can do given that you are my pre-eminent customer.'

Carmichael ignored Stock's comments – he was too anxious to get his team together in the garden.

'What time did we release Napier and Lazarus last night?' he asked the three officers.

'Napier was released at about nine thirty,' replied Cooper.

'And Lazarus at about ten,' added Rachel.

'So allowing them just over half an hour to get here, in theory that means her murderer could be any of our suspects,' confirmed Watson.

'Bugger,' said Carmichael through gritted teeth. 'I hope to God the murderer isn't Napier or Lazarus. If it is, I'll never forgive myself for letting them both go last night.'

The three officers glanced sideways at each other but said nothing. 'OK,' said Carmichael after a few seconds had elapsed. 'I want the three of you to remain here and make sure we get detailed statements from all of these houses, and the ones across the street. Then get yourselves back to the station for a debrief at four.'

Without waiting for a reply, Carmichael slowly and rather despondently walked back to his car.

'He'll never forgive himself,' repeated Watson as soon as the boss was out of earshot. 'It's not his conscience he should be worried about. This could be the end of his career if it is one of those two. He had enough to hold both of them, especially Napier.'

Cooper and Dalton remained silent, but they knew Watson was right.

Chapter 34

Carmichael's normal emotional default setting was silent contemplation. With the realisation that he had, in all probability, released the killer of Geraldine Ramsey the previous evening, he reverted to this state and pondered how this would play out for him in the days ahead. The whole situation troubled him greatly; especially as in reality he knew he had ample evidence to hold them both overnight.

He decided to gather his thoughts at home rather than back at Kirkwood Police Station, a decision which was made all the more easy given that his house was no more than ten minutes' drive from the crime scene.

'This is a nice surprise,' remarked Penny as he sauntered into the kitchen, his shoulders hunched and chin down.

On seeing the demeanour of her husband, Penny rushed over and gave Carmichael a consoling hug. 'Why the glum face?' she asked.

'There's been another murder,' replied Carmichael gloomily. 'It's a woman called Geraldine Ramsey. She lives down Rose Bush Meadow.'

'Oh my God!' exclaimed Penny, her hand instinctively shooting up to cover her gaping mouth. 'What dreadful news.'

'What's worse,' interrupted Carmichael, 'she may have been killed by one of the suspects we released last night or, rather, that *I* released last night.'

'Sit down,' said Penny, who had over twenty years'

experience of hauling her husband out of similar troughs of despair. 'I'll make us a nice cup of tea and we can talk this through. Whatever happened to poor Miss Ramsey, I'm sure you're not to blame.'

* * * *

Having received their orders, Watson, Cooper and Dalton spent the next two hours knocking on doors in the surrounding area, but with little success.

'It's unbelievable,' exclaimed Watson when the three officers met up to compare notes. 'I've got absolutely nothing. Nobody heard or saw anything.'

'Me neither,' said Rachel. 'What about you, Paul?'

Cooper shrugged his shoulders. 'The old dear in number nine did say she heard a car driving away at speed at around ten twenty, but she didn't look out of the window so she has no description of the car, and to make matters worse, she said she can't be one hundred per cent sure it was at ten twenty. She said it may have been a bit earlier.'

'So, as I said before,' added Watson. 'We've got the best part of bugger all!'

'So what do we do now?' asked Rachel.

'We've got a few hours before we need to meet Carmichael at the station,' said Cooper. 'Let's go and visit a few of our main suspects and find out if they have an alibi for last night.'

Watson nodded. 'Good idea,' he concurred. 'We definitely need to talk with Napier and Lazarus. If we can prove neither of them could have done this one, the boss might not be in it so deep.'

'But what about Miranda Coyle and Ernest Walker?' Rachel said. 'We need to talk with them, too.'

'Miranda Coyle's out of the question,' continued Cooper. 'There's not enough time for us to get to Manchester and back before four. So I propose we just focus on the other three.'

'OK,' replied Watson. 'I suggest Rachel talks with Lazarus, I'll do Napier, and you do Walker?'

'Sounds like a plan,' said Cooper, who was already heading off in the direction of his beaten-up wreck of a car. 'I'll see you both at four.'

*   *   *   *

It took rather longer than normal for Penny to drag her husband's spirits back to a more even keel, but once he had emerged from his haze of self-pity, Carmichael's mind started to analyse the murders in a detached and more logical fashion; an area of policing that he enjoyed and at which he excelled.

'I think we need to focus on the letters,' he announced, having pondered in silence for over twenty minutes. 'I also think that we may be looking for more than one murderer here.'

'Why do you say that?' asked Penny, who was mighty relieved to get her husband back in an altogether more optimistic frame of mind.

'Well,' replied Carmichael enthusiastically. 'These letters have to be the key.' At that juncture, Carmichael pulled out from his briefcase the three letters he had collected from Napier, Coyle and Walker.

He laid them on the table, and against the letters for Napier and Coyle he also rested the envelopes in which the letters were sent.

Penny leaned over him as she gazed at the exhibits.

'Well, there are three things that strike me about these letters,' she remarked. 'Firstly, they are exactly the same apart from the addressee; secondly, only two have their original envelopes, and thirdly, the ones to Coyle and Napier are addressed to them by their first names, whilst the other is more formal in that it's addressed to Dr Walker.'

Carmichael pondered for a moment. 'Well yes, they are all identical and we don't have the envelope for Walker's letter as he must have just binned it. I don't see that as relevant. However, your last observation is interesting. I hadn't picked up on that,' he said with a sense of intrigue in his voice. 'So what does that tell us?'

'It tells me that the sender did not know Dr Walker as well,' replied Penny. 'In fact, he may have not even known his Christian name.'

'Yes,' exclaimed Carmichael, who had now got over his previous downer. 'I think you may be on to something there.'

Penny felt a sense of pleasure in being able to help her husband, and moved even closer to him.

'So why do you think there may be more than one killer?' she asked, recalling her husband's words from a few moments earlier.

'It was something Marc said earlier,' replied Carmichael. 'Having argued for days with good cause that Napier is the killer, he's now convinced that Miranda Coyle is our killer; but she has a cast-iron alibi for Ardleigh's death. If she did kill Kenyon, someone else has to be involved. And the more I think of it, the more I'm starting to come to the conclusion that we may well be looking for two killers.'

Chapter 35

Having finally managed to successfully eject Spot On from his house and, more importantly, from his mother's subtle but effective interrogations, Robbie decided that he'd take Brooke to Southport for the day. Cheerfully buoyed by the news that his job was safe, he'd called his girlfriend within seconds of the door shutting behind Spot On, and within an hour, he and Brooke were already sitting in the tired empty train carriage en route to the seaside.

'I saw something really strange last night,' said Brooke as she snuggled up close to him.

'What was that?' replied Robbie who was concentrating hard on the game he was playing on his iPhone and only half listening to what she was saying.

'I'll tell you later,' said Brooke petulantly as she saw that his attention was not wholly on her. 'You just carry on with your game.'

'OK,' replied Robbie as he focused his attention on the small screen, blissfully unaware of the irritation that this was causing. 'Look, Brooke, I'm nearly on level four.'

'Fantastic,' replied Brooke sarcastically before theatrically turning her shoulder away from her boyfriend and gazing grumpily out of the carriage window at the miles and miles of flat farmland that stretched out as far as the eye could see.

* * * *

As he made his way down the quiet winding country lanes, that bright summer's afternoon, Carmichael's mood was much cheerier than a few hours previously. As he drove, Carmichael listened to some of his favourite tunes which his youngest daughter, Natalie, had loaded up on the small portable player, a present the children had all chipped in to buy him for his last birthday.

Carmichael often thought how wonderful it would be if he could have Penny in the team, as she frequently seemed to be able to find new angles on his cases. And, once again, her observations relating to the way that Ernest Walker's letter had been addressed were interesting and certainly made his mind go into overdrive. His deliberations, however, were rudely interrupted by the loud ringing of the hands-free phone.

'It's Stock here,' said the unmistakeable voice on the line. 'Just thought I'd let you know that I've finished the post-mortem on Geraldine Ramsey and I can confirm that she was killed by a single blow to her head. It was definitely the cast-iron door stop that was used and I can now narrow down the time of death to between ten and midnight last night.'

'Thanks,' replied Carmichael. 'So do you think it was the same person who killed Kenyon?'

'That's not my call,' responded Stock curtly. 'That's what you're paid to find out. I just provide the forensic and medical facts.'

Carmichael sighed deeply. 'I should have known better than to ask you that, I suppose,' he said. 'So we are not really much further than we were when we were at the murder scene.'

'Actually, we are,' replied Stock with a sense of an impending revelation in his voice.

'Really?' replied Carmichael eagerly. 'What else have you learned from the autopsy?'

'I'm fairly certain that our man is a leftie,' he said with a great deal of delight in his voice.

'Do you mean a Labour supporter,' remarked Carmichael, who knew full well what Stock actually meant. 'There must be tens of thousands of them in this part of Lancashire, so that won't help much.'

'No, a left-handed person,' replied Stock in exasperation. 'The blow to Miss Ramsey's head was made by someone who was standing behind her and was left-handed. It could not have been made by anyone other than a left-handed person. That would be impossible.'

In the years Carmichael had known the portly Dr Stock, he had never known him to claim certainty unless his statement was indisputable, so if Stock said the killer was a left-hander, the killer was a left-hander!

'Thanks, Stock,' responded Carmichael gratefully. 'That piece of news is going to be a big step forward for us.'

'My pleasure,' replied Stock. 'You'll have my full report on your desk later today, but there's not going to be anything spectacular outside what I've told you already.'

As soon as the phone had been replaced, Carmichael keyed in Cooper's number. 'Paul,' he said, 'are you with Rachel and Watson?'

'Err, no,' replied Cooper, who was just about to ring Ernest Walker's doorbell. 'We split up earlier. I'm at Dr Walker's house, Marc's gone to talk to Napier and Rachel's with Lazarus.'

'That's good,' he said excitedly. 'I'll explain more at the debrief later, but our killer is left-handed, so get hold of them and ask them to check out their two. You do the same with Walker and I'll phone the police in Manchester and get them to check out Miranda Coyle.'

'OK, sir,' replied Cooper dutifully. 'I'll get on to it right away.'

*　*　*　*

After making his call to the police in Manchester, Carmichael spent the remainder of his journey to Kirkwood Police Station considering what the chances were of having two left-handed individuals out of a random group of four people.

His head concluded that the probability was almost certainly quite low, but with the way his luck was going, he'd probably find all four of his prime suspects were left-handed.

*　*　*　*

After taking almost twenty minutes completing his calls to Rachel and Watson, Cooper finally rang Dr Walker's doorbell.

Within seconds the maid, Tatiana, answered the door.

'Can I help you?' she asked in her strong Eastern European accent.

'I would like to talk with Dr Walker,' he said.

'They are both out working,' replied the maid in her pidgin English.

'Where can I find him?' enquired Cooper, speaking very slowly and emphasising the *him,* so she could understand.

'He is at his work,' replied the maid with a dismissive expression on her face.

As Cooper attempted to make himself understood and discover exactly where he could find Dr Walker, a familiar car sped into the drive. It was the Mercedes belonging to Mrs Walker.

'Can I help you?' Mrs Walker asked as she carefully extracted herself from the car.

'I'm trying to locate your husband,' replied Cooper.

'He's away working, I'm afraid,' she replied, as she walked awkwardly across the gravel drive to the front door. 'Can I help?'

209

'No, it's really your husband I need to talk to,' he confirmed.

'If you come inside, I'll check his diary, as to be honest I can't remember where he's gone this time. He's away so much, you know,' continued Mrs Walker nonchalantly.

Cooper followed obediently behind Mrs Walker as she entered the house.

'Have you hurt your leg?' he heard himself ask her once they were inside.

Mrs Walker smiled. 'I did,' she replied. 'I broke it skiing earlier in the year. It was a nasty break and I've only just come off crutches. It seems to have mended well but the muscles are a bit weak, so I'm limping around like an old woman at the moment. I really should have more physio, but it's a case of finding the time.'

Cooper smiled back. He was relieved that the limp was due to an accident, as after asking the question, he had a sudden fear that Mrs Walker may have some awful condition that she was embarrassed about, or worse, would be totally unaware that she had a pronounced limp at all.

'If you come with me, we can look at his desk diary,' continued Mrs Walker. 'It's in his study.'

As they walked down the hallway and past the dozens of large paintings that festooned the walls, Cooper noticed the empty space he had remarked upon to Dr Walker in his earlier visit was now occupied.

'I see that you've got the painting back,' he remarked.

'I'm sorry?' replied Mrs Walker, who clearly had no idea what Cooper was talking about.

'The other day when I was here, I remarked to your husband about there being a space on the wall,' explained Cooper. 'He told me that the picture had been dislodged and was at the mender's.'

'Oh the Hoffmann,' exclaimed Mrs Walker. 'I suppose he told you I did it, too, didn't he?'

'I can't remember if he said that,' replied Cooper tactfully. 'He did say that you had taken it to be mended though.'

Mrs Walker smiled again. 'Very diplomatic,' she said. 'I got it back yesterday. You'd never know it had been damaged. Mind you, for the cost of repair, it *should* look in mint condition, too.'

Mrs Walker led Cooper into a small room at the end of the hallway. Once inside, it was clear to Cooper that this was Dr Walker's study.

In keeping with the rest of the house there were pictures covering the walls, but in this room they were smaller in size and mainly pencil drawings and watercolours.

'Get off, Thursday,' Mrs Walker said as she pushed a large tortoiseshell cat from its comfortable resting place smack bang in the middle of the writing desk. 'You know you're not allowed on his desk.'

The indignant cat let out a loud meow and leaped off the desk and scurried quickly out of the study. 'She'll be a bit cross with me for the rest of the day now,' continued Mrs Walker. 'It's Ernest's cat and she's spoilt rotten. In fact, I think he likes her more than he likes me. He feeds her prawns, you know!'

Cooper smiled and remained silent, but could not help thinking to himself that if Mrs Walker was right and the cat was the major recipient of her husband's attention, then Dr Walker certainly needed his eyes testing.

'Ah here it is,' she said, oblivious to Cooper's secret thoughts. 'Now let me see.'

Cooper gazed around the room as Mrs Walker flicked through the diary. His eyes suddenly became fixed on a photograph of Dr Walker sitting behind a desk, apparently signing a document of some description.

'What's your husband doing in that photo?' Cooper asked.

Mrs Walker looked down at the photo.

'Oh that was taken about ten years ago when my husband

was on the council. He's signing the agreement with the consortium who built the new shopping precinct in Kirkwood.'

Cooper looked intently at the photograph. Dr Walker was holding the pen in his right hand.

'Ah here it is,' continued Mrs Walker, oblivious to Cooper's fixation on the photograph. 'He's in Chester today. He stayed over last night and will be back this evening.'

'Thanks,' replied Cooper, who, having completed his mission, was eager to get away.

'Don't you want his number?' Mrs Walker said in astonishment as Cooper headed off down the hallway.'

'No, it's all right,' replied Cooper. 'I'll maybe try and talk with him tomorrow. Many thanks for your assistance.'

Tatiana the maid and her employer watched as Cooper's clapped-out car spluttered and belched its way out of the drive and down the lane.

'How peculiar!' said Mrs Walker. 'I'm a bit bemused by all that.'

Tatiana shrugged her shoulders. Having lived in Moulton Bank for about two years, there was little that she now found surprising about the English – their ways were a complete mystery to her.

Chapter 36

'So out of our four prime suspects only Napier's left-handed,' announced Carmichael as he and his three officers sat in the incident room at Kirkwood Police Station. 'He's our man then.'

'Shall we arrest him now?' enquired Watson, half expecting to be told no.

'Yes,' replied Carmichael as if it was the most dim-witted question he had ever heard. 'I want him in custody right away. I'm not leaving him out there to commit more murders. I want you and Cooper to go and arrest him immediately.'

The two officers rose and walked over to the door.

The news that only Napier was left-handed was a great result for the team. In short it meant that Hugo Lazarus, Ernest Walker and Miranda Coyle could not have killed Geraldine Ramsey and effectively implied that they were also all innocent of the other two deaths.

This news was of course a personal disaster for Carmichael and he was starting to feel very nervy. He knew for certain he would come under intense pressure in the days that followed, given he had released Napier the previous evening and, in so doing, had allowed him to murder Geraldine Ramsey.

'When you get back and while Napier's sorting himself out a lawyer, we'll finish off the debriefing,' continued Carmichael before Cooper and Watson had managed to get through the doorway. 'But I want Napier safely behind lock and key before we do that.'

* * * *

Once the two sergeants had departed, Carmichael leaned back in his chair and, with his hands clasped firmly behind his head, stared across the room, as if he had all the world's problems resting on his shoulders.

'It's a great result, sir,' remarked Rachel, who felt obliged to remain and boost her boss's spirits. 'At least we've now got the killer. I was certain it would be one of the others; Napier would have been at the very bottom of my list.'

Carmichael smiled. 'That's really kind of you, Rachel,' he replied with genuine appreciation. 'But I should have been more diligent last night. I'll get slaughtered for this once it gets out.'

Rachel knew he was right, but felt compelled to try and lighten his mood.

'I think you're being very hard on yourself, sir,' she continued. 'Last night we had four suspects and there was a strong case for all of them. It was only when we discovered the killer was left-handed that we could narrow it down to Napier. Before, then it could have been any one of them; and you couldn't detain them all.'

Carmichael nodded. 'Actually you are right,' he said. 'But I'm not sure that's how others will see it. It's a bloody good job Hewitt is off on leave; if he was here, it would be a nightmare.'

Rachel smiled. 'Shall I get you a coffee, sir?' she asked.

'Yes please,' replied Carmichael. 'Make it a strong one with two sugars.'

* * * *

Robbie and Brooke arrived back at Moulton Bank railway station at 5:50 p.m. In spite of their small spat on the train going to Southport, they had enjoyed a fun day messing about like youngsters do in the warm summer sunshine.

'Do you want to come back to the house?' Brooke asked. 'We could have some tea there and then maybe do something later.'

Robbie didn't need to be asked a second time. He was keen to avoid further questions from his mother about his confrontation with Spot On, and the chance to spend more time with Brooke was OK with him.

'Great,' he replied. 'That sounds like a cool idea to me.'

It took them about fifteen minutes to arrive at Brooke's house, by which time most of the vehicles that had swamped the area earlier in the day had gone; however, there was still a couple of police cars parked outside Geraldine Ramsey's house and the blue and white tape that was cordoning off her driveway was still in view to indicate all was not as it should be.

'I wonder what's going on,' Brooke remarked nosily.

'I've no idea,' replied Robbie. 'It looks like there may have been a burglary or something.'

Brooke's mind instantly went back to what she had observed the night before. She went to tell her boyfriend, but something inside her stopped her from sharing with Robbie what she'd witnessed.

'Actually, Robbie,' she said as they stood by the garden gate. 'Do you mind if we just call it a day for today. I've got a blinding headache. I think I may just go to bed.'

Robbie's heart sank. 'OK,' he said reluctantly. 'That's fine.'

'I'm really sorry,' continued Brooke, who could see how disappointed Robbie was. 'It's just so painful. I think the best thing is if I get some sleep.'

Robbie forced a smile and gently kissed her, before heading off in the direction of his house.

'Remember we're going to the Prom Night tomorrow with Mum and Dad,' he shouted back at her. 'You need to be at ours at about six, I think.'

Brooke waved back and disappeared up her drive to consider what she should do next.

*　*　*　*

Knowing it was going to be another late night at the office, Carmichael decided to call Penny.

'Oh hi, darling,' Penny replied as she realised who was calling. 'How are you getting on?'

'We've just arrested Gordon Napier,' he replied. 'Cooper and Watson have just brought him in. We're certain it's him and, with everything we have to do, it may be midnight before I get home.'

Penny could tell by his voice that he was less than happy with the outcome. 'Are you sure it's definitely him?'

'It's pretty much cut and dried,' he replied. 'Anyway, I'll see you later.'

Without giving his wife a chance to reply, Carmichael hung up.

*　*　*　*

Gordon Napier was getting used to being interrogated by the police, so much so that he no longer exhibited the nervous signs that had been so evident earlier in the week.

Immediately after he was arrested and Cooper had explained why he was being held, Napier had maintained an unnatural silence. After being formally charged with the murders of Marcus Ardleigh, Ruben Kenyon and Geraldine Ramsey, Napier declared quite calmly that he wanted a solicitor present at any interviews and that he was not prepared to cooperate at all from now on.

'Suit yourself,' retorted Watson, when he heard Napier state his position of silence. 'In my experience, silence just proves your guilt.'

Having made this profound observation, Watson left the custody sergeant and his small team of PCs to deposit Napier in a cell.

'What was all that claptrap?' enquired Cooper. 'There are numerous cases of innocent people refusing to talk. Why did you tell him all that rubbish?'

'Because I'm annoyed and he just got on my nerves,' replied Watson. 'I knew my initial gut feel about him was right, but I let Carmichael make me question myself and I was starting to believe Miranda Coyle was the killer, but the left-handed development from Stock means I was right all along.'

Cooper smiled. 'Come on, we'd better get ourselves up to the incident room and complete the debrief.'

'Now that is a waste of time,' remarked Watson curtly. 'As we now have Napier banged to rights, who cares about what we have or have not found out about Ardleigh and the others?'

'Carmichael cares,' replied Cooper calmly. 'And he's the boss.'

'He's also deep, deep in the mire and is probably hoping to hell that Napier is not the killer,' observed Watson with a hint of malicious pleasure.

* * * *

Brooke felt a little guilty about lying to Robbie, and as soon as she knew he would be back at home, sent him a text:

Does your Dad know anything about what had happened over the road?

She got his reply a few minutes later:

According to Mum there was a murder, but she says Dad has caught the killer already.

On receiving the text message from Robbie, Brooke was unsure what she should do. Her first thought had been to call Robbie and tell him what she'd seen; but she was worried about getting involved. And anyway, she figured, if the killer had already been caught, what she saw was now irrelevant. So, like many girls of her age, she decided to ask her mother for advice.

Unfortunately for Brooke, her mother was not like most mothers and the advice she received was not the sort of advice most mothers would give in those circumstances.

'I thought you said that Robbie's dad has caught the killer,' said Brooke's mother. 'It's not our problem, Brooke; just stay out of it.'

Despite feeling uncomfortable with this advice, Brooke was always respectful of her mum and decided, albeit reluctantly, that on this occasion she should follow her counsel.

Chapter 37

It was 6:15 p.m. by the time the debrief resumed.

'OK,' said Carmichael. 'First things first. Is Napier under caution?'

'Yes,' replied Cooper. 'He's demanding a brief this time and has said that from now on he will refuse to cooperate.'

'He does sound as though he's guilty then,' remarked Carmichael glibly, much to the animated delight of Watson, and the astonishment of Cooper. 'But I'm glad he's asked for a brief; I don't want him to be able to claim that we denied him his rights.' Carmichael then looked over in the direction of Cooper and Watson. 'And as you are the arresting officers, I'll let you do the interview with Napier. Rachel and I will observe from next door.'

'Fantastic,' replied Watson, who was delighted to be conducting the interview without Carmichael in the room.

'Yes, thank you, sir,' added Cooper, who was happy enough with the honour, though as always his excitement was far less noticeable than that of his colleague.

'OK, that's settled,' concluded Carmichael. 'Now let's make sure we close out the case without leaving any lines of investigation open. I want to make absolutely sure we have the right man. I don't want a smart barrister or anyone else for that matter, picking holes in our procedures here. Let's keep this nice and tidy.'

'Who is he kidding?' whispered Watson out of the side of

his mouth. 'He's hoping and praying that Napier's not our man as Carmichael's neck is still on the block if he is.'

Carmichael didn't hear Watson's comment, but seeing the look on Rachel's face, guessed it was probably made in bad taste and most likely aimed at him. 'OK, Marc,' he said loudly, 'you go first.'

'Right you are, sir,' replied Watson, trying hard to appear as if nothing had been said. 'Where would you like me to start?'

'Why don't you fill me in on the results of the house-to-house enquiries that were made today? Then you could outline how you discovered that Napier was left-handed,' said Carmichael as if he were talking to a small child.

It was not the first time that Watson had irritated his boss, but on most of the previous occasions Carmichael would be out of sorts with him for only a few moments. By the expression on Carmichael's face, Watson surmised that this time he may have overstepped the mark and forgiveness for his aside might not be so quick in coming.

'The house-to-house wasn't very successful, I'm afraid,' he said nervously. 'Paul spoke to one old dear who said she heard a car driving away at speed at around ten twenty, but she didn't look out of the window so she has no description of the car.'

'And to make matters worse,' Cooper added, 'she said she couldn't be one hundred per cent sure it was at ten twenty. She said it might have been a bit earlier.'

'That was it!' exclaimed Carmichael. 'Out of a dozen or so houses only one person heard anything and that's it.'

'We still have to get back to a couple of houses as there was no answer when we called,' added Rachel.

Carmichael shook his head. 'So who is following up on those houses?' he asked despairingly.

The silence that followed answered his question.

'This is not good enough, guys,' Carmichael shouted. 'We

may think we have the killer downstairs but we cannot get sloppy here.'

Carmichael looked up at the clock. 'Rachel, call the desk downstairs and get them to send a couple of PCs to the houses we missed today. I want all the residents of the surrounding houses to have been spoken to before we go home tonight.'

Rachel scurried off to carry out her instructions.

'So what about your meeting with Napier earlier today?' Carmichael asked, his eyes fixed intently on Watson. 'What did he have to say for himself?'

Watson was feeling very uncomfortable with the atmosphere in the room, but endeavoured to keep his composure.

'I tracked him down in his shop as usual,' replied Watson. 'He was unable to give much of an alibi for his movements after we released him last night. He said he went straight home, had three or four stiff whiskies in front of the TV, and then went to bed. But of course on his own.'

'And how did you deduce that he was left-handed?' enquired Carmichael.

'I asked him to write down the programmes he watched,' replied Watson self-righteously.

'Clever ploy,' remarked Carmichael. 'And have you checked out the programmes to make sure they tie up with the time we'd expect him to get home?'

'Err, well no,' replied Watson, his smug grin now vanishing. 'It's not needed now surely!'

'If I were you, Marc,' said Carmichael angrily. 'I'd check out whether the programmes he wrote down were on, what times they started and finished, and I'd also ask him some detailed questions about what happened in them. If he can successfully give a strong account of the programmes he claims to have watched, his guilt will be all the more difficult for us to prove.'

'Yes, sir,' replied Watson meekly. 'I'll do that right away.'

'Actually, Marc,' continued Carmichael. 'You may want to try and watch them, or at least some of them before you interview him. It might help your questioning later.'

Knowing he had dropped the ball badly, Watson exited the interview room as quickly as he could. As he did so, he almost knocked Rachel over as she made her way back from giving the duty sergeant Carmichael's instructions.

'If I'm interviewing Napier, too, maybe I should go and watch the programmes,' suggested Cooper.

Carmichael held his head in his hands. 'Yes, you should, but first I want you to tell me what you learned about Dent and Boutilier this morning and also what happened when you went to talk with Ernest Walker.'

*   *   *   *

Brooke hid herself from sight at the top of the stairs while her mother talked to the two police officers. She could not make out all that was being said, but clearly heard her mother say that she had not seen anything and to her knowledge, neither her husband nor her daughter had either.

'My husband's out and my daughter's in bed,' Brooke's mum said loudly. 'However, I'll speak to them and, if they did see or hear anything, I'll let you know.'

As soon as the police had gone and the door had been closed, Brooke appeared at the top of the stairs. 'I think I should tell Robbie's dad what I saw; I think it's the right thing to do.'

Brooke's mother scowled at her. 'It's your choice, my girl,' she shouted at her. 'But my advice is to keep quiet. It's none of our business. However, you're a big girl now, so if you're willing to be dragged into court then go straight ahead.'

Brooke chose not to continue with the conversation. She

now did have a headache and went back into her bedroom to think things over for herself.

* * * *

Cooper had made little progress in finding out more about either Dent or Boutilier. He was unable to trace any of Dent's relatives in such a short time and, with the Boutilier family being located in Canada, he had drawn a blank trying to contact them, too. Once he'd explained about his meeting with the maid and Mrs Walker, and described how he had established that Dr Walker was right-handed, he asked if he could leave to join Watson.

'Unless you've anything else to contribute then, yes, you can go,' remarked Carmichael, who was pretty frustrated with the contributions of both his senior officers.

'Actually, there were a couple of things,' said Cooper. 'They may mean absolutely nothing, but the other day when I was in the house Dr Walker told me his wife had knocked a picture off the wall and it had been broken and had been sent to the repairer's.'

'And?' said Carmichael who was totally oblivious to the relevance of this piece of information.

'Well, today it was back,' he continued.

'Yes, so what's so remarkable about that?' Carmichael enquired, his irritation now quite palpable in his voice.

'Well, I'm certain Dr Walker said it was only sent away a few days ago and that it would be weeks before it was back,' continued Cooper. 'However, Mrs Walker said she picked it up yesterday. It looked in perfect condition, and one would assume it would take a long while to restore a broken picture, so why did Dr Walker lie to me about when it was sent to be repaired?'

Carmichael and Rachel exchanged a brief look of bewilderment.

'I've no idea, Paul,' replied Carmichael. 'But I doubt it has any relevance to the case.'

'I tend to agree,' remarked Cooper as he sauntered away. 'But I just thought I'd mention it, though.'

'You said there were a couple of things,' remarked Carmichael. 'What was the other?'

'Just that I found out that the Boutilier family had funded the college boathouse,' replied Cooper. 'It was something they were doing at about the time Alain Boutilier went missing.'

'Maybe he's under the foundations,' Rachel said jokingly.

'That's all we need,' replied Carmichael. 'Anyway, thanks for sharing your findings with us, Paul. You can go and join Watson now and do some prep before your interview with Napier.'

'Thanks, sir,' replied Cooper as he quietly disappeared out through the door.

* * * *

'Remember, we're all going to the Prom Evening tomorrow at Rivingham Hall,' said Penny, as the Carmichael family (minus Steve) were sitting at the dinner table.

'Actually, Mum, do you mind if I don't go to the Prom Evening tomorrow?' asked Natalie. 'It's really not my thing and I was planning to spend the day at the stables. If I go to the Prom, I'll have to come back at around three to get ready.'

'Well, if you don't fancy it, that's OK I suppose,' replied Penny. 'But it means I have a ticket going begging that's been paid for.

'Really?' said Jemma. 'If that's the case, can I bring someone?'

'Who?' Penny asked.

'It's just someone I met in the pub the other night,' replied Jemma vaguely.

'I suppose it's yet another in the long line of your boyfriends,' remarked Robbie.

'You're taking precious little Barbie!' retorted Jemma angrily. 'So why can't I take someone if a ticket is going spare.'

'Brooke is not my little Barbie,' Robbie replied firmly. 'Just because she takes pride in her appearance, that's no reason to call her names.'

'Pack it in, you two,' snapped Penny. 'Of course you can bring someone, dear,' she continued while shooting a dark scowl in the direction of her son. 'Who is this young man? Do I know him?'

'He's called Chris,' replied Jemma. 'And no, you won't know him.'

* * * *

'Can I get you another coffee?' Rachel asked once she and Carmichael were alone in the incident room.

'Is it me or are those two on a different planet sometimes?' remarked Carmichael. 'What on earth was Cooper on about there? It was totally beyond me.'

Rachel smiled. 'It's been a long week for all of us, sir,' she remarked tactfully. 'I suspect everyone's getting a bit tired.'

'I guess you're right,' replied Carmichael. 'Yes, I'd love a coffee. Then maybe you can tell me what you found out about Ardleigh this morning and also how your meeting with Lazarus went earlier today.'

Rachel strolled away to get the drinks, leaving Carmichael alone to gather his thoughts.

Within a few minutes she was back; and having laid Carmichael's coffee mug in front of him, sat herself down and started to recount what she had uncovered that morning.

'It's amazing what you can find out about someone like

Ardleigh on the Internet,' she remarked. 'Apart from everything we know already about his time in the Thatcher government and also working with the Blair administration, he was also an accomplished yachtsman in his youth. He apparently sailed in races all over the place, won many of them, too. And he wrote several books on mathematics, the most notable one called *The Random Behavioural Walk*.'

'And what is that exactly?' enquired Carmichael.

'It's to do with probability,' replied Rachel. 'As far as I can gather he used a financial model normally used to predict share price movements to try and predict human behaviour and other non-financial occurrences.'

Carmichael looked bemused. 'Say that again!' he said.

Rachel laughed. 'I'm not totally sure myself,' she admitted. 'However, I have ordered his book from Amazon, so when it arrives I will show it to you. But the example I saw online was of the probability of a virus spreading within an area based upon weather conditions and the prevailing winds. Actually, it was really interesting and gave some pretty exact predictions of outcomes, based upon certain variables being present.'

This was all too complicated for Carmichael to take in, but he was mildly interested.

'So Ardleigh would have been an expert on knots,' he said, casting his mind back to Rachel's initial comment. 'If so, then maybe his death *was* suicide.'

'It's possible,' replied Rachel. 'But why would he do that? And how and why would he get his own hands tied up? Also how would he get the rope into Napier's van after he had died and why would he want to frame Napier? And, most bizarre of all, if he was going to hang himself, why set up the elaborate charade with the letters and the meetings at The Lindley?'

'All very good questions,' replied Carmichael. 'And I'm afraid, at the moment, I cannot answer any of them.

* * * *

'So tell me about Chris,' enquired Penny as soon as she was alone with her eldest daughter. 'How old is he and where does he work?'

'He's about twenty something,' replied Jemma. 'He's tall and well built, good-looking, too, and he lives in the village, though he is originally from Cumbria or Newcastle; somewhere up there anyway.'

Upon hearing this scant description, Penny's face suggested to her daughter that she may have an inkling who the new boyfriend was.

'Does he often say "Spot on?"' Penny enquired.

'How do you know that?' exclaimed Jemma, who was gobsmacked by the accuracy of her mother's question.

'He works with Robbie,' replied Penny. 'It was him Robbie punched yesterday.'

* * * *

'So how did you get on with Lazarus?' Carmichael enquired.

'He was his usual very amiable self,' replied Rachel. 'I met him at his house and he said he did understand how it looked with him getting payments from Ardleigh, but he is sticking fast to his story that these were payments made out of kindness with no strings attached.'

'And do you believe him?' asked Carmichael in disbelief.

'Yes I do,' she replied almost apologetically. 'I think he's quite harmless.'

'Did he have an alibi for last night?' added Carmichael.

'Not really,' replied Rachel. 'He was also in alone, or so he claims.'

'And how did you establish he was right-handed?' said Carmichael.

'I just asked him,' Rachel replied. 'He said he was right-handed, then proved it by signing his name. He used his right hand and it matched the signature on his statement from Monday.'

Carmichael nodded his satisfaction at what Rachel had managed to unearth. 'I'm not convinced he's telling us the truth, but well done!'

'So what now?' Rachel asked.

'You make me one more mug of coffee and we wait until our two sergeants are ready to conduct the interview with our left-handed, toupee-wearing antiques dealer.'

Rachel laughed. 'You noticed the toupee, too. Marc already commented on that when you interviewed him the other day.'

'Well, as rugs go it's not the best one I've seen,' replied Carmichael, with a massive childish grin on his face.

'Two sugars, sir?' Rachel asked, trying hard to stifle her laughter.

'Actually, just one,' replied Carmichael. 'I'm feeling far more calm and composed than I was before.'

Chapter 38

It was 8:45 p.m. by the time Watson and Cooper started the interview with Gordon Napier.

'So, Mr Napier,' began Watson, who was keen to take the lead in the interrogation. 'Can you tell us what you did last night after you were released from Kirkwood Police Station?'

Napier sat back in his chair, arms folded and stared directly into Watson's eyes. 'No comment,' he said firmly.

'When we arrested you earlier today you told us you had gone straight home and watched TV,' continued Watson. 'Is that correct, Mr Napier?'

'No comment,' said Napier once again.

'Remaining silent won't help you, Gordon,' interjected Cooper. 'We have evidence that links you with Marcus Ardleigh's death – namely the rope we found in your van – and we have established that you have a very strong motive for killing him. We know he had been blackmailing you for decades, and your alibis for all three murders are very weak. Given all that evidence against you, I think you should seriously consider your decision to remain silent, don't you?'

'No comment' came back the response as resolutely as on the previous two occasions.

Behind the two-way mirror Carmichael and Dalton watched the proceedings.

'Do you think he's guilty?' Carmichael asked, without taking his eyes off the events on the other side of the window.

'The evidence points to him and him alone,' replied Rachel.

'Yes, that's true,' remarked Carmichael. 'However, I'm still not convinced. What if Ardleigh did commit suicide and the only two murders we are investigating are those of Kenyon and Geraldine Ramsey?'

Rachel paused to consider Carmichael's hypothesis. 'Well, if that was the case, then we probably have as much on Lazarus as we do on Napier; and for me, Miranda Coyle would then make the most likely suspect but they're not left-handed.'

Carmichael nodded. 'Yes, you're right,' he concurred.

'Whichever scenario we pick though, Dr Walker does not seem to figure as a suspect,' continued Rachel. 'It seems odd that he even got a letter. It's almost as if it was sent to the wrong person.'

'I agree,' replied Carmichael, who could not help but smile when he heard Rachel's comment. He found it interesting that the two women he had discussed the case with, Penny and now Rachel, had both commented about Walker receiving a letter as being peculiar. 'Dr Walker's association does seem to make him the odd one out,' he continued. 'However, I think that's because as yet we haven't discovered his secret. Maybe if we knew that we would think differently.'

'You're probably right,' remarked Rachel. 'So what do you think, sir? Do you think Napier did it?'

'I don't honestly know,' replied Carmichael. 'We certainly have enough evidence to push for a trial, but my gut feeling is that this case is not as straightforward as that.'

On the other side of the glass Gordon Napier remained unyielding. 'No comment,' he replied for the umpteenth time.

'I was interested in what you found out about Ardleigh,' continued Carmichael his eyes still fixed on Napier. 'What sort of man do you think he was?'

'A successful man,' replied Rachel, 'and for sure a very clever man, too.'

Carmichael nodded. 'That much is certain, but what about his character?'

Rachel thought about the question for a few moments before providing her considered opinion. 'He was someone who liked to be in control, but probably not that pleasant.'

'I agree,' replied Carmichael. 'I see him as a control freak, someone who hates to lose. Someone who was jealous, even maybe intimidated, by people who were more popular or cleverer than him. I think Boutilier was one such person, and I think he was probably capable of killing Boutilier.'

'Do you think so?' enquired Rachel.

'Why not?' replied Carmichael. 'I suspect he was probably OK with people who he could dominate, like poor Geraldine Ramsey but someone like Boutilier and also people more gutsy like Miranda Coyle, he would have struggled with. I bet he could not believe his luck when he found out she'd had a bigamist marriage. The power that gave him would have been immense, I suspect.'

*　*　*　*

After fifteen minutes and over thirty 'No comments' from Napier, the two frustrated officers brought the interview to a conclusion.

'OK, Gordon,' said Watson as the detainee was led away from the interview room. 'We've got better things to do than waste our time on you. I think you'll regret being so uncooperative.'

Napier didn't even bother to look back at Watson as he walked slowly away down the corridor. 'No comment,' he shouted.

*　*　*　*

'What do you think, sir?' asked Cooper as the four officers gathered in the incident room.

'He may well be implicated in the deaths,' replied Carmichael. 'But I find it hard to believe he killed all three on his own. I think this is a more complicated case than that.'

'We're both on duty tomorrow,' announced Watson, at the same time pointing in Rachel's direction. 'Do you want us to interview him again?'

Carmichael shook his head. 'Unless he decides to talk, I don't see any point in you doing that. No, you need to check again on the houses around Geraldine Ramsey's home. Someone must have seen something. You can also see if Miranda Coyle has a good alibi for last night, and then if you've time, you might also want to do some research into Dr Walker. I need to know why he got a letter.'

'Right you are, sir,' replied Watson, who was already working out in his head which of the tasks he would delegate to Rachel.

Chapter 39

Saturday 21st August

Carmichael was woken by the bright rays of dawn, as they pierced their way through the bedroom curtains. His slumbers that night, though short in hours, had been deep and peaceful, and as he slowly stirred he felt calm and relaxed. On the pillow next to him Penny remained motionless with only the quiet sound of her breathing to confirm her presence. Carmichael glanced at the clock on his bedside cabinet – it was 7:45.

For the next twenty minutes, he lay there silently admiring his beautiful wife, who tranquilly lay so close to him that he could feel her warmth. He studied her face, that small nose, the lovely cheeks that would rise like mountains and light up her face when she smiled, and her gorgeous lips that he had kissed so many times. And as the early-morning light caught her hair, making it gleam like highly polished mahogany, Carmichael could not help thinking how lucky he was to be married to such a wonderful, attractive woman.

Eventually, the sounds of the morning as they crept through the open window and the beams of sunlight which bounced around the bedroom made Penny start to stir. Gently she opened her eyes, at first squinting as the sharp rays dragged her to consciousness, then, after a few moments as she started to become aware that her slumbers were over, she slowly turned her head towards him and smiled at her husband.

'Hello, you,' she said, as she snuggled closer to him. 'What time did you come to bed last night?'

Carmichael could not remember, but guessed that he must have spent at least two hours in front of the TV sipping his favourite whisky before he had finally joined his wife in bed. 'I think it was around one,' he muttered.

'So what's the plan for today?' Penny asked.

'Not sure,' replied Carmichael. 'I'll probably take a walk to buy the papers then I may just ...'

'Don't tell me,' interjected Penny. 'You'll come home, have a cooked breakfast, read the paper, then at about eleven thirty you'll go to The Railway for a couple of pints, and then at around two you'll come home, where you'll most likely fall asleep.'

Carmichael jabbed his wife hard with his elbow. 'Am I that predictable?'

'At weekends you are,' she replied. 'And that bloody hurt!'

'Well, today I might just surprise you,' Carmichael announced indignantly.

'How's that?' asked Penny, trying hard to stifle her laughter.

'I may just have toast and cereal today!' he replied. 'And I may have it *before* I get the paper.'

Penny pulled the duvet around her ears and rolled away from her husband. 'Mr Predictability,' she teased, 'that's what we should call you.'

Carmichael smiled and clambered out of bed. 'Do you really think it's possible to predict what people do?' he asked.

'If you know someone well enough, I would imagine it's quite easy,' replied Penny. 'They may do one of a couple of options, like have cereal rather than a cooked breakfast, but yes, I reckon it is.'

'The Random Behavioural Walk,' muttered Carmichael to himself as he recalled the conversation he had had with Rachel the day before. 'I wonder.'

* * * *

Brooke had spent an anxious night wrestling with her conscience. She definitely did not want to disregard her mother's advice, but in her heart she knew what she had seen was important. She decided she would talk to Robbie; she felt sure he would know what to do.

She picked up her iPhone and started to text him.

* * * *

'Predictable,' muttered Carmichael to himself as he strolled slowly towards the newsagents. 'How on earth can she call me predictable?'

'Hi, Steve,' shouted Robbie Robertson who was walking rather briskly towards him on the opposite side of the road. 'Will you be in the pub at lunchtime as usual?'

Carmichael raised his hand to acknowledge his friend. 'Of course,' he replied.

The irony of his statement struck home almost immediately, making Carmichael first smile and then stop in his tracks as he reflected again on what he'd been discussing with Rachel the day before.

He reached for his mobile and dialled Dr Stock's number.

The phone rang three times before Stock picked up the receiver.

'I wondered whether you'd be working today,' bellowed Carmichael, who was trying to be heard over the din of the traffic.

'Just this morning,' replied Stock gloomily. 'I've a backlog, so I thought I'd catch up without any interruptions. How wrong I was.'

'I need a couple of questions answered,' announced Carmichael, totally ignoring the words of the glum forensic expert. 'Could you tell me whether Ardleigh could have made those rope marks on his wrists himself,' shouted Carmichael as a van noisily passed by. 'Secondly, I'd also like to get an idea of how advanced Ardleigh's cancer was and how long he had to live.'

'I'd have to relook at the body again to answer your first question,' replied Stock. 'But, on the second point, I'd say he had no more than six months to live, a year at the very most. It was pretty advanced.'

'How soon can you get back to me on the rope marks?' enquired Carmichael.

On the end of the line, Stock rolled his eyes skyward in desperation. 'Give me an hour, Carmichael,' he replied. 'I'll call you back.'

'Thanks, Stock,' replied Carmichael. 'I really appreciate your help.'

Both men ended the call, one with a sense of impending triumph, the other with a sense of exasperation in the knowledge that his already heavy workload had just been augmented.

Chapter 40

Rachel never relished working on Saturdays; she hated the thought of them even more when she was on duty with Marc Watson.

It wasn't that they didn't get on. In fact, in many ways Rachel admired Watson. However, it was the constant smart-arse, sexist remarks he would make that irritated her most, and these always seemed to be more prevalent when Carmichael and Cooper weren't around.

'Morning, your ladyship,' bellowed Watson as he saw her walking down the corridor. 'Does Gregory have to do his own breakfast this morning?'

'It's Gregor,' corrected Rachel moodily, as she reached her work station and slammed her bag on the desk. 'You've met him at least a dozen times; you'd think you could remember my boyfriend's name by now.'

'Now who's a little tetchy then?' Watson replied with a devilish grin on his face. 'You and Gregor have a falling-out this morning? Is he jealous that you're spending your Saturday with me rather than him?'

There was a small fragment of truth in what Watson was alluding to but there was no way Rachel was going to allow him the pleasure of knowing that her boyfriend was the jealous type. She took a deep breath.

'Sod off, Marc,' she replied. 'I'm getting a coffee – do you want one?'

Not wanting the coffee tipped over his head, Watson

decided to temporarily discontinue his tormenting quips. 'Yes and you couldn't get me a bacon roll, too, could you?'

'You're unbelievable,' replied Rachel with an air of total resignation in her voice. 'Come on, give me a tenner!'

'A coffee's only a quid and a bacon roll can only be two or three quid, so why a tenner?' Watson enquired.

'Cos your buying mine, too, if I'm getting them,' replied Rachel firmly. 'And I'm having a bowl of cereal as well – I'm starving.'

Watson took out his wallet and handed Rachel a ten-pound note. 'This is blackmail,' he said as the note was snatched out of his hand.

'No, Marc, it's extortion,' said Rachel as if she were a teacher admonishing a small boy. 'You'll never make an inspector if you don't know the difference.'

Pleased with the outcome of their first verbal encounter of the morning, Rachel marched off down the corridor, totally oblivious to her colleague's lecherous eyes that were transfixed on her small round bottom.

* * * *

Brooke had been checking her text messages every few minutes to see if Robbie had replied. This went on and on until almost ten thirty when she clambered out of her bed and headed for the shower feeling totally exhausted after having had very little sleep. She had a hair appointment at twelve forty-five so she knew she'd have to get a move on as, after her shower, she needed to have breakfast and then make herself presentable to go out – a set of tasks she figured would take her all of the two and a bit hours that remained.

She checked her texts again. There was nothing from Robbie.

238

She sent him another. This time Brooke highlighted the word 'urgent' by underlining it. As soon as she could see it had been sent, she threw down the iPhone on her bed and dashed into the bathroom.

With absolutely nothing to do that day, and having spent until the early hours of the morning playing computer games, Robbie would not be emerging from his slumbers until that afternoon. And it would be after 1 p.m. before he read Brooke's texts, at which time she would already be at the hairdresser's.

*   *   *   *

True to his word, Stock called Carmichael back with some answers.

'You're not as foolish as you look, Carmichael,' he said. 'I checked Ardleigh's wrists again and I'd say that, not only was it *possible* he made the rope burns himself, but in my opinion it's actually quite *probable*.'

'Really,' replied Carmichael, who was now predictably in the lounge of The Railway Tavern, with a half-empty pint of best bitter in front of him. 'Why do you say that?'

'To be honest, I'm kicking myself for not spotting it before,' continued Stock. 'But the marks are heavier on the right-hand side of his right wrist and on the left-hand side of his left wrist. He also has some grazing on the inside of both wrists.'

Carmichael's silence told Stock that he needed more information.

'If his hands had been tied behind his back, the marks would be fairly uniform on both hands but only on the outside of the wrists. The insides would be bound together so would not have made any contact with the rope.'

'So how do you think the marks were made?' enquired Carmichael.

'I can't be one hundred per cent sure,' replied Stock. 'However my best guess is that they were made when the hands were in front of the body. They are consistent with the rope being rubbed vigorously against the wrists in a saw-like motion. As this was done prior to death, I'd say most likely by Ardleigh himself, too.'

'Thanks, Harry,' replied Carmichael, who ended the call as he'd now got the news he had been waiting for. 'You cunning old bugger,' he said out loud, before downing his beer and heading for the exit.

'Only the one today?' remarked Robbie Robertson in amazement.

'Sorry, my friend,' replied Carmichael. 'I've got to see someone.'

Carmichael didn't hang around; he was out of the door within seconds.

'It must be important,' Robertson remarked to the handful of locals stood at the bar. 'He's a creature of habit is our Inspector Carmichael. He normally has at least three pints most Saturday lunchtimes.'

* * * *

After three hours of door knocking in the vicinity of Geraldine Ramsey's house had yielded no more information, Watson decided to end the house-to-house.

'Come on, Rachel,' he said despondently. 'We're wasting our time here; let's get off and talk again with Miranda Coyle. Let's see what sort of alibi she has for the other night.'

Rachel didn't argue; she just nodded and followed Watson to his car.

They had just clambered in when Carmichael phoned.

'Where are you?' he asked.

'We've just finished the house-to-house again,' replied the

dejected Watson. 'We are just about to go and see Miranda Coyle to see if she has an alibi for Thursday evening.'

'You're only a few minutes away from me,' announced Carmichael.

'I'm outside The Railway Tavern. Come and meet me; there's been a breakthrough.'

The line went dead, leaving the two police officers to exchange a glance. 'What do you think that's all about?' enquired Rachel.

'God knows,' replied Watson. 'But whatever it is, it's got the boss excited.'

* * * *

Penny's day, so far, had been somewhat hectic. She and Jemma had booked appointments at the hairdresser's for 2:30, so her morning had been spent desperately trying to get the house tidy, not to mention finishing some washing and making sure that any clothes the family would be wearing that evening were pressed and ready to be worn. Natalie had got herself up and out very early so she could spend the maximum amount of time with her horse. Jemma and Robbie, however, had yet to emerge from their respective rooms even by the time Penny decided to take a short break for some lunch. Under normal circumstances she would not have been happy with Steve being at the pub and her two eldest children languishing in their beds. However, on this particular Saturday she was actually quite pleased to have the house pretty much to herself. At least she could get on with her jobs without being interrupted.

This peaceful state was shattered within two minutes of her sitting down when her dishevelled-looking son materialized in the kitchen, yawning widely and scratching himself vigorously, before rummaging in the fridge for something to eat.

'Afternoon, darling,' remarked Penny in as cheerful a

voice as she could muster given the objectionable vision that stood before her. 'Did you sleep well?'

'Yeah, I think so,' replied Robbie, who plonked himself down next to his mother, placing his mobile and a half-full carton of milk in front of him.

'What are you up to today?' Penny enquired, hoping he would be going out with Brooke rather than bumming around the house under her feet.

Robbie shrugged his shoulders and took a large swig of milk from the carton.

'I really wish you wouldn't do that,' Penny yelled at him. 'It's not only disgusting and unhygienic, but also means that nobody else will want to use that milk.'

'Chill out, Mum,' replied Robbie. 'There's nobody here and I'm going to finish it all anyway.'

'That's not the point,' replied Penny indignantly, 'and anyway *I'm* here.'

Robbie placed the now empty milk carton in the bin, returned to the table and started to read his text messages. Penny didn't have time to get into a long debate with her son about his table manners, so she proceeded to flick through a magazine while she nibbled at her sandwich.

Having read both messages from Brooke, Robbie sighed deeply and switched off the phone. 'Mum, do you like Brooke?' he asked.

'Well yes, I think she's a very nice girl,' replied Penny, carefully choosing her words. 'Why do you ask?'

'Well, I'm not sure I want to carry on going out with her,' said Robbie. 'She's fun to be with and she's really fit, but sometimes I'm not so sure I want to be with her.'

'Why do you say that?' Penny asked.

'Well, she's a bit of a drama queen, isn't she?' he replied. 'She's always making out she's in the thick of things and she knows what's going on, but she doesn't. Take those nasty rumours about you and Mr Robertson; she was sure she knew

242

more than she did. If I'd believed everything she said, I could have quite easily thumped him and made myself look a right idiot.'

'Instead of thumping poor Chris,' said Penny with smile. 'Anyway, what did Brooke tell you about me and Robbie Robertson?'

'Nothing specific,' replied Robbie, not wanting to upset his mother unnecessarily. 'But she was making out that she knew more than she did and that she was not telling me so as to spare my feelings.'

'Well, she's quite young for her age,' Penny said, trying to be as tactful as she could. 'Maybe she's just trying to keep your attention. That's not uncommon in girls. I'm sure she's not a malicious person, just a bit immature for her age.'

Penny put her arm around her son's shoulders in an attempt to reassure him.

'Anyway, what's brought all this on?' she asked.

'She's sent me two texts saying she has to talk to me and that it's urgent,' Robbie said. 'I'm sure it's just her trying to be the centre of attention again, but I guess I should try and get hold of her.'

Penny wasn't sure what to suggest, but felt she needed to impart some sort of wisdom to her son. 'Why don't you just text her back and ask her if it can wait until tonight. You're seeing her at six; I'm sure it can wait until then. If she replies and says it can't wait, then call her and find out what she's so het up about. How does that sound?'

Robbie considered what his mother had said. 'Yep, that works for me,' he replied before walking back to the fridge to find something to eat.

Chapter 41

It took only a few moments for Watson's car to pull up outside The Railway Tavern. Carmichael flung open the back door and quickly clambered inside.

'Get over to Lazarus's, Marc,' he ordered. 'Hugo Lazarus has some explaining to do.'

On the short journey to Fiddlesticks Cottage, Carmichael told Rachel and Watson about Stock's revelations and what he had concluded from them.

'So do you think Lazarus is our murderer?' enquired Watson.

'I'm not sure, Marc,' replied Carmichael, 'but I do know that he has a lot more to tell us and I'm going to insist he stops messing us about and tells it to us today, before anyone else gets killed.'

* * * *

Brooke was in the hairdressers reading a magazine when she received Robbie's text reply:

Can it wait til I c u later? Remember to be at ours for 6.

She desperately wanted to talk with him, but figured that a few more hours would not make any difference; after all, apart from talking it through with her mother, she'd kept silent for nearly two days already:

OK but we do need to talk at the Prom ... B xxx☺

* * * *

'Good afternoon, Mr Lazarus,' announced Carmichael with a broad smile, as soon as the door opened. 'May we come in?'

Lazarus's frustration at seeing three police officers at his door was undisguisable. 'For goodness' sake, Carmichael, haven't I told you enough?' His agitation was palpable in his voice.

The look on Carmichael's face suggested the answer was 'no', so begrudgingly Lazarus beckoned the three officers to come inside.

'I don't have a lot of time,' continued Lazarus. 'I'm on the organising committee for this evening's Prom, so I really will have to insist that you let me get about my duties in the next ten minutes.'

'Well, how long we remain here depends entirely on you, Mr Lazarus,' remarked Carmichael calmly. 'If you cooperate fully with us this time, you may make the Evening Prom, but if what I believe to be the case is true, I think your attendance at the Prom this evening should be the least of your concerns.'

Lazarus pointed at a couple of sofas in the small cosy sitting room of his pretty cottage but was not about to offer his visitors refreshments, not this time. Once his unwelcome house guests had sat down, he tried to make himself as comfortable as he could in his favourite arm chair.

* * * *

'Where on earth is your father?' remarked Penny, her exasperation clear in her voice. 'It's two fifteen – we've got to be at the hairdresser's at two thirty and he's still in the bloody pub.'

'Chill out, Mum,' replied Jemma. 'He'll be along soon. All

245

he needs to do is have a shower and put his suit on. If he gets here at five, he will still make it.'

'But he has to pick the suit up from Tissard's first,' replied Penny. 'He's hiring a dinner jacket and Tissard's close at four.'

'I'll get it,' interjected Robbie. 'Just leave me the money.'

'Thanks, dear,' replied Penny with relief. 'Here's fifty pounds. That should be enough.'

On that note she handed her son the money, planted a big sloppy kiss on his forehead and marched out of the house with Jemma trying to keep up behind her.

Once he had the house to himself, Robbie sauntered into the kitchen. He opened up the fridge, removed another milk carton, took a deep swig, belched loudly, wiped his mouth with his shirt sleeve and returned the carton to the safety of the fridge.

*   *   *   *

Carmichael stared intently at Lazarus who, by now was visibly nervous.

'There are a few things that keep puzzling me about this case, given your relationship with Ardleigh,' he announced confidently.

'Really?' replied Lazarus in a faltering voice

'First of all,' continued Carmichael, 'I have always found it hard to understand how someone as close to Ardleigh as you could not have known about the letters. For me that is inconceivable. And, if he was planning to commit suicide, as now looks likely to have been the case, I can't understand why Ardleigh would have invited you to the pub on that evening, knowing full well, as he must have done, that he would not be turning up.'

Lazarus gave a faint shrug of his shoulders but elected not to answer.

246

Carmichael could see that he had his quarry worried and kept his piercing stare fixed on Lazarus's eyes. 'I don't think you've been telling us the whole truth,' he said gently. 'Don't you think it's about time you got everything off your chest?'

Lazarus mopped away a small bead of sweat from his hairline. 'It's true I may have been a little economical with the truth up to now,' he said, his voice stumbling as he spoke. 'But I want to be clear on a few things, Inspector Carmichael. I knew nothing of the letters that Marcus sent out and I have no idea whether he died by his own hand or not. Also I swear to you that I've never killed anyone, not all those years ago in Oxford and not now either.'

*   *   *   *

By the time Lazarus had finished unburdening his conscience to the three police officers it was almost 4 p.m., which gave Carmichael two hours to collect his suit and get ready for the Evening Prom. He instructed Rachel and Watson to take Lazarus back to Kirkwood Police Station and charge him with perverting the course of justice, and to get him to make a full and detailed statement.

Chapter 42

The annual Prom Evening at Rivingham Hall was one of the major events of the year in that part of Lancashire. Its origins could be traced back to the nineteenth century when it was a showcase for the local army regiment to dazzle the local people with their smart uniforms and horsemanship. However, over the years this military spectacle had developed into a much grander affair. This year it boasted a full orchestra, a fly-past by some surviving planes from the Battle of Britain and countless sponsored marquees full of the well-to-do sipping Pimm's, fine wine and Champagne, and eating all manner of delights from the humble hot dog (though at this event, of course, they were made from locally reared free-range pigs) to smoked salmon and delicate exotically flavoured canapés.

The military theme was not totally lost, with the inclusion of some thirty or forty men on horseback dressed as hussars from the Napoleonic Wars, who at various times during the evening were required to re-enact famous battles from the period.

* * * *

'I feel a right prat in this,' muttered Carmichael as he sauntered across the field in his black tie.

'By the way, have you thanked Robbie for kindly collecting it for you? enquired Penny, who was clinging on to her husband's arm to avoid falling over in her high heels. 'If it wasn't for him, you'd have had to wear one of your awful work suits. Anyway, I think you look so smart, dear, and I think it's nice to get dressed up for once.'

Carmichael didn't reply. This was not his sort of thing, but he knew Penny really loved it and as such was trying as best he could to keep his misery in check.

Behind Penny and Steve marched Jemma and Spot On, both of whom had also made a big effort to look smart. Jemma was wearing her new summer dress, an expensive purchase she had made the week before and which made her feel very glamorous. And, although Spot On had elected to wear a smart grey suit, black shirt and a normal black tie rather than a dinner jacket, he too looked quite the gentleman.

At the back of the group came Robbie and Brooke. Like Jemma, Brooke wore a pretty summer dress and, with her delicate, shapely figure and her blonde hair blowing in the wind, she was certainly getting noticed, particularly by the younger males – much to her delight and Robbie's displeasure.

Robbie hated dressing up even more than his father and, to emphasise his refusal to conform, he had decided not to wear a tie. Although he was wearing his smartest trousers and shoes, he had chosen not to don a jacket at all, despite the protestations of his mother that he would be cold later in the evening.

'Well,' said Brooke as she tottered gingerly over the uneven field in her high heels. 'Do you think I should tell your dad what I saw?'

'I don't know,' snapped Robbie, who was more concerned about who might see him than what Brooke thought she had seen the night Geraldine Ramsey was murdered.

'That's not very helpful,' replied Brooke. 'I thought you'd at least be able to say yes or no.'

'In that case I suppose you should,' replied Robbie and to

try and get some closure, shouted over to his father. 'Dad can Brooke have a quick word with you?'

His father, however, did not hear Robbie as he had been distracted by a group of people whom Robbie did not recognise and had started up a conversation.

'Are they friends of your dad's?' Brooke enquired.

'I've no idea,' replied Robbie. 'I've never seen them before in my life.'

'Please allow me to introduce you to my wife, Inspector,' said Ernest Walker. 'This is Harriet.'

'Pleased to meet you, Harriet,' replied Carmichael, shaking Mrs Walker's hand. 'Let me introduce you to my wife, Penny,' he said as soon as he had released his hand from Dr Walker's wife's quite firm grip.

Dr Walker then introduced the Carmichaels to the other people in his group, whose names were instantly forgotten by Carmichael, since his interest lay only with the Walkers.

'And these are two of our children and their partners,' added Penny, when she realised her husband was not about to do the necessary introductions. 'This is Jemma and her friend Sp … Chris,' she spluttered. 'And this is Robbie, our son, and his girlfriend Brooke.'

The four youngsters smiled but didn't attempt to shake anybody by the hand or start a conversation.

At that moment a few small droplets of warm summer rain started to fall.

'Oh I do hope the weather holds up,' remarked Harriett Walker. 'It would be such a shame if it rained.'

As she spoke, the rain started to fall a little heavier, prompting her husband to signal to a largish tent some ten yards away. 'We've hired that one for our party tonight – why don't you join us, Inspector? We've plenty of space.'

'Oh yes, please join us,' added Harriet. 'We've got plenty of everything to go around – meats, sandwiches and drink. There's more than enough for six more.'

'You've forgotten my trio of desserts, dear,' added Dr Walker proudly.

Harriett shook her head gently. 'He bought them from Marks and Spencer's this morning. They do look very nice, but to hear him you'd have thought he'd prepared them himself.'

Seeing that the skies were becoming ever darker, and without much else around to give cover, Carmichael decided to accept the Walkers' kind offer. 'That would be very much appreciated,' he said, looking up to the heavens. 'It doesn't look that promising, I must say.'

As if to authenticate his remark, the rain now started to fall quite heavily.

'I'm sure it's just a shower,' remarked Penny. 'However, I think it would be wise if we got under cover.'

The group scurried across the now-wet grass and beneath the cover of the marquee.

'That's who I saw,' Brooke whispered to Robbie, 'coming out of Geraldine Ramsey's house. It was Dr Walker.'

'Are you sure?' enquired Robbie, who recalled Brooke's last apparent 'certainty', namely that his mum and Robbie Robertson were having an affair.

'A hundred per cent positive,' she replied.

'Then we need to tell dad, and pretty quickly, too,' said Robbie. 'If he has too many glasses of Pimm's, he'll be in no fit state to arrest anyone.'

'I just need to go to the ladies,' said Brooke, who was clearly looking anxious.

'You are joking!' exclaimed Robbie. 'It's pouring down out there. Can't it wait a few moments?'

Brooke shook her head. 'I'll be five minutes.'

Bemused and bewildered, Robbie stood mouth gaping open as his girlfriend rushed out of the tent.

Having overheard some of Brooke and Robbie's conversation and seeing that the young girl was going to get soaked, Harriett Walker shouted after her, 'Wait! Take this umbrella.' With that she produced a sturdy green golfing umbrella, with a thick wooden handle, and dashed across to where Brooke was now waiting for her.

'Actually,' she added. 'I'll come with you. There's plenty of room under here for both of us.'

By the look on Brooke's face it was clear she was not comfortable with the arrangement, but Harriett was so quickly by her side that she had no time to object.

Holding the umbrella firmly in her left hand, Harriett clamped her free arm around Brooke and within a flash both women disappeared into the increasingly wet and gloomy evening.

Once they were out of sight, Robbie got himself a glass of beer from the ample stocks that had been loaded onto one of the two large tables. He then stared at Dr Walker as he chatted calmly and in a friendly manner to the rest of the group. He found it hard to believe that this man could be a killer, although he wasn't too sure what a typical killer actually looked like.

As he studied Dr Walker, he noticed out of the corner of his eye, Spot On filling his paper plate with sandwiches, tiny pork pies and a whole range of nice-looking food.

'Get stuck in,' instructed Spot On. 'It's free scoff, man.'

Robbie was hungry so he did as Spot On had suggested, but with a little less enthusiasm.

For the next ten minutes Robbie munched slowly, keeping his eyes firmly on Dr Walker, only occasionally breaking off to either look at his watch or to give a monosyllabic response to a question that either Jemma or Spot On had asked him.

'She's taking ages,' he said when his girlfriend had not returned after fifteen minutes.

'Maybe there's a big queue,' remarked Jemma. 'There always is for us ladies.'

Jemma's response placated Robbie for a further two minutes, after which time he started to get very worried.

'Bugger this!' he said out loud. 'We can't hang around anymore; *I'll* tell Dad.'

'Tell Dad what?' enquired Jemma.

'That Brooke thinks Dr Walker over there is the killer,' replied Robbie in a hushed voice. 'And his wife's now taken Brooke off to God knows where.'

Robbie rushed over to his father and grabbed him by the arm. 'Dad,' he whispered in his ear. 'I need to talk to you urgently.'

Carmichael could see his son was serious, so broke off his conversation with Dr Walker and a couple of men and wandered over to the side of the tent.

'What's so urgent?' he asked with an alcohol-induced smile.

'Brooke has just told me that she saw Dr Walker coming out of Geraldine Ramsey's house on the evening she was murdered,' said Robbie, in a voice that was a little less muted than he had desired.

'What!' exclaimed Carmichael 'Is she sure?'

'Yes,' replied Robbie, who could see that at least three or four people were now eavesdropping on their conversation. 'She's adamant that she saw him.'

Carmichael could not believe what he was hearing. 'So where is Brooke?' he demanded.

'Oh she's not yet come back from the toilet,' said Robbie meekly.

'Well, bloody well go and find her and bring her back here at once,' Carmichael ordered. 'Why the hell didn't she mention this to me before. I need to talk to her.'

As he was speaking, the skies erupted with the sound of a loud clap of thunder. And with the thunder came an even heavier downpour of rain, which within seconds turned into a deluge.

'Put my jacket over your head,' said Carmichael as he quickly disrobed and flung his smart dinner jacket in his son's direction.

Robbie held the jacket above his head and, with his friend Spot On by his side, disappeared out into the dark evening and the drenching summer downpour.

As soon as his son had gone, Carmichael looked back to try and locate Dr Walker. He spied him at the other side of the tent, smiling, laughing and very much the amiable host, surrounded by a posse of devotees who appeared to be hanging on his every word.

Carmichael took his mobile out of his trouser pocket and dialled the station, and as he dialled he kept one eye firmly fixed on Dr Ernest Walker. There was no way he was going to let Walker out of his sight.

Chapter 43

The torrential rain had completely cleared the throng of well-heeled ladies and gentlemen who, just an hour earlier, had covered practically every inch of the grounds of Rivingham Hall.

A large number of the crowd had decamped to one of a number of large tents that had been erected around the main viewing area, but even more had decided to call it a day and were now scurrying off in the direction of the car park, soaked to the skin and with shoes and legs caked in mud.

In that watery chaos Robbie and Spot On attempted to find Brooke.

'I think the toilets are over there,' shouted Spot On, pointing over to the left of the field. 'Come on, follow me.'

He didn't wait for Robbie to reply and marched purposefully in the direction where he had just pointed.

Robbie, who had already abandoned using his father's saturated jacket as a makeshift umbrella, followed close behind.

* * * *

'Get a police car down to Rivingham Hall right away,' ordered Carmichael, trying hard to conceal the fact he was making a call. 'I think we have our murderer here.'

The duty sergeant at Kirkwood Police Station didn't ask any questions. 'Right away, sir,' he replied.

'And get hold of Cooper, Watson and Dalton and tell them to get themselves down here, too!' added Carmichael.

* * * *

'Brooke,' Robbie shouted loudly, as the two sodden figures finally arrived at the ladies' Portaloos.

With the rain falling so heavily, it was no surprise that the toilets looked deserted. The two young men looked at each other.

'Come on, Robbie, let's go inside and see if she's there,' shouted Spot On. 'Now's not the time to be bashful.'

Spot On clambered up the three steep steps that led to the ladies' toilets and once inside yelled out Brooke's name.

Within seconds Robbie was by his side.

'She's not here,' announced Spot On. 'Actually there's nobody here.'

'Brooke,' yelled Robbie, just to make doubly sure.

'Come on,' said Spot On. 'Let's see if there's another toilet block somewhere.'

As they turned away Robbie heard a faint groan coming from one of the cubicles. 'What was that?' he said.

'What?' replied Spot On, who had heard nothing.

'It's coming from over there,' replied Robbie, pointing towards the end cubicle.

Robbie ran over and, seeing the door was slightly ajar, gently pushed it open.

* * * *

'What on earth is happening?' enquired Penny, who had only caught some of what her husband had been saying on the phone.

'Shh,' said Carmichael, 'I'm trying to hear what they are saying.'

'Who?' enquired Jemma, joining them with a glass of white wine in one hand and a plateful of sandwiches in the other.

'It's tremendous to see dear "H" back on her feet again,' said one of the sycophants in Walker's set.

'Yes, she's well on the mend now,' replied Walker. 'She came off the crutches this week. It was a nasty break, but apart from a slight limp, you wouldn't know she was laid up for nearly six months.'

'Mind you, being a doctor, I suppose she got priority treatment at the hospital,' remarked another of the group, who then let out a pompous forced laugh.

'Doctor!' repeated Carmichael on overhearing this bombshell. 'Walker's wife's a bloody doctor, too!'

Not getting the relevance of what her husband was saying, Penny shrugged her shoulders.

'Keep your eyes on him,' Carmichael ordered. 'Don't let him out of your sight while I make this call.'

Carmichael turned away from Walker's group and started to dial.

'You don't intend to eat all those sandwiches, do you?' Penny asked, before stealing a couple from her daughter's plate.

*   *   *   *

'Is she alive?' asked Spot On, as he peered down at Brooke's seemingly lifeless body.

'I'm not sure,' replied Robbie, who had put his ear to Brooke's chest trying to locate a heartbeat. 'Get help, Chris, quickly!'

Spot On did not need to be asked twice. He rushed out of the Portaloo and sprinted at full pelt back towards Dr Walker's tent. En route he had the foresight to stop and dial 999 to ensure that medical help was despatched.

'Brooke's been hurt!' gasped Spot On as he entered the

tent. 'Robbie's with her ... She's lying in the ladies' toilets ... It looks really bad.'

'What?' replied Penny anxiously. 'Have you called for an ambulance?'

Spot On nodded and then led Penny and Jemma back through the evening rain in the direction from where he had come.

'What about Harriett?' enquired Dr Walker, the concern palpable in his voice. 'Is Harriett OK?'

'It will have been Harriett that did this,' snapped Carmichael. 'And until I am satisfied that you're not implicated, too, I am placing you under arrest.' Carmichael grabbed the stunned doctor and pushed him out into the rain. 'Follow them down to the toilet block,' he ordered. 'And don't even think of making a run for it.'

* * * *

Harriett Walker's car screeched to a halt on the gravel drive, sending fragments of sharp stones high into the air. Soaked to the skin with her feet caked in mud, she threw open her car door and ran towards the house. Harriett's hands were shaking so much that at first she struggled to successfully insert the key into the lock, but once she had managed to open the door she rushed inside, slamming it shut behind her.

Harriett headed upstairs, discarding first her shoes and then the saturated dirty rag that hours earlier had been a pretty summer dress. She knew she had only a small amount of time to get changed, pack a bag and be away, before the police would be at her door. She had no time to shower.

By the time she had reached the bathroom she was naked. She grabbed a large bath towel and quickly rubbed herself down before heading into the bedroom.

* * * *

Upon her arrival at the toilet block, Penny assumed control.

'She's still alive!' Penny exclaimed after checking Brooke's pulse. 'She's really cold, though. Has anyone got anything that's not soaking wet that we can wrap around her while we wait for the ambulance?'

For a few seconds the group of five who now stood behind her just looked at each other. No one had a coat on, so all were drenched.

'I'll sort it,' shouted Spot On, whose resourcefulness in the last thirty minutes was proving to be invaluable. He rushed out of the toilet block, returning moments later with two large table cloths, which he had liberated from the nearest tent, much to the annoyance of the ladies of the Women's Institute.

'Will these do?' he asked upon making his triumphant return.

'Perfect,' replied Penny, who then started to gently cover poor Brooke.

Ernest Walker had not said a word since being bundled out of the tent and frogmarched across the sodden grass. 'Where's Harriett?' he asked with genuine concern. 'I don't understand.'

Carmichael ignored Walker's question and dialled Watson's number.

'Where are you, Marc?' he enquired as soon as the call connected.

'Rachel and I are in Cooper's car,' replied Watson. 'We should be at the hall in about fifteen minutes. What's happening?'

'You need to find Harriett Walker,' Carmichael shouted. 'She's a doctor, too. If I'm right, it was her that received Ardleigh's letter; it was her that killed Kenyon and Geraldine Ramsey, and if the bloody ambulance doesn't get here soon, I'm afraid that she may be responsible for another murder.'

'Where is she now?' asked Watson.

'I don't know, but my guess is that she will have already made a run for it,' replied Carmichael. 'Try their house. She'll be soaking wet, so my guess is that she'll have gone there first.'

'Will do, sir,' replied Watson, who ended the call and ordered Cooper to change direction and head over to the Walkers' house.

* * * *

Harriett Walker was only inside the house for fifteen minutes, during which time she had changed her clothes and stuffed her passport and as many garments as she could into a large holdall. She slammed shut the door of her now-filthy red Mercedes sports car, manoeuvred it around so it was facing the road, and sped out of the drive.

Harriett was doing almost forty miles an hour down the narrow country lane when she saw Cooper's battered Volvo come around the corner.

Eyes bulging and heart pumping, Cooper managed to slam on his brakes and bring his car to a halt. Harriett was less fortunate. She thumped her right foot hard on the brakes, but her sudden reaction, coupled with the car's momentum, served only to put her into a long screeching skid, which led first to her hitting the high grassy bank and then veering across the road, inches away from Cooper's stationary car, and through a dry-stone wall.

* * * *

The Carmichael family eventually left Kirkwood General Hospital at 2:30 in the morning. Cheerless and exhausted, they clambered into the people carrier and remained silent for the forty-minute taxi drive back to Moulton Bank.

On its arrival in the village the taxi stopped at Spot On's house.

'You played a blinder this evening, Chris,' Carmichael said as the young man got out of the car. 'If she does recover, Brooke has to thank you and Robbie for finding her and being so swift in getting assistance.'

'I hope she pulls through,' replied Spot On before disappearing into the night.

'Do you think she's going to die?' Robbie asked as the taxi set off again.

'She's in the best place and will certainly get the care she needs,' replied Penny as tactfully as she could. 'I'm sure she will be fine.'

When the taxi finally arrived at their house, Carmichael paid the driver before wearily following the rest of the family into the hallway. Tired and forlorn, Jemma and Robbie went straight to their rooms, leaving Carmichael and Penny alone.

Penny gently embraced her husband as they stood silently in the hallway. 'Are you OK?' she asked, although she knew the answer was no.

'I'm fine,' replied Carmichael. 'I'm just so annoyed with myself for not considering that Dr Walker was *Mrs* Walker. It seems so obvious now.'

'Don't beat yourself up,' replied Penny. 'You weren't to know. Anyway I'm off to my bed, I'm so worn out. Are you coming?'

Carmichael shook his head. 'You go – I'll be along shortly; I need a large scotch first.'

Penny kissed him gently on the lips and slowly clambered up the stairs.

Chapter 44

Sunday 22nd August

Carmichael was woken by the wonderful sight of a steaming hot-mug of coffee being placed on his bedside cabinet. He glanced at the clock – it read 9:25 a.m.

'Good heavens,' he said as he awkwardly lifted his still-tired torso into a sitting position. 'I'll need to collect the car from Rivingham Hall; hopefully the tyres won't be too stuck.'

Penny smiled sweetly back at him, opened the bedroom curtains a few inches and peeked out. 'Well, the rain has stopped and the sun's out, so you may be lucky. Do you want me to run you there?'

'Thanks,' replied Carmichael, as he raised the coffee mug to his lips. 'That would be great.'

Penny sat down beside him. 'With all that went on yesterday I'm a bit confused,' she confessed. 'Is Harriett Walker responsible for all these deaths?'

Carmichael thought long and hard before he answered. 'Actually, in a way she's not,' he replied. 'She killed Ruben Kenyon and Geraldine Ramsey; she certainly tried to kill poor Brooke last night too, but the person who's really responsible is Marcus Ardleigh. His sick, controlling mind is behind all this.'

Penny's perplexed expression signified the need for more information.

'I don't have all the facts yet,' he continued. 'But Dr

Harriett Walker should provide me with those as soon as I am able to talk to her.'

'That might be a while given the state she was in last night when they admitted her to the hospital,' Penny remarked.

'That's nothing compared to the state she will be in when I've finished with her,' replied Carmichael, who took a large mouthful of coffee before launching himself out of bed.

*　　*　　*　　*

Carmichael's black BMW was one of dozens of cars that had been abandoned in the car park at Rivingham Hall the evening before.

As luck would have it, he found his car neither blocked in by other vehicles nor stuck in mud. With a small amount of careful manoeuvring he was able to head through the imposing entrance gateway and off in the direction of Kirkwood, some thirty miles away.

*　　*　　*　　*

As instructed, Paul Cooper was waiting for Carmichael at the hospital entrance.

'Morning, Paul,' said Carmichael. 'What's the latest update?'

Cooper had been at the hospital for two hours already. 'Brooke is stable but still unconscious,' he replied. 'They've done a brain scan which has revealed that, although her skull is cracked, there are no signs of any bleeding. However, the doctors all seem to be very concerned about her.'

'At least there appears to be some hope then,' replied Carmichael. 'Is her mother with her?'

'Yes,' replied Cooper. 'She's been here all night. I spoke with her briefly this morning and she's told me Brooke had told her about seeing Harriett Walker coming out of

Geraldine Ramsey's house the other evening, but she had advised her daughter not to tell the police.'

'Why?' exclaimed Carmichael. 'That is such a dim-witted piece of advice. And in hindsight it may well prove to be fatal for poor Brooke.'

Cooper nodded. 'Believe me, sir, her mother is painfully aware of the terrible cost of her misguided counsel.'

'What about the other patient?' enquired Carmichael.

'She's conscious but in a pretty bad way,' replied Cooper. 'The doctors say we can talk to her but will only allow us in there for fifteen minutes.'

'That's all I'll need,' Carmichael responded. 'Lead on, Cooper; let's see what Dr Walker has to say for herself.'

* * * *

Carmichael and Cooper entered the small private room where Harriett Walker had been admitted after her accident.

At her bedside sat Ernest, who had tenderly held his wife's hand all night, and one of the specialists attending to Harriett. Also present was a WPC who, on Carmichael's instructions, had remained in the room throughout the night, while outside the door was a PC whose job it was to prevent anyone other than the clinical staff from entering the room and to ensure that Ernest Walker did not make a dash for it.

'Good morning,' Carmichael said. 'I need to ask you some questions, Mrs Walker. Are you up to talking?'

Ernest Walker looked up from where he was sitting, his face tired and drawn. 'Can't this wait until my wife is feeling a bit better?' he snapped. 'Can't you see she's in a lot of discomfort?'

'It's all right, Ernest,' Harriett said. 'I'm ready to tell the inspector everything. The sooner I do so the better.' She smiled gently as if the confession she was about to make would actually be a relief to her.

264

'How is the girl?' she asked. 'Will she be OK?'

'We don't know,' replied Cooper. 'She's stable but she's still in a critical condition.'

Harriett closed her eyes for a second, as if she were thinking. Then she opened them widely and stared at Carmichael. 'I suppose you've been told,' she said with seeming indifference, 'I'm now totally paralysed, from the neck down – no feeling at all.'

Despite her horrendous crimes, Carmichael could not help feeling some pity for her. 'I was told,' he replied.

'Where do I start?' said Harriett impassively.

'Why don't you start by telling us how and when you first met Marcus Ardleigh?' suggested Carmichael.

'We've known him for a couple of years,' replied Ernest. 'He was introduced to me at a party and he seemed interested in my art collection so I invited him home.'

'Which is when I first met him,' added Harriett. 'Then, about eighteen months ago, when one of the consultants retired from the practice, I inherited Marcus as a patient, not that he ever needed me until about eight months ago.'

'And what happened then?' enquired Carmichael.

Harriett cleared her throat before answering. 'He came to see me about some abdominal problems he was having. I did a few basic tests and when they were not as good as I had hoped, I referred him to the hospital for a full body scan.'

'And what did that reveal?' enquired Carmichael.

'That he had cancer,' replied Harriett.

'And how did he take the news?' asked Carmichael.

Harriett's eyes moved sideways to catch her husband's attention. 'That's where things started to go wrong,' she said quietly with a hint of foreboding in her voice.

'How do you mean?' enquired Carmichael.

'Well, as fate would have it, I had another patient, an American businessman called Chuck Armstrong, who was of a similar age to Marcus and had a similar set of symptoms,' continued Harriett, her voice now trembling. 'Their results both arrived on the same day, which was the day my new car was due to be collected. Foolishly, rather than call Marcus, which is what I'd normally do in these circumstances, I instructed one of the nurses to make sure letters were sent to the two men. Armstrong's was to say that he was completely clear, while Marcus Ardleigh's was to ask him to contact the practice for a consultation.'

Carmichael sensed what was coming next but chose to wait to see how Harriett was going to explain the obvious mix-up.

'In short, the nurse messed up,' continued Harriett. 'She got the letters the wrong way around.'

'But surely you picked that up almost immediately?' enquired Cooper with a puzzled expression on his face.

Harriett closed her eyes for a few seconds before she replied. 'That's the infuriating irony in all this. In normal circumstances we'd have picked that up very quickly. You'd probably be shocked and surprised how often these sorts of mix-ups occur. But on this occasion, two unforeseen factors meant it wasn't spotted.'

'And what were those two factors?' enquired Carmichael.

Harriett Walker took a deep breath. 'Firstly, my wonderful husband decides to take me for a marvellous surprise holiday, skiing in France. Unbeknownst to me, he had organised the time off for me with my colleagues at the practice, so on the evening I came home with the new car he whisked me off to Chamonix, leaving one of my partners at the practice to pick up my cases. He didn't know either of the men and he just assumed that the letters they'd received were the correct ones.'

'But surely the fact that this Chuck Armstrong was clear would have been easily detected once he'd been to get treatment?' remarked Cooper.

'Yes and, although you had a surprise holiday, surely you

266

were away for just a few weeks at the most?' added Carmichael.

Harriett smiled ruefully. 'Under normal circumstances yes, but on this occasion it was different. On receiving his letter, Armstrong decided that he'd return immediately to the US to get treatment. Some very expensive private clinic in Reno, paid for by his company. And as for my wonderful holiday, it lasted just two days before I had a very bad fall and broke my fibula and femur. I was laid up in a French hospital for three months before I could even travel home. I've only been back at work for the last two months.'

'I see,' said Carmichael, trying to soak up what he was hearing.

'So the first I knew of the mix-up was when I received a letter from Chuck Armstrong, when I returned to work, threatening legal action against the practice and me in particular, for the worry and stress that the catastrophic muddle had caused him,' continued Harriett. 'When I read that letter I felt sick to my stomach. I knew immediately what had happened.'

'When was this?' Carmichael enquired.

'About six weeks ago,' replied Harriett.

'Why didn't you tell me about this?' Ernest asked, the shock and disappointment clear in his trembling voice. 'That must have been such a dreadful burden for you to shoulder.'

Harriett smiled. 'I didn't want to worry you my dear,' she replied. 'And initially I thought I could still sort the mess out myself.'

'So what did you do?' Cooper asked.

Harriett took another deep breath. 'I contacted Armstrong and after a couple of conversations, he finally agreed not to follow through his threat of litigation; and I dismissed Anna Porter, the nurse who had fouled up.'

'But I suspect Marcus Ardleigh was more difficult to placate,' suggested Carmichael. 'After all, it was he who had been left without treatment for six months because of the error.'

'Twenty weeks to be precise,' replied Harriett sadly. 'And yes, he was, I suppose quite rightly, angry. Actually, he was furious. The truth is his cancer was so advanced that, even if he had been properly diagnosed, it's highly unlikely he could have been successfully treated. But that is of course, as his solicitor put it, pure conjecture.'

'So Ruben Kenyon was aware of the mix-up?' remarked Carmichael.

'Oh yes,' replied Harriett despondently. 'After my initial visit to Ardleigh's house all contact went through that unpleasant man.'

'My poor dear,' Ernest lamented. 'You should have told me!'

Harriett ignored her husband. 'After a lot of discussion Kenyon finally made what seemed to me to be a very bizarre proposal.'

'Which was?' probed Carmichael.

'Kenyon said that Marcus would drop any action against me and would agree to remain silent about the error if I gave Geraldine Ramsey one of Ernest's paintings.'

'Which one?' enquired Ernest, who was clearly amazed by his wife's revelations.

'The Hoffmann,' Harriett replied. 'The Hoffman in the hallway that Marcus always commented upon when he visited.'

'Which is why it wasn't there when I visited with Sergeant Watson that first time,' added Cooper.

'Yes,' replied Harriett. 'I told Ernest I had knocked it off the wall and the frame was being repaired, but in fact I had given it to Kenyon to stop Ardleigh from going public.'

'I see,' replied Carmichael. 'But how were you going to cover that up from Ernest. Sooner or later he would have expected the painting back. How were you going to resolve that conundrum?'

'My plan was to borrow the painting from Geraldine and try and get it copied,' replied Harriett. 'I hadn't totally figured out how I'd do that; after all, I only handed it over to Kenyon a couple of weeks ago. Restoring does take time, so I figured I would have a few weeks to find someone to do a good copy.'

Carmichael, Cooper and Ernest Walker were all stunned by the story they were hearing and it took a few moments before any of them spoke.

'So how did you feel when you received the letter from Marcus?' enquired Carmichael. 'I take it that the Dr Walker Marcus wrote to was you and not your husband?'

'I was livid,' replied Harriett. 'I couldn't believe he could be so deceitful. I'd carried out my side of the bargain, but he was still determined to go public.'

'I suspect you felt like killing him,' remarked Carmichael mischievously.

Harriett sighed. 'If he had been with me in the room, I would have killed him; make no mistake about that,' she replied fervently. 'But he wasn't and within hours I heard on the local news that he was dead.'

'You must have been relieved to learn of Ardleigh's death,' suggested Cooper.

'I was,' replied Harriett. 'However, I did not trust that snake Kenyon, so I went to see him after work on the Monday evening to find out what he planned to do, now Marcus was dead.'

'You went to his office?' enquired Carmichael.

'Yes,' replied Harriett. 'But when I got there he was just driving away. You couldn't miss that pretentious Bentley he drove. I didn't want to risk leaving it to the next day, so I followed him.'

'And where did he go?' Carmichael asked.

'He drove to the church car park on Ambient Hill,' replied Harriett. 'He waited there for twenty or thirty minutes. Then he was joined by a stylishly dressed woman in her early fifties. She was driving a tangerine Lotus. She got into his car, but after no more than five minutes she got out and rather angrily stomped back to her car and quickly drove away.'

Carmichael smiled. 'We know who that was,' he replied in a way that signified he wished Harriett to continue with her story.

'By the manner in which she departed,' continued Harriett, 'I guessed she was one of the three people mentioned in Marcus's letter.'

'So what did you do then?' Carmichael asked, deliberately avoiding any further dialogue about the driver of the Lotus.

'I followed him,' replied Harriett. 'And he drove back to his office.'

'I take it that you finally got to speak with him in the car park of the practice,' said Carmichael.

Harriett paused for a few seconds to collect her thoughts and consider what the implications would be of continuing her story. 'Yes,' she replied forcefully, her eyes now fixed at a point way beyond the police officers. 'He saw me follow him into the car park but remained in his car. I parked next to him and walked around to his car. The arrogant sod didn't even get out. He merely wound down the passenger window for me to talk to him.'

'And how did the conversation go?' Cooper asked.

'It was short,' replied Harriett. 'I asked him what the hell he and Ardleigh were playing at, sending me the letter when we had an agreement. He just sniggered. I then enquired what he was planning to do, now that Marcus was dead.'

'And what was his reply?' Carmichael asked.

'He said that the meeting the next evening would go on as planned, that he would host it and unless I gave him another of Ernest's paintings, he would reveal everything about the mix-up over Marcus's diagnosis. He also showed me a letter that Marcus had written to him outlining the details of the three so-called secrets.'

'You read this letter?' asked Carmichael, who was eager to find out more about the note.

'Not then,' replied Harriett. 'I did later.'

'After you had killed Kenyon,' Carmichael stated.

'Yes,' confessed Harriett. 'After I'd silenced that weasel, I took all his papers. His car was full of them.'

'What papers were these?' Carmichael enquired.

'Various things,' continued Harriett. 'The letter he had received from Marcus, which outlined the secrets of the three of us – Miranda Coyle, who I guess was the person he had met earlier that evening, a man called Gordon Napier and me. Then there was a copy of his will and also some files on his marriage to Miranda, a file relating to the car crash when he and Napier were at Oxford, and one on me with his all-clear letter and notes he made after I had visited him.'

'Do you still have these documents?' Carmichael enquired eagerly.

'Sorry, I don't,' replied Harriett. 'I decided to have a bonfire at home that evening and they all went on it.'

Carmichael was clearly disappointed by this latest revelation, but wanted to get Harriett's full confession while she was in the mood to talk. 'So how did you kill Kenyon?' he asked.

Harriett laughed. 'I still had my crutches in the car. I opened up the back door and took one out. I removed the rubber stopper from the end and, as the window of his car was still open, jabbed it through with all my might.'

Harriett paused briefly at that point as if she was reliving the experience with some pleasure. 'I caught him on his left temple, just above his left eye. He must have been totally unaware of what was coming. I suspect the first blow killed him, but I hit him several times to make sure he was dead.'

The lack of either compassion or remorse expressed by Harriett left Carmichael and Cooper amazed, but it was also undoubtedly a bolt from the blue for Ernest, who immediately released his wife's hand – an involuntary action that did not go unnoticed by Carmichael.

'So having killed Kenyon, and removed and destroyed his papers, what did you do next?' enquired Carmichael.

'I knew the existence of the letters was likely to come out,' continued Harriett. 'So I decided to try and make out that mine was actually for Ernest. The letter itself made no mention of my full name, did not indicate that I was a female and, with Ernest being away on Monday evening, I thought he would have a cast-iron alibi. The only reference to me was on the envelope, which was addressed to Dr Harriett Walker. I had to destroy that.'

'So let me get this straight,' interjected Carmichael, 'are you telling us that when Ernest got home you just told him he had a letter? You didn't mention to him anything about the mix-up, nothing about the painting you had given to Kenyon, or about your fateful meeting with Kenyon on Monday evening?'

'That's correct,' replied Harriett. 'There was no need for him to know. In fact, my judgement was that by his *not* knowing, you would be less likely to see him as a serious suspect.'

By this time the colour from Ernest Walker's face had disappeared completely and he had been struck speechless.

'So why did you kill Geraldine Ramsey?' enquired Carmichael.

Harriett stared back at Carmichael with incredulity in her eyes, then without emotion she replied. 'She had Ernest's painting. I had to get that back. On Thursday our housemaid Tatiana had heard one of your officers on the phone saying that Geraldine was returning home from her holiday that afternoon. When Tatiana told me this I went round to talk

272

with Geraldine. My plan was to buy it back, but when I arrived she refused to let me have it. She also said that she had posted the letter and had seen my name on the envelope, and was going to tell the police the next day. I swear I had no idea she knew about the letter being addressed to me before I went round. But once she told me that, what else could I do?'

A chill spread throughout the room where Harriett Walker lay. Ernest Walker could now not bear to look at his wife, his amazement at her behaviour and the seemingly relaxed and callous way she was now recounting her exploits left him feeling rigid and cold towards her; a feeling that he could never had dreamed possible a mere ten minutes earlier.

'That leads us to the events of last night,' continued Carmichael, eager to ensure that Harriett made a clean breast of all her crimes. 'Tell me what happened with Brooke at the Prom last night?'

For the first time, Harriett showed some compassion. 'I regret what happened with her,' she insisted. 'I just panicked. I sincerely hope she pulls through.'

'When did you realise you'd been spotted coming out of Geraldine Ramsey's house?' asked Carmichael, keen to get Harriett back on track.

'I had no idea until last night,' she replied sadly. 'I overheard her talking to your son. Then when she needed to go to the ladies I went with her to find out exactly what she'd seen.'

'And did she tell you?' enquired Carmichael.

Harriett hesitated. 'She refused to say anything at all, and although I couldn't quite place her surname, I did recognise her as being a patient of ours at the practice. I'd treated her a few times for minor ailments. I hadn't heard everything she'd said to your son earlier, but I'd heard enough to realise that she'd seen me that night at Geraldine Ramsey's. And I was frightened about what she would tell you.'

Harriett's eyes moistened as she recalled the evening before. 'Oh my God, what has that evil man done to me?' As she spoke, her voice hardened and her bitterness broke through. 'Six months ago I was a successful well-respected doctor, enjoying my job and proud of being able to make the lives of others more bearable. Now look at me – I'm nothing but a murderer, someone who thinks nothing of trying to bludgeon a poor young girl to death with an umbrella handle, and what's more a paraplegic, too.'

Despite her hideous crimes, Carmichael nevertheless felt sorry for Harriett. He was in no doubt that her previous character would prove to be impeccable and that her actions in the last week had been the result of the malevolent machinations of first Ardleigh and then Kenyon. But murder was murder, he said to himself, and her crimes were so heinous that it was difficult to feel too much pity for her.

'We'll need a full statement from you, Dr Walker,' he said before beckoning to Cooper to join him outside. 'Given the circumstances, we will arrange for it to be done by video. Sergeant Cooper will organise that when you are ready.'

'What will happen to me?' Harriett asked, her fear audible in her voice.

'That's not for me to say,' replied Carmichael sympathetically with a faint smile. 'It will be for the court to decide.'

The two police officers turned to leave the room.

'One last thing,' Cooper asked, just as he was about to close the door behind them, 'are you left-handed?'

'I was,' replied Harriett gloomily. 'But I'm not sure I can make that claim any longer.'

Without another word, Cooper followed his boss out into the corridor.

Chapter 45

Penny Carmichael was sitting quietly in the kitchen. Except for making herself a coffee, she had scarcely moved since her husband had left for work. In spite of having a reasonable night's sleep she still felt exhausted, and no matter how hard she tried, Penny could not extinguish her worries about poor Brooke and the impact her death would have on Robbie, if that most awful fear became a reality.

None of her three children had emerged so far that morning, which was a surprise to Penny, but a welcome one. It gave her the time she needed to work out how she was going to manage the inevitable sadness that had engulfed the Carmichael family.

The silence which had been her only companion since her husband had left was rudely interrupted by the sound of the front doorbell. Penny gazed up at the clock on the wall – it was 11:35 a.m.

Slowly, Penny rose from her chair and with little urgency in her step she ambled down the hallway and opened the door.

'Hello, Katie,' she said, upon seeing Katie Robertson at the door. 'Come in.'

'No, I can't stay long,' replied Katie. 'I just wanted to give you this.'

Katie handed Penny a white envelope with 'The Carmichaels' carefully written in Katie's best handwriting.

'It's an invitation to the wedding,' said Katie excitedly, not that the contents were ever going to be a mystery to Penny.

'Thank you, my dear,' replied Penny with a broad smile. 'It's so kind of you to invite Steve and me.'

'It's for all of you,' replied Katie. 'Jemma, Robbie and Natalie, too!'

Penny's smile broadened. 'That's very thoughtful of you, Katie. I'm sure they will all be thrilled to come.'

Katie looked at her watch, and gave the impression that she was already short on time. 'I'll have to rush. I'm meeting Barney after he's finished the morning service.'

Penny watched as the excited young woman dashed away down the road. Katie's joyfulness and her infectious energy was just the tonic Penny's spirits had needed.

'Be positive,' she whispered to herself as she turned and went back inside.

*   *   *   *

'What a mess!' exclaimed Carmichael once he and Cooper were safely out of earshot.

Cooper nodded in agreement. 'It sounds absurd but I can't help feeling sorry for Harriett Walker,' he said. 'It's ridiculous I know, but the thought of her being like that for the rest of her life does make me feel some sadness for her.'

Despite having similar thoughts, Carmichael didn't want to let Cooper see how he felt. 'You're getting soft in your old age,' he remarked flippantly. 'I understand what you're saying, Paul. However, I doubt Kenyon's widow or poor Brooke's mother would share your kind-heartedness. She's a killer and, although her injury may help her lawyer plead her case, I can't see her being given too much sympathy when she's finally sentenced. And, to be honest, it's not our problem.'

Carmichael looked deep into Cooper's eyes as he delivered his final sentence, as if to drive home his message.

'Anyway, I promised Penny I'd drop in on Brooke,' he continued. 'Fingers crossed, her condition has improved since last night.'

Cooper nodded. 'She's down the corridor,' he said, his eyes glancing in the direction they needed to take.

'Lead on, Cooper,' instructed Carmichael. 'Let's go and see how she's doing.'

The two officers sauntered down the corridor towards the small private room where Brooke and her anxious mother had spent the last thirteen hours.

* * * *

Once back inside the house, Penny had wasted no time in taking command. Her plan was straightforward; she would take a positive approach and, in so doing, deny the family the opportunity of fretting over Brooke's plight. Penny was determined to keep them occupied and was unwavering in her desire to be positive. She knew it was important to appear optimistic about Brooke's chances of recovery, even though, after seeing the condition of the poor girl the night before, Penny secretly feared the worst.

'Jemma,' Penny announced cheerily as she burst into her eldest daughter's bedroom, 'I need you to get up, my dear.'

'What?' exclaimed Jemma, who was totally confused and disorientated.

'I want to spend some time with Robbie today,' Penny explained as she perched herself on the side of Jemma's bed.

'What time is it?' Jemma enquired as she wiped the sleep from her eyes.

'Never mind the time,' replied Penny. 'I'm waiting for an update on Brooke's condition from your dad,' she continued, while at the same time stroking her daughter's long strawberry-blonde hair. 'I suspect that Robbie may want to go and see her later; and if he does, I need to go with him so I'll need your help to look after Natalie.'

Under normal circumstances the prospect of having to look after her little sister would have sent Jemma into a tailspin, but she knew the score and nodded back at her mother. 'OK, Mum, I'll get a quick shower and be down in a few minutes.'

'Thanks, dear,' said Penny before planting a tender kiss on her daughter's forehead then moving away towards the door.

'Do you think Brooke will pull through?' enquired Jemma, hardly daring to ask the question.

Penny looked back with as natural a smile as she could muster. 'We have to believe so,' she replied. 'I think Brooke's quite sturdy for her size, so I'm confident she'll be OK.'

Having successfully recruited her eldest daughter to help her, Penny took a deep breath and headed towards Robbie's bedroom door. She knew full well that getting him into a positive frame of mind was not going to be quite so easy.

* * * *

Carmichael and Cooper entered the room as quietly as they could. The curtains by now had been opened by the nursing staff, so the room was brightly lit.

Brooke lay serene under the neat bedclothes. With the exception of the constant repetitive rhythms of the oxygen machine which was aiding her breathing and the regular bleeps from the monitor which measured her responses, the room was silent.

As the two officers arrived, a worried grey face looked around at them from next to the bed. Brooke's mother was still just on the right side of forty and, as a rule, people told her she looked young for her age. Unfortunately, at that moment she looked far from being a young thirty-something. Her hair was tangled and unkempt from the constant nervous fiddling over the past thirteen hours, and her normal healthy complexion had deserted her, leaving her face looking sallow and tired.

'How is she?' asked Carmichael in a whisper.

'The doctor says she is stable,' she replied in a feeble voice. 'But she's not come round and they say she may never gain consciousness.'

Carmichael felt awkward, but wanted to try and do all he could to reassure the poor woman.

'She's in the best place,' he heard himself saying, a sentence that struck him as being wholly inappropriate and totally inadequate, almost as soon as it had been uttered. Nevertheless it appeared to do the trick, as it brought a smile to the face of Brooke's mother.

'I'm Sarah, by the way,' she said almost apologetically. 'I didn't introduce myself properly last night.'

Although Robbie and Brooke had been seeing each other for several months, neither Penny nor Carmichael had yet met Brooke's mother.

'I'm Steve,' Carmichael replied as he approached the bed. 'And this is Sergeant Cooper.'

Cooper smiled, but remained at the back of the room.

'I blame myself,' remarked Sarah, her eyes now starting to fill. 'Brooke saw the bitch coming out of Geraldine Ramsey's house and I told her to keep her mouth shut. Now look where that brainless piece of advice has brought us.'

Carmichael fully agreed with Sarah's summation, but sensitively elected not to say anything that would create more distress for her. 'It wasn't your advice that did this, Sarah,' he replied, placing a caring hand on her shoulder. 'It was a desperate and evil act that brought Brooke here last night. And something that will not go unpunished, I can assure you.'

'I hear she's paralysed,' commented Sarah, her eyes fixed on her daughter.

'Yes,' replied Carmichael. 'That's correct. Her car came off the road last night when she was trying to escape.'

'Good,' exclaimed Sarah, with unveiled hatred in her voice.

Chapter 46

Carmichael and Cooper stood quietly in the hospital corridor for a few minutes before Carmichael broke the silence.

'So which one do you feel pity for the most?' he asked caustically, 'Sarah or Harriett?'

Cooper pondered the question for a few seconds. 'To be honest, sir, I pity them both,' he said candidly. 'I also feel sorry for Ernest Walker, too, and for your poor boy. I feel sympathy for Geraldine Ramsey's family and of course for Kenyon's wife, too. In fact, there are so many victims here, sir, that it's impossible to decide who I feel sorry for the most.'

Cooper's sage-like summing-up impressed Carmichael and allowed him to enjoy a faint wry smile. 'You're absolutely right,' Carmichael replied. 'And while you're sorting out Dr Harriett Walker's video confession, I have to go and talk to another victim.'

'Who's that?' enquired Cooper.

'Miranda Coyle,' replied Carmichael. 'It's time she was put out of her misery.'

*   *   *   *

It was already mid-day when Carmichael's car left the car park at Kirkwood Hospital. He estimated that it would take him fifty minutes to get to Miranda Coyle's swanky Salford Keys apartment; enough time for him to call Penny and give her the update on Brooke's condition and also time to call

Rachel and Watson to bring them both up to speed. He elected to call Penny first.

*   *   *   *

Penny had succeeded in organising the young team at home and, although the general mood was still one of quiet apprehension, the fact that all three were trying to sound as positive as they could was a victory of sorts in Penny's eyes. The surprise arrival of Spot On just as the family were about to start their late-morning breakfast, served only to lift everyone's spirits further.

'Have you eaten, Chris?' Penny asked as the young man plonked his bulky carcass down at the table.

'Not yet,' replied Spot On, who had actually already consumed a large bowl of cornflakes before he had left home, a fact that he chose to discount given that the smell of cooking bacon and eggs was something he found appealing.

'We're waiting for Steve to call us from the hospital,' Penny informed Spot On, who had already helped himself to a slice of toast, which he was buttering liberally. 'If she's doing OK, Robbie and I might go up and see her later.'

'Spot on,' replied Spot On, his mouth now full of toast. 'I reckon she'll be fine.'

'And how do you arrive at that conclusion?' enquired Robbie sceptically, being a little put out, firstly by the way this person was merrily tucking into what he saw as *his* breakfast, and secondly by the apparently nonchalant way the imposter had come to such a flippant conclusion.

Oblivious to Robbie's frustration, Spot On grabbed a second slice of toast and started to layer it with butter. 'Well,' he said as if he was just about to make an earth-shattering statement. 'If there was bad news, we would have known by now,' he remarked. 'So my theory is that she must be doing OK.'

Although his comments were as far from profound as

made no difference, and although Penny could see no sense or logic behind his announcement, his words remarkably appeared to have some resonance with her three offspring, which in turn seemed to raise their spirits.

'It makes sense,' remarked Natalie. 'I bet when Dad calls he'll tell us she's doing well.'

Pleased that the mood was improving, Penny turned her attention to more mundane issues. 'Would you like some bacon and eggs, Chris?' she asked with a kindly smile.

'That would be spot on,' he replied before thrusting half a slice of toast into his gaping mouth.

By the time Carmichael called, the table was laden with bacon, eggs, sausage and even more toast, all of which were now rapidly being demolished.

'That'll be Steve,' exclaimed Penny.

Jemma, Robbie, Natalie and Spot On all listened intently as Penny answered the phone. For a minute she said nothing, which increased the tension in the kitchen. However, having been informed by her husband that Brooke was stable, and fully aware that her responses were being closely monitored by the four people sitting around the kitchen table, Penny tried to sound as upbeat as she could. 'Well, that's good news,' she remarked loudly.

'Not necessarily,' replied Steve on the other end of the line. 'She's still in a serious condition.'

'Do you think that Robbie and I should go and see her today?' Penny enquired.

'I see no reason why not,' replied Carmichael, 'but don't expect miracles. She may never come out of her coma.'

There was no way that Penny wanted to use the word 'coma'. 'Even if she's still sleeping, it may help us being there. They say that sometimes the sound of people can bring them round.'

Carmichael twigged what Penny was doing. 'Are the kids listening?'

'That's right, dear,' replied Penny. 'So it's looking a bit better than it was last night?'

'Actually it probably is,' Carmichael replied honestly. 'But as I said, don't expect miracles.'

'So what are you doing this afternoon?' Penny enquired.

'I'm going to see a bigamist to tell her about her first love,' replied Carmichael.

'I assume you mean Miranda Coyle,' replied Penny, who had been brought up to speed about Miranda's guilty secret, during an earlier tête-à-tête.

'Yes,' replied Carmichael. 'And it's bad news, I'm afraid.'

* * * *

As soon as the conversation ended, Carmichael called first Watson and then Rachel. Although they were both officially off duty, Carmichael felt they needed an update.

Penny, meanwhile, took a deep breath and marched confidently into the kitchen.

'She's still not come round,' she said hastily. 'But it sounds as though she's in a reasonable state and I think it might be good if you went to see her,' she suggested to Robbie.

Penny's optimism worked. For the first time that morning she could see a sign of hope on her son's face.

'OK, Mum,' he replied with a forced smile. 'I'll take my iPhone, too, for her to listen to. She hates the stuff I like, so that might wake her up.'

Penny smiled broadly and tried to persist in her strategy of acting positively, even though inside she was still very concerned about poor Brooke's chances of recovery.

Chapter 47

It was early Sunday afternoon when Carmichael arrived at Miranda Coyle's apartment. He'd managed to complete the journey in forty-eight minutes, a feat that pleased him immensely as it was two minutes under his estimated time. He parked his black BMW next to one of the expensive high-performance cars that littered the car park.

'At least it will be safe here,' he muttered to himself. 'I can't see anyone wanting to nick mine with all these around.'

Carmichael strolled over to the front entrance and pressed the shiny stainless-steel button located next to Miranda's nameplate.

'It's Inspector Carmichael,' he announced as loudly and as confidently as he could. 'May I come up for a few moments?'

The last person Miranda Coyle wanted to see was a policeman.

'Can't we do this tomorrow?' suggested Miranda, her frustration quite clear in her voice.

'I've not come to talk to you about the recent murders,' Carmichael assured her. 'I have some news about Alain Boutilier that I feel you should know.'

There was a moment's silence before the door clicked open and the intercom fell quiet. Carmichael entered the lobby and made his way over to the lift.

*　　*　　*　　*

It was 12:50 p.m. when Penny and Robbie entered Brooke's room.

Sarah looked up from Brooke's bedside and, seeing Robbie and his mother, manufactured a friendly welcoming smile.

'How is she?' asked Penny in a whisper, handing Robbie the huge bunch of flowers she had bought on the way, as she quickly went over to Brooke's mother to give her a reassuring embrace.

'She's battling away,' replied Sarah just before she was engulfed in Penny's all-consuming hug of motherly support and sympathy.

Robbie loitered at the back of the room, flowers in hand and his eyes now watery as he spied his girlfriend lying peaceful but motionless on the hospital bed.

'Robbie's brought Brooke his iPhone,' said Penny. 'He thought it might help to bring her round. Do you think it would be OK if he played it?'

Sarah smiled and nodded. 'I'm certain Brooke would like that,' she said with genuine gratitude for some support in her vigil at Brooke's bedside.

Robbie handed back the flowers to his mother, who by now had released Sarah from her bear hug. He sat down on the opposite side of the bed from the two women and took his iPhone out of his jeans pocket.

Carefully he uncoiled the earphone cables that he had earlier scrunched up in his pocket. Using his good hand, he gently placed one of the earphones into Brooke's right ear. The other earpiece he pushed into his left ear. As the two mothers looked on, Robbie switched on the iPhone.

Holding Brooke's warm dry little hand tightly in his, Robbie would remain in that chair for the next three hours, listening quietly with Brooke to his favourite tunes.

*   *   *   *

286

It had taken a few minutes for the lift to arrive, but by the time Carmichael finally reached Miranda's apartment he found the door ajar. Anticipating this had been done deliberately, he didn't knock, electing to just walk inside.

Miranda was perched on a high stool at her breakfast bar when Carmichael entered the room.

'Would you like a drink, Inspector?' enquired Miranda, holding up a large glass tumbler containing what Carmichael believed could be either gin or vodka.

'No thank you,' replied Carmichael. 'As they say in all good police programmes on TV, I'm on duty.'

Miranda did not acknowledge Carmichael's attempt at lightening the mood.

'So what's the news on Alain?' she enquired bluntly. 'I assume he's dead.'

'I'm afraid he is,' replied Carmichael. 'Based upon information received very recently, we now believe he has been dead for over thirty years.'

'It was that bastard Ardleigh, wasn't it,' Miranda stated rather than asked.

Carmichael nodded his head. 'If what we have been told is true, and I have no reason to discount this information, I think that is correct.'

Miranda took a large swig from the glass and stared aimlessly out of the panoramic ribbon window across towards the skyline of Manchester.

'I was just seventeen when I first met Alain,' announced Miranda, still deep in her distant trance. 'He was good-looking, charming, clever and ever so charismatic, and that first time when he sauntered over to me at the club, I felt like the luckiest girl in the world. For a young unsophisticated girl, who had never ventured too far from her little terraced house in Cowley, he was quite simply the most wonderful person I had ever met. He was a gentleman, too. He was witty and I loved his soft Canadian accent. He was simply the love of my life … my only true love.'

Carmichael could see the anguish in Miranda's eyes as she poured out her story.

'We believe he was killed in Oxford,' said Carmichael, attempting to give an outline of what they knew as humanely as he could. 'We believe it was Ardleigh who killed him, but we're not really sure how that came about.'

'So how have you come by this news?' enquired Miranda, who was still looking nostalgically into the distance.

'Someone who knew him back then has admitted helping Ardleigh bury Alain's body,' replied Carmichael. 'He has given us a good idea where it was buried and early next week our colleagues in Oxford will try to exhume the body.'

'This *somebody*,' Miranda said sourly, 'I assume this was one of the damn Quintet.' Miranda turned and looked directly into Carmichael's eyes as she spoke.

Carmichael could feel the bitterness exuding out of Miranda as she directed this question at him.

'You know I can't tell you that at this time,' Carmichael replied.

'It will be Lazarus,' she muttered. 'It was him, wasn't it?'

'Why do you think it was him?' Carmichael answered, trying hard not to give anything away.

Miranda raised her eyes skyward. 'You don't have to have an Oxford education to know that it would have to be one of the Quintet,' she continued. 'And as there's only Gordon Napier and Hugo Lazarus still alive from the Quintet; it has to be one of them.'

Carmichael said nothing.

'And it won't be Gordon Napier – Marcus didn't like him,' added Miranda.

'Why was that?' enquired Carmichael.

Miranda smiled. 'I thought initially it was because he was

quite good-looking, a bit flash in his fancy sports car and was popular with the girls. However, when I married Marcus he told me that the first time he'd met Gordon in Oxford he'd made fun of his more modest background,' replied Miranda.

'And that was enough for Marcus to bear a grudge for over thirty years?' replied Carmichael, who was totally astonished by such a feeble basis for such a deep-rooted hatred. 'I can't believe a small thing like that could be the sole cause of his extreme dislike for Napier; there must have been something more.'

Miranda smiled and shook her head. 'You didn't know him, Inspector,' she replied.

'Clearly not,' added Carmichael. 'So what was Marcus Ardleigh really like?'

Miranda took a large gulp of the clear liquid from her glass. 'He was a bitter, twisted, odious little man, and he could bear a grudge for a lifetime. In short, he was evil and capable of anything.'

Carmichael was shocked by the venom in Miranda's words, which was all too apparent to Miranda, who smiled and changed the subject. 'So you can see why I don't think it was Gordon he confided in,' she continued. 'So it has to be Hugo Lazarus.'

'As I said before,' Carmichael reiterated with a smile, 'I simply cannot say.'

Miranda nodded gently. 'I understand,' she replied. 'And to be honest, it doesn't matter anymore. Whether it was Lazarus or Napier, it makes no odds to me; I just want to know for sure what happened to Alain and, if he is dead, find his body.'

Carmichael could see that Miranda was very anxious to conclude the mystery of her missing boyfriend from all those years ago. 'I'll keep you informed,' he continued with sincerity. 'I know it's important to you.'

'Thank you, Inspector,' replied Miranda with genuine

warmth. 'I really appreciate you taking the trouble to tell me. When Alain's body has been found I'd like to give him a proper funeral,' she added. 'Would that be possible?'

Carmichael shrugged his shoulders. 'It's really the next of kin that should do that,' he said uncomfortably.

Miranda smiled broadly. 'Well, that will be me,' she replied. 'That's another little secret of mine. Alain and I married quietly in Oxford, just weeks before he disappeared. I thought I was pregnant and my gallant Canadian gentleman did the right thing. Well, as it happened, I wasn't pregnant,' Miranda added rather sadly. 'I told Alain just a few days before he disappeared. I had always thought he might have run off because he thought he'd been trapped. It may sound odd, but now I know for sure he's dead, in a strange way I'm pleased, as I know he didn't leave because he thought I'd ensnared him.'

Carmichael found this latest confession of her marriage to Boutilier difficult to comprehend. 'Did Ardleigh know?' he asked.

'Good God, no,' replied Miranda. 'We told none of them. At the wedding ceremony, such as it was, there was just me and Alain, the registrar in Oxford and two people we dragged off the street. We were the only ones who knew.'

Carmichael could not prevent his mouth from gaping open with astonishment.

'So before you ask,' Miranda continued indifferently, 'until today I had no way of knowing whether my marriage to Andrew Coyle was my only bigamous one.'

'You do realise that we will have to charge you with that offence, Mrs Coyle,' announced Carmichael. 'But, to answer your question, if you can prove you were legally married to Alain Boutilier then, if we do find his body, you will be able to give him a proper burial. That's of course once his body is released by the police in Oxford.'

'I understand, Inspector,' replied Miranda.

Carmichael nodded back at Miranda Coyle and wandered towards the door.

He had taken just a few paces when he turned back to face Miranda.

'If you were already married to Alain Boutilier, what possessed you to accept Ardleigh's marriage proposal?'

Miranda shook her head gently. 'I was young, Inspector. I was an innocent and I was seduced by these clever vibrant freethinkers. My world up until then had been limited to "little old Cowley", a drab nothing suburb of Oxford. My background was modest, to say the least. My mother was a cleaner at the local school and my father worked nights at the car factory. Being associated with an Oxford scholar was my ticket out. You have to remember, Inspector, to a young unsophisticated girl they were dynamic free-spirited people and I guess I just became intoxicated by the whole Oxford thing. It's hard to imagine now, but back then Ardleigh was, as my nan would say, a real catch.'

Carmichael found it hard to imagine Miranda as a naive and innocent young woman, but of course that was many years before.

'Different times,' he replied with a smile.

'One last thing from me, Inspector,' exclaimed Miranda. 'Where exactly in Oxford did Marcus bury him?'

Carmichael saw no reason to hide this from Miranda. 'Down by the River Cherwell. A place called Isis Meadow,' he replied.

'The nasty creep!' spat Miranda angrily. 'That's the place where Marcus asked me to marry him. I bet he got some sort of sick kick out of asking Alain's girl to marry him on the spot where he'd buried Alain. Even by Marcus's low standards that was a really vile act, don't you think, Inspector?'

'I do,' replied Carmichael. 'It's about as wicked as it gets.'

*   *   *   *

After he'd concluded his meeting with Miranda Coyle, Carmichael had no desire to return to the office; instead he drove back to the Kirkwood Hospital, where he fully expected to see Penny and Robbie at Brooke's bedside.

It was a beautiful warm sunny day, a perfect day for driving. The soft white clouds, such as they were, drifted serenely in the sky. It was over thirty degrees, but the day was made much more tolerable by the faint breeze that brought some welcome relief from the summer sun's rays.

As he clambered into his car, Carmichael's thoughts wandered to the callous way in which Ardleigh had treated Miranda all those years ago. In the course of his work, Carmichael had met some truly evil characters, but he was hard pressed to remember many that had engendered such feelings of hatred in him as Marcus Ardleigh.

He was still pondering the extent of Ardleigh's depravity when his phone rang.

'Carmichael,' he announced, not noticing it was Penny's number that was displayed on his mobile.

Chapter 48

The Railway Tavern was heaving that warm summer evening and by 9:30 p.m. it seemed like all of the village were in there celebrating.

'Who says miracles don't happen?' Penny shouted over the noise.

'I thought you said it was Robbie's awful music that brought her round?' replied Carmichael, who was already well on the way to becoming inebriated.

'Whatever it was, Brooke's conscious and they seem optimistic she'll make a full recovery.'

'Well, I'll drink to that,' shouted Carmichael as he raised his half-full pint glass.

'Before you get totally smashed,' said Penny, 'come outside where it's less noisy. I've got something to tell you and I also need you to explain a few things to me about what's been going on here.'

'What did you say?' enquired Carmichael, who could not fully make out what his wife was saying.

Penny grabbed his arm and guided her husband to an empty bench in the beer garden.

'What a day!' she remarked, the relief plainly audible in her voice. 'I thought she might not make it, didn't you?'

Carmichael nodded. 'Given the state she was in last night, I'd have never believed she'd pull through, and certainly not so quickly.'

'Anyway, tell me about the case,' enquired Penny. 'I'm not sure I fully understand what's been going on.'

Carmichael smiled. 'It's hard to know where to start,' he said. 'I suppose I should start at the beginning, back in Oxford in the early 70s.'

Carmichael spent the next twenty minutes trying to explain how he thought events had unfolded.

'So let me get this straight,' said Penny as soon as her husband had finished. 'Dent, one of the Quintet, dies in a car accident, the other three in the car cover up the fact that Napier was driving, and then, when Boutilier says he is going to tell the truth, he's murdered by Ardleigh?'

Carmichael nodded. 'So far so good.'

'Then Ardleigh and Lazarus bury the body, and Ardleigh marries Miranda,' continued Penny. 'However, Miranda was already, unbeknown to anyone else, married to Boutilier.'

'So she says,' replied Carmichael.

'Then Ardleigh spends the next thirty or so years paying Lazarus to maintain his silence about Boutilier's murder and at the same time is blackmailing Napier, whom he hates due to some insignificant remark he made when they first met.'

'So I'm told by Miranda Coyle,' confirmed Carmichael.

'And later, Ardleigh also blackmails Miranda Coyle when he discovers she has married again without getting a divorce from him.'

'Spot on,' replied Carmichael, cheerily raising his glass in the air. 'I've been itching to say that for days.'

Penny thought for a few moments. 'It's like something from an Agatha Christie novel.'

Carmichael smiled. 'I guess it does sound a bit implausible, but this whole case is a strange one.'

Penny was still trying to get the story clear in her head. 'OK, I understand and I get why Harriett Walker killed Kenyon and also poor Geraldine Ramsey,' she continued. 'And, terrible though it sounds, I also get why Harriett beat

294

poor Brooke half to death with the handle of her umbrella last night. But what I am struggling with are those three letters. What were the letters all about and also, who actually killed Marcus Ardleigh?'

Carmichael smiled. 'Let me answer your second question first,' he said with the air of smug superiority. 'In short, it was Marcus Ardleigh that killed Marcus Ardleigh. He committed suicide – there's no question in my mind about that.'

'But why?' enquired Penny incredulously.

'My guess is that, as soon as he realised his cancer was too advanced, he decided – true to character – to try and cause as much pain as he could to the people he hated most.'

'I'm sorry,' interrupted Penny, 'you're going to have to explain it in a bit more detail than that, I'm afraid.'

Carmichael took a sip from his glass of beer. 'What I've discovered in the last week is that Ardleigh was essentially evil. He was a control freak and it looks like, even when he knew he was dying, his last thoughts were about how he could continue to control events and hurt certain people, even from beyond the grave. We know he spent his life as a scholar of probability – he was an expert when it came to predicting likely outcomes; after all, he'd done it for the government. I believe he planned his death meticulously. He wanted to implicate Napier as his potential murderer. Although he could not have known for sure, I suspect he had a clear idea of the repercussions his letters would bring about and how we would react when we found his body. As I say, his planning must have been scrupulous in its detail. I think the timing of his suicide and the timing of when the letters were posted was carefully orchestrated.'

Penny's face suggested that she still needed greater clarity from her husband.

'Go on,' she begged. 'Explain about his timing.'

'Of course, I can't be certain,' continued Carmichael. 'However, I'm as sure as I can be that Ardleigh left Lazarus the money in his will so that Lazarus would remain loyal to him. He would not have wanted Lazarus to reveal anything about Boutilier's death, and to keep him sweet he let Lazarus know that he would inherit half his estate.'

'OK,' said Penny. 'Go on.'

'He timed his death to be when Lazarus and Geraldine both had alibis,' continued Carmichael. 'Which he did perfectly – Lazarus was in the pub supposedly meeting him and Geraldine was in Italy on holiday.'

'So explain about the timing of the letters and also how the rope with fragments of Ardleigh's skin managed to get into Napier's van?' Penny asked.

'From what Harriett told us we know that Ardleigh got Geraldine Ramsey to post the letters,' said Carmichael. 'She posted them on the Friday evening after the last post had gone, and before she went on holiday.'

'So?' enquired Penny.

'Well, the timing is really important,' replied Carmichael. 'I think he got her to do this so that the letters would arrive on the Monday. Getting Geraldine to post the letters after the last post had gone was critical to his plan for two reasons. Firstly, he knew he was going to commit suicide on the Sunday and he wanted to make sure that the letters arrived *after* he was dead. He did not want any of the recipients confronting him before he had committed suicide. However, he also needed them to be able to attend the meeting at The Lindley on Tuesday evening, so that meant they really needed to get them on the Monday.'

'Clever,' commented Penny.

'And secondly', added Carmichael, 'he got Geraldine to post them for him, since he must have known that she would look at who they were addressed to and would be able to tell us, should we struggle to identify the three recipients after he had died.'

'Very clever,' remarked Penny.

'Yes, but what he didn't allow for was Dr Harriett Walker trying to pass off her letter as her husband's,' added Carmichael. 'I think he missed that one, which, as it turned out, proved fatal for Geraldine.'

'What about the rope?' Penny asked.

'Oh that was easy for Ardleigh,' replied Carmichael. 'I spoke with Stock yesterday and he confirmed that not only was it possible but, in his view, it was most likely that the rope burns on Ardleigh's wrists were self-inflicted. I think he created the burns deliberately to make us think his hands were tied up by Napier. He would have known that Napier always kept his van unlocked, so it would have been easy that Sunday to plant the rope in his van before he went home and hanged himself.'

'My God!' exclaimed Penny. 'How wicked is that?'

Carmichael nodded in agreement before draining the last dregs of beer from his glass.

'It's certainly been an eventful week, Steve,' continued Penny.

'That's an understatement,' replied Carmichael with a self-righteous smirk. 'I've solved my case and I've got so many people to charge, it's hard to know where to start.'

'I suppose you're right,' remarked Penny. 'To start with you've a murderer and attempted murderer in Harriett Walker. Then a bigamist in Miranda Coyle, and you're not going to be hauled over the coals for releasing Lazarus and Napier on the evening poor Geraldine Ramsey was killed.'

Carmichael nodded vigorously. 'And I can charge Napier for misleading the police in Oxford back in the 70s.'

'And of course Lazarus for being an accessory to murder,' added Penny, as she rested her head on his shoulder.

'And it's just a shame that Ardleigh's dead really,' said Carmichael. 'I could have really hit the jackpot with him.'

Penny laughed. 'Yes, that's right, but apart from your great triumphs as a sleuth, we've also found out that Robbie

Robertson doesn't have cancer, and that Brooke will be OK. To me, they are much more important.'

'And there's your reputation restored,' added Carmichael with a wry smile. 'The village no longer thinks you're a fallen woman.'

'You never believed that, did you?' enquired Penny, the tone of her question indicating that there was really only one sensible answer he could give.

Carmichael smiled and put his arm around his wife's waist. 'Absolutely not,' he remarked as he kissed her cheek. 'Don't be ridiculous. With a husband like me why would any woman even think about another man?'

Penny gave her husband a sharp and painful dig in the ribs and a look of utter incredulity.

'Dream on,' she sniggered. 'The Columbo of mid-Lancashire you may be, but you're certainly no George Clooney.'